AVARICE'S HOARD

Brent A Stratford

Avarice's Hoard is a work of fiction. While actual geography of the greater New York City area is referenced, all names, characters, and incidents are completely fictitious or are used fictitiously. Any resemblance to actual persons or incidents living or dead is entirely coincidental.

In remembrance of
my mother,
who taught me that love is the answer,
no matter the question.

ACKNOWLEDGEMENTS

Thanks to all my family and friends who have encouraged me throughout the writing process. I'm grateful to Studio Di Modica for allowing references to the history of the Charging Bull. Thanks to the Aurora Writer's Group. Thanks to Brian T for bringing me back to earth on the cover. Special thanks to those who helped edit the book, Christian, Heather, Josetta, Jackie and Shalissa. But above all, thanks to Stephanee, without whom none of this would have been possible. You are amazing.

1

I lay in the gutter, staring at the bridge that spans 24th Street between the Credit Suisse buildings, and wondered if I was ever going to make it through high school. Today was the last day. I just had to get through my Government final exam and I'd be finished with school forever. Mr. Morgan failed anyone who wasn't there for the start of the test and I was definitely late.

The bike messenger who just plowed into me had sent me sprawling into the gutter. The precious few seconds I had to get to class were ticking away. My head throbbed and my ears screamed with pain. That, or a car was about to slide over me. I sat up. My head felt too sloshy to do more than that.

A black SUV screeched to a stop just short of crushing the bike messenger in the middle of the street. Two guys in black suits jumped out. Neither was very tall. Both had shoulders too broad for their height.

They jerked the messenger from the pavement. His feet barely touched the ground as they dragged him back to the vehicle. He shouted in some language I didn't understand. I didn't need to. It sounded like he was being taken to his death.

"Hey, leave him alone!" someone close by yelled. I

flinched at the pain of the sound. The gathering crowd rumbled a low agreement and hesitantly advanced on the SUV.

One of the suited men held up his wallet. The small gold shield flashed in the morning light. "FBI. It's all right. We're FBI." The advancing mob froze as the FBI shoved the messenger into the back seat.

I grabbed my back pack, anxious to get to class. It was empty. The books and notes it had contained now littered the sidewalk.

I cringed at the sound of twisting metal and crunching plastic. The bottom of the SUV's grill cracked as the vehicle mangled the messenger's bike. The tires squealed as the FBI sped away, up Madison Ave.

There was no time to sit around. With some help from the crowd I gathered my things and stuffed them into my bag. Several people asked if I was ok. I shrugged off their questions. I had to get to class.

My head spun when I tried to run, so I staggered to class as quickly as I could.

My high school occupied the first five floors of a high rise on 25th. If Mr. Morgan's classroom had been on the fifth floor I would have failed. When I walked into his second floor room, the stack of tests was still being passed through the class, each student grudgingly taking one.

Mr. Morgan stood in front of the class leaning on his cane. His hand opened and closed on the chromed top that matched his white hair. He was much too young to have white hair and far too agile to need a cane. I figured it was mostly for intimidating students.

He slowly turned to give me that look, the look of frigid contempt that he reserved only for me. I admit to taking some small pleasure at seeing that look evaporate into one of shock when he saw me. "Are you OK Mr. Jones or do you need to go to the nurse?" he said with more compassion than I thought he possessed.

"I'm fine Mr. Morgan." I replied laying the back of my hand on my forehead like an actress trying not to faint from the drama. "Just a near death experience with a bike messenger."

The class chuckled. Mr. Morgan scowled. "Take your seat then Mr. Jones," he said in his sternest voice. The hairs on the back of my neck stood on end. I hated being ordered to do anything. It was my long standing policy to do things only because I wanted to, and not because I was told to. I wanted to graduate, so I knew I would take my seat, but I wasn't going to move until the hairs on the back of my neck relaxed. Mr. Morgan went back to glowering at the class before I headed to the only empty seat.

Not surprisingly, it was in the back of the class, next to my best friend Dillon. He was the shortest and skinniest kid in our class. His mess of brown hair looked like it hadn't seen a brush in years and he wore clothes that looked and smelled like they hadn't been laundered in a week. He was still wearing his new glasses, the kind that were supposed to be tinted in sunlight and clear indoors, but they never seemed to clear up the way they should. I wondered why he hadn't replaced them in the past month.

I would've said Dillon was your stereotypical computer nerd but that didn't quite fit. He was more like a hacker savant. In a high school that has a lower acceptance rate than Harvard there are a lot of smart people and a lot of them know their way around computers. Dillon didn't only know his way around computers, he lived them. This singular focus, his lack of personal hygiene, and an extremely flexible view of the rules meant most kids kept their distance.

"Morning JJ," he said as he happily drummed on the desk and danced in his seat.

I plopped into my chair where a copy of the test was already waiting and stared at him. "What's with you?" I asked. I thought the only thing he hated more than mornings was this class. There was no reason for him to be happy.

"Begin!" bellowed Mr. Morgan cutting off whatever answer Dillon would've given.

The test was excruciating. Between the incessant pounding pain in my head, and Dillon tapping his feet like a dancer, I struggled to focus. To my astonishment, Dillon finished first. He beamed as he bolted from the room. One by one, everyone finished before me, until I was the last one in the room. Mr. Morgan seized the opportunity to hover, standing just behind my desk. I wondered how someone who spent his life preaching about freedom could be such a taskmaster.

I'd just finished answering the last question, "Which branch of the federal government does the Constitution grant control of coinage and taxation?" when the bell rang and Mr. Morgan snatched the paper from my desk. He shook his head as he walked to the front of the class. "This was an easy test Mr. Jones. The easiest I have given in my entire time at this school," he scolded.

I picked up my bag and dragged my aching body toward the door. "Does that mean I didn't pass?" The thought of listening to any more of his lectures made me nauseous.

"It means you'll have to do better in college."

A wave of relief washed over me. I snorted a laugh as I reached the door. "Yeah, you thought you were real slick telling my mom about that cheap Mormon school in Utah, but I'm not going to college. I'm staying here and working construction."

The horror in his face was very rewarding. "But you were accepted. I even helped secure a partial scholarship for you."

It was my turn to be surprised. My mom hadn't told me about the scholarship. I paused by the door. "Your mistake then; even if I did go to college I wouldn't waste my time at some religious school in the middle of nowhere. But I'm done with useless lectures and ridiculous conspiracy theories. I'm never going to school again." I immediately regretted my retort, but escaped through the door before the better part of me could apologize.

Nikki waited for me just outside the classroom. She always wore jeans and a t-shirt and they were always too big for her. Today, she was wearing a light blue shirt that said "Got Sarcasm?"

I'd known Nikki since my freshman year. We weren't boyfriend/girlfriend, and we weren't best friends. I would say we were "look-out-for-each-other-friends." Or more accurately, she looked out for me.

"What happened?" she asked. Not for the first time, I noticed her enormous eyes. They were the largest I'd ever seen and seemed to change color from day to day. When we first met, they creeped me out a little. Eventually, I only noticed them when she stared at me intently, usually because I'd done something wrong. Today the ring of blue around the outside and several shades of green in the middle were more than intense.

She was only a little taller than Dillon, but her protective side could get a little scary so I replied, "Bike messenger" as flatly as possible.

"Yeah, I got that," she said as she delicately picked some dried blood out of my eyebrow. I closed my eyes and flinched when she pulled out one of the hairs. "Did you at least get his contact information in case you need stitches?" she asked.

"No, and I don't need stitches," I said defensively. She took a deep breath and I knew a lecture on my safety was coming. "I barely even saw the guy before the FBI picked him up," I said.

She paused for a moment. "Yeah right," she said sarcastically. "Like crashing into Michael Jefferson Jones is a federal offense."

I smiled. Not only had I escaped the lecture but she'd used my full name. For some reason that always improved my mood. "Of course it is," I teased as we headed toward the library. "I think that was question five on the test we just took."

She smiled. I wondered how much it cost to get her teeth so straight and white. I was pretty sure between that and her perfect studio tan her father had spent more than my mom made in a year.

"Well I'm glad you're OK, JJ" she said brusquely, then quickly looked away.

"Me too," I said, baffled at her reactions.

"Hey, are you doing that traditional end of year note burning thing with Dillon?" she asked. She must have been desperate to change the topic if she was bringing up Dillon. He and I usually celebrated the end of each school year by burning all our class notes. It was more ceremonial than malicious since we periodically used his high speed scanner to create digital copies.

"I think so. At least that's if he didn't bail on me after class. Did you see how quickly he finished?" I replied.

"It's all about preparation," Dillon said from behind us. We both jumped. "And of course we're on for," at this point he mimicked a movie announcer, "the ritual sacrifice of the unholy remains of the evil educational empire's failed attempt to indoctrinate us."

Nikki rolled her eyes.

"Yes! The first eye roll of the day," Dillon cried, pumping his fist in celebration.

I just chuckled. Dillon was prone to random outbursts with questionable applicability to what was actually happening. It was one of the things I liked best about him. After such a bizarre morning it was comforting to fall into familiar patterns.

When we reached the library, Nikki pulled out a neat stack of books to be returned and gave them to the librarian. I opened my backpack and groaned. After stuffing all the books and papers into my backpack it looked like a garbage pail.

"Here, hold this" I said shoving the open bag at Dillon. He held it while I started to dig.

"What's all that?" he asked, looking at my bag like it was something you'd find in the boys bathroom.

"My bag must've been open when I got leveled by the bike messenger because everything flew all over," I explained.

By the time I unearthed my books there was a ring of wrinkled papers on the floor. Nikki turned from the librarian, smiled at me, and started picking them up without a word.

Dillon helped while I handed in my books. I was elated when the librarian took them. It was the type of joy felt only by prisoners being set free from a ball and chain.

"Dude, the high speed scanner isn't gonna work on all these crumpled papers," said Dillon. "'Twill foul the mouth of the beast!" he said with his best Shakespearean accent. I turned around to watch him celebrate another eye roll from Nikki but he was staring at her in disbelief. "Not even a blink?" he said, disappointed.

"What's this?" asked Nikki holding up a piece of paper she'd been examining. It was a plain white envelope I'd never seen.

"I don't know," I said as she handed it to me.

It was exactly the same size as a normal piece of paper and was so thin I wondered if there could be anything in it. The address was written in a fancy script that almost vibrated on the page. It read:

> *Mr. Chan Long*
> *Plaza Suite*
> *Plaza Hotel*
> *New York*
>
> *Special Service*
> *Hand Deliver to Mr. Chan Only*
> *Collect on Delivery*

"It must have come from the messenger," I said trying to remember picking it up.

"Let me see," said Dillon and I handed it over to him as we made our way out of the library and headed toward the elevator.

"Dude, I bet the collect on delivery amount would be pretty sweet on this. I think we should deliver it," he said.

I just looked at him with what I hoped was consternation. He knew that wasn't my style. What he didn't know was that the past month I had been avoiding him for this very reason. Every time I did something dishonest it left me feeling hollow inside, somehow less defined as a person. When he branched out from breaking school rules and got into some seriously illegal hacking, I couldn't hang with him anymore. Not and feel like myself.

"JJ isn't a cheat and thief like you." Nikki snatched the envelope from him as we stepped into the elevator. Dillon was the only person I had ever seen her snap at and I had a feeling it was because every story about me getting in trouble started with, "I was with Dillon and..."

"He'll just call the delivery company and let them know he found it," she said.

I smiled at how well she knew me. Dillon scowled at her as she turned the letter over in her hands.

"That's weird, there's no sender or messenger company, just this weird mark on the back," she said handing it back to me.

Sure enough the only mark, other than the address, was a tiny coat of arms that had been drawn like a seal over the flap of the envelope. It had a curly border and two panels, one with a small dragon, the other with a sword. "Alright Mr. Hacker," I said to Dillon as we walked through the lobby. "Are you good enough to discover what this seal means?" I hoped to goad him into helping.

He looked at me like I had insulted him. "Five minutes tops," he replied.

I enjoyed seeing him squirm a little so I pressed the challenge, "From the time we walk through your door or after you're at your computer?"

He thought a moment before replying, "Ten minutes from the time we walk through the door." He switched to a mock British accent and said, "I must have time to use the loo."

Nikki rolled her eyes.

"Yes! Another eye roll," Dillon celebrated.

We stepped out of the building and onto the sidewalk. A slight tingle of joy ran down my back. I paused, closed my eyes, and took a deep breath. Despite the beautiful sunny day and slight breeze, the city air was too stale. It did not match the fresh freedom I felt at stepping out of the building that had been my personal prison for the last four years.

"What's wrong?" asked Nikki.

"Nothing's wrong. That is the last time I will ever be in that building," I said. They looked up at the building while I looked up and down 25th Street for what I hoped was the last time. A black SUV was parked in front of the Appellate Court building on the corner. Normally only police cars parked there.

"I guess they were FBI," I said absentmindedly.

"What?" Nikki and Dillon said in unison.

"That SUV looks just like the one that picked up

the bike messenger," I said pointing at it.

"But you can't know for sure," Nikki said.

"Should we run down there and see if the plastic below the bumper is broken from where they ran over his bike?" I replied a little offended.

"The FBI doesn't just run over private property. There are rules of evidence you know." Nikki sounded like she was a lawyer.

"Oh dude, maybe they were after that letter," said Dillon. His eyes glazed over and I knew he was coming up with something really off the wall. "Maybe it's a message from the head of the Ukrainian crime syndicate to the leader of one of those super-secret government conspiracies that Mr. Morgan is always talking about," he said in a very mysterious voice. He looked at Nikki expectantly.

I think that was the first time I heard Nikki giggle at Dillon. I also think it was the first time Nikki's reaction really bothered him.

"Don't you have some place you need to be?" he asked her angrily.

"Oh no! I'm going to be late for my first day of work," she cried pulling out her phone to look at the time. "You're coming to my graduation party on Saturday, right?" she asked me in a panic.

"Yeah, I'll be there," I replied.

"See you then," she called as she ran toward Madison Square Park.

"I'll be there too," shouted Dillon after her.

She stopped to turn and glare at him, "You're not invited." She glanced at the front of the SUV then back at me with a concerned look before turning to run again.

"Well that wasn't very nice," Dillon said as we watched her go.

My stomach growled. "We need to pick up some Rafiqi's before we go to your place," I said as we turned the other direction, toward Park Ave. Rafiqi's was only a little food cart but it had the best gyros in the city. The thought made my mouth water.

"You know, someone must have been in an awful hurry to get that letter delivered." Dillon pretended to be thoughtful. That usually meant he was hatching a plan that would get us in trouble.

"So?" I replied warily as we rounded the corner onto Park Avenue.

"So if we go all the way to my place, then figure out what company that logo belongs to, then call them and figure out who sent it, it could be tomorrow before the message gets delivered," he said rapidly.

"So what? We are *not* snaking someone else's delivery fee," I replied with more contempt than intended. The image of some nervous dignitary pacing his luxury suite, waiting for the message, flashed through my mind. Dillon actually had a point.

"That and the fact that looking up that logo in less than ten minutes will require the use of some systems I've commandeered through less than conventional means," he said smiling.

I looked at him from the corner of my eye but was having a hard time focusing. The heavenly smell wafting from Rafiqi's cart called to my hunger but my pockets were empty. "Oh no."

"What's wrong?" Dillon asked.

"I was in such a hurry this morning I threw my wallet in my backpack." We stared at each other for a long moment as the realization that someone had taken my wallet set in. I stared at the meat sizzling on the griddle that my stomach ached for but would not be mine.

"How about I buy you lunch and we deliver it together."

All I heard was "How about I buy you lunch?" I'm not sure I even acknowledged the offer before ordering a gyro with everything on it and grabbing an iced tea.

The rest of the world vanished the moment the warmth of the foil-wrapped gyro hit my hands. I held the pita bread with two hands trying to contain the succulent meat, onions and spicy sauces as I ate. We'd passed through Madison Square Park before I wanted a drink. I looked around in a daze, realizing I'd forgotten the iced tea. Then Dillon handed it to me. The sauce dripped down my arm to my elbow as I held the pita in one hand and drank with the other. I vaguely remember Dillon rummaging through my backpack for my MetroCard and swiping it when we entered the subway. I chased the last swallow of gyro with a long swig that drained the last drops of my iced tea and sighed, perfectly content.

Only then, I realized we weren't on a 4 train headed toward Dillon's apartment. "Why are we on an N train?" I asked.

"Because you agreed to let me deliver your letter and this is the fastest way to get there," Dillon replied.

"Oh yeah, I forgot," I said. My recently contented stomach churned uncomfortably. No doubt I was going to regret my agreement with Dillon. I began licking sauce from my fingers and lamented the fact that it is impossible for humans to lick all the way to their elbows.

"Here," Dillon said, handing me a small pile of napkins he must have taken from Rafiqi's. "I'm surprised you have all your fingers left after the way you scarfed that thing down."

It took a while to clean myself up. I just finished wiping down my hands and arms when we emerged from the 59th/5th Ave station just across the street from the Plaza Hotel.

It was easy to see why this was THE hotel for the wealthiest and most powerful visitors to New York. The granite edifice reeked of money. It looked like someone had plopped a French chateau on the southeast corner of Central Park and stretched it until it was twenty stories high. The islands of flowers and statues that interrupted the streets around it were well maintained and teemed with tourists and people on their lunch break. Everything from the Central Park horse drawn carriages to the way the bell hops carried themselves screamed opulence.

We tentatively walked up the red carpet steps of the hotel. I half expected someone to stop us and ask if we were guests the way ushers at a baseball game ask to see your ticket before letting you into the nice seats. No one did. We were able to walk right into the main lobby. The shapes in the high ceiling were covered with gold leaf and enormous crystal chandeliers hung over the marble floor.

I felt underdressed and turned to ask Dillon to reconsider. He was already striding across the lobby toward the concierge. Dillon in this lobby was like a grease stain on an otherwise clean white shirt. After briefly considering mutiny, I hurried to catch up. He stepped up to the concierge and said, "I have a delivery for Mr. Chan Long in the Plaza Suite".

The man behind the desk looked at us like we were worse than grease stains. "I'm sorry, for whom do you have a delivery?" he said.

"For Mr. Chan Long," said Dillon holding up the envelope and pointing to it.

"Yes, I can read Chinese too, one moment please," said the man as he picked up the phone. Dillon and I looked at each other and then at the envelope. The characters 斩龙 now appeared where the name Mr. Chan Long had previously been. Dillon and I looked at each other in disbelief.

"Yes, the package you've been expecting has arrived," said the man behind the desk followed by a short pause. "Yes, as you said they do not appear to be executive couriers."

Another pause.

"Yes, there are two of them."

Another short pause.

"Yes, I will inform them." He hung up the phone and said to us "Your party will be with you shortly if you would care to wait over there." He motioned to a small bench that was out of the way. I got the impression he didn't want us diminishing the appeal of the lobby so was hiding us on this bench the way you might stuff a closet full of clutter when expecting guests.

We took our seats and watched as men and women walked in and out of the lobby. The women had perfectly colored hair, pristine makeup, and wore suits I'm sure cost more than my mom's monthly rent. The men wore suits that must have been custom tailored because not one fold was out of place. They were all clearly comfortable in the too lavish setting of the Plaza lobby.

A woman walked out of the elevator that was younger and even more striking than the other guests. She couldn't have been more than a couple years older than Dillon and me. She wore a white pant suit with an over long jacket over a white blouse. Her chestnut brown hair was short and spiky. Brilliant blue eyes shown from her alabaster heart shaped face. While she looked like a super model gliding across the lobby, there was deliberateness in her movements that betrayed the training of a powerful athlete. Every man in the lobby stared at her in lust and every woman in disgust.

We watched her walk to the concierge. He pointed at us and Dillon's mouth dropped open.

I stood as she sauntered over to us. "Hello, I am Kari. I understand you have a letter for Mr. Chan?" she asked in a tender British accent.

Dillon remained seated. His mouth hung open as he stared at her. I kicked him in the shin, annoyed that he was fumbling his own scheme. "Ow!" he said glaring back at me. I motioned toward Kari.

"Oh yeah! We have this letter for you," he said and started to hand it to her.

"Wait!" I said snatching the letter just before it reached Kari's hand. They both looked at me like I had sprouted six heads. "It is to be hand delivered to Mr. Chan Long only," I said as firmly as I could manage. If I was going to let Dillon deliver the letter I was going to make sure it was done right.

"And... and... we are to collect on delivery,"

stammered Dillon, the bravado in his tone betrayed by his faltering words.

"Oh, that's all right," Kari said in a tone that was too sticky sweet to sound genuine. "I am his assistant and will give it to him right away."

Dillon was gone again. His mouth hung open as he stared at her. He looked like a lost puppy, eager for a handout. It was embarrassing.

"I'm sorry ma'am," I replied in my most polite tone, "but the delivery instructions are clear. This is to be hand delivered to Mr. Chan Long only." I hoped I was doing the right thing and not getting us into more trouble.

Kari scowled at me. I'd seen that look before. I was in for a lecture. She knew we weren't the messengers and was going to make sure we paid for being difficult.

Then she paused, looked around the lobby and let out a little sigh. Apparently, she didn't want to make a scene more than she didn't want to play along with our charade. She gave me one of those fake, forced smiles and turned to face away from us. I thought I heard her mumble something under her breath as she dialed her cell phone, but the only word I could make out was "ma'am", spoken as if it were a profanity. It briefly occurred to me that I may have offended her.

I'd had enough of Dillon's lot puppy act and pulled him to his feet. "Come on dude. This was your idea." I hissed.

"Mr. Chan will be with you shortly," Kari said in her over sweet tone as she put her phone away.

"Thank you," I said.

We stood there watching each other. I shifted my weight back and forth and tried to look at anything other than Kari.

"So, what's your sign," said Dillon in the worst possible "'I'm a sleazy pick up artist" tone. I groaned inside. Kari just shook her head, turned her back on us, and made that sound all women do when they suck on their teeth. That sound that means, "you disgust me."

Then I *knew* we had offended her.

A moment later the elevator opened and the largest man I have ever seen stepped out. He was nearly seven feet tall and three feet wide with solid black hair that hung in a ponytail below his shoulders. His eyes were so dark you couldn't tell where the iris started and the pupil began. His sallow skin was a stark contrast to the black pants and button up shirt he wore under an enormous black leather trench coat. I thought it must have taken three cows to get enough leather to make that coat. But even the coat couldn't completely hide his muscles when they rippled with suppressed rage as he headed toward us.

"Mr. Chan," Kari stated in a very businesslike tone, "these are the messengers

2

Mr. Chan loomed over Kari as if he would rip the arms off anyone who dared look at her. I couldn't speak. I was too scared he would squash me like a bug.

"Are you Mr. Chan Long?" Dillon said in an authoritative tone that startled me. I thought he had gone comatose looking at Kari. Mr. Chan gave a quick nod. He glared at Dillon with such intensity I thought he might burst into flames.

"May I see some ID please?" said Dillon maintaining his tone and returning as scorching a glare as a hacker savant can muster. I was too terrified to laugh. The corner of Mr. Chan's mouth twitched ever so slightly before he reached into his trench coat without revealing where his hand went. Visions of him pulling out a gun and killing us where we stood flashed through my mind. But when his hand reappeared it held only a small red booklet. He opened it to the first page and turned it toward us. It was a Chinese passport.

Dillon took the passport and compared it with the address on the envelope. Not only did the Chinese characters match but the envelope now included the name Mr. Zhan Long, the Anglicized name that appeared on Chan's passport. I was too scared to imagine any explanation for the sudden change.

"That appears to be in order," Dillon said as he handed it back to Mr. Chan. "And the payment for delivery?" he said holding out his hand.

Mr. Chan smirked. He held open his trench coat so we could clearly see under it as he reached into one of the inside pockets. A long wide scabbard hung from his belt. The leather handle on the polished hilt of the sword looked worn from use. My blood ran chill. I looked around the lobby to see if anyone noticed the sword toting giant in front of us. No one paid any attention. They couldn't see the sword under his trench coat.

I clenched my teeth at the thought that one of Dillon's schemes was about to lead to our death. Right then I decided, if we got killed, I was going to wait at the pearly gates to make sure he didn't get in.

Mr. Chan looked at what he had pulled from his pocket as if deciding whether to give it to us. His smirk turned into wide smile that did not match the clinched teeth it revealed. He dropped three gold coins into Dillon's outstretched hand and closed his trench coat.

Dillon was stunned.

Kari plucked the letter from his hand. "Cheers then" she said as they headed toward the elevator.

I stood frozen, waiting to see if they would change their mind. Only my eyes moved as I watched them stride across the lobby and into a waiting elevator.

The elevator door closed. I let out a long sigh of relief. I hadn't been murdered. The thought of my demise sent a shiver down my spine and propelled me toward the closest door. I'd already taken five steps before I realized Dillon wasn't next to me. He was still staring at the elevator. I clenched my fists trying to restrain the frustration building in my chest and arms.

"Dillon!" I hissed as I walked back to him. He shook his head and looked at me as if he was surprised to see me there. "Let's get out of here before they come back," I said grabbing his sleeve and dragging him toward the exit.

"She might come back?" he said hopefully. He wheeled to look at the elevator again. His turn caught me off guard. I don't know if the way I jerked his sleeve was a reflex reaction or my arm flexing in anger, but I almost pulled him off his feet.

"Yeah, along with the guy who almost killed you." I tried to sound menacing. Somehow I had to get him to realize the seriousness of the situation.

"No way, the guy's a renaissance wannabe." His nonchalance added fuel to my frustration and I practically threw him through the revolving door. "I mean, come on, who wears a leather trench coat in June or carries a ridiculous sword."

"That guy could have killed us as easily as swatting a fly," I spat as we reached the sidewalk.

"Maybe, but she's too smart to let him do that in the middle of a public lobby," he replied with a dreamy look on his face.

"Just the fact that we are debating the likelihood of our death is a problem!" I yelled at him in fury.

He turned to reply but thought better of it when he saw my face.

We walked to Lexington Ave and caught the first uptown train that pulled into the subway station without saying a word. It was a local 6 train rather than an express 4 or 5. Dillon opened his mouth to complain but shut it when I glared at him. I was too anxious to be farther away from those psychopaths to listen to Dillon's typically flawless recommendations for navigating the city. I felt my shoulders relax and the tension of the adrenaline rush fade as we pulled out of the station.

"What's she doing with a Neanderthal like that?" Dillon mused to himself.

"What were you doing trying to stare him down?" I was still annoyed with him.

"I was trying to protect my turf. I'd have gotten her number if he hadn't shown up."

I couldn't repress my laughter at Dillon's obviously skewed view of the situation. It erupted as a big belly laugh. Everyone on the train looked at me like I was nuts. I didn't stop; it felt wonderful to laugh after such a horrifying experience.

Dillon was indignant. "What are you laughing about? I was working my magic," he said.

"She could barely … stand … being in the same room with you," I said between suppressed laughter and gasps of breath. Dillon looked like I had knocked the wind out of him. I stopped laughing. "Dude, there was no way you were going to get her number." He hung his head and pursed his lips. I knew I'd hurt his feelings and felt a small pang of guilt at pulling him back from his fantasy.

"Come on Dillon, 'What's your sign?'" I said trying to lighten the mood with my best impression of him.

"Lay off, OK? She flustered me," he said dejectedly.

"Sorry man." I actually did feel bad for him. I knew

how it felt to like a girl and know she was unattainable. It was the story of my uneventful high school career.

Neither of us spoke the rest of the ride.

As soon as we got out of the subway station on 86th my cell phone vibrated. The text from my mom read, "how was the test?"

I'd been waiting to tell her I wasn't going to college and wondered if Mr. Morgan had told her about my plans. I decided not to bring it up. "I'll graduate," I replied as Dillon and I walked down Lexington Ave.

"awesome :-) U going 2 Dillons?"

"Yep"

"C u tonight" was her final reply.

It was a rare treat to eat dinner out but we both agreed it was an appropriate celebration for the completion of high school. After such a bizarre day, telling her I wasn't going to college over a nice quiet meal sounded almost relaxing. I smiled.

We turned onto 84th. Like most streets on the upper west side, it tried to look like a nice suburban street but failed. The scraggly trees that punctuated the sidewalk reached high above the perpetual line of parked cars. They stretched hungrily toward the sunlight but only their tips extended past the shadows cast by the tall brick apartment buildings. The small patches of dirt at the trunk of each tree had been planted with flowers. It was trash day. The low iron railings protected the flowers from being crushed by the piles of garbage. Nothing protected our noses from the stench.

"Mr. Gottschalk," the doorman greeted Dillon as we entered his building.

"Hey Ed" he replied somberly and slopped toward the elevator.

"It's a pleasure to see you again Mr. Jones," Ed said with surprising sincerity as he held out his hand.

"Yeah, it's been a while," I said shaking his hand and trying to remember the last time I'd been there.

He pulled me a little closer and whispered, "Perhaps you can keep him out of trouble for a day?" I forced a smile and hoped it didn't come out as the grimace I felt inside.

The elevator door opened and I hustled to catch up with Dillon. He looked puzzled as he groped in his pocket for the key. He pulled out the contents of his pocket and held them in his open hand. Along with his key, were the three coins Mr. Chan had given him.

"I can't believe I let him intimidate me into taking a couple coins," he lamented as he put his key in the elevator panel and pressed the button for the 4th floor.

"What are they?" I said nodding toward the coins in his hand.

He glanced at them quickly at first. Then a curious expression came across his face as he looked more closely.

The elevator stopped and we stepped from it into a small alcove with a heavy metal door opposite the elevator. Next to the door were a key pad and a sensor pad. The only other door was marked by a sign that read "emergency exit only."

Dillon absentmindedly passed his wallet next to the sensor pad and entered a long set of numbers on the key pad as he continued to look at the coins. The lock in the door buzzed.

"I'm not sure what they are but they're heavy," he said, testing their weight as we pushed inside.

Dillon's father had purchased all the units on the

4th floor and turned it into a single apartment that was the most spacious I had seen in New York. It had every possible amenity and the décor was so perfectly orchestrated it looked like a showroom. Like a showroom, it also felt unnaturally sterile and unfriendly. We stopped in the open gourmet kitchen and grabbed some Reese's and Mountain Dew before making our way to Dillon's room.

Dillon's room was more like NASA ground control than an actual bedroom. Only the king sized bed, that sat under the windows looking out over 84th street, betrayed it. A big screen TV hung on the wall opposite his bed. It would have been suitable for tracking the orbit of satellites but as far as I had seen was only used for video games. One side of the bed had a desk with six different monitors on it. On the other side, two black cabinets full of computer servers stood like sentinels on either side of the door to his walk in closet.

I dropped myself on his bed and opened a Dew, expecting him to plop down in his normal place at the desk and start typing away. Instead he walked straight into his closet. I watched as he opened what looked like a vault door and stepped into the safe room. His father had it installed in case of an emergency. From the assorted electronics that lay in disarray on the floor it was clear Dillon was using it for more than that.

A moment later he emerged without his shoes or glasses. I hadn't seen Dillon without glasses since he slept over in elementary school. He sighed heavily and leaned against the closet doorway.

"You're not still hung up on what's her name are you?" I asked.

"Kari, her name is Kari," he corrected in an acid

tone.

I shook my head and said, "I am never gonna be that whooped."

"Sure, you say that now," he replied. "Wait 'til you find that Aphrodite you've been dreaming of," he said in an airy voice. "She'll have you dancing like a marionette." He did a little dance, tapping his feet and flailing his arms like a puppet.

"Oh, that reminds me. What was with all the foot tapping during the test today? It was driving me nuts," I accused.

"Like I said before, it is all about preparation," he replied.

I waited. I knew he couldn't leave it at that. He walked over to his desk and plopped into the chair. "I've been working on this project for months," he said. I hadn't noticed the small black box he plugged into his computer. The six screens came to life. "I put all our notes and the entire government textbook on this," he said as he held up the black box and began unraveling some small wires from it.

I recognized the US Constitution on one screen in tiny dim orange writing, but the other screens were filled with images I only recognized as electronic schematics. "Unless those wires attach to a brain implant I don't see how that would help."

"Actually, I've had contact lenses for over a month. Those glasses are a full 3D high def display." His fingers flew across his keyboard and an image of his glasses popped up on one of the screens.

"No way," I said, trying to take in the fact that his glasses weren't broken but part of an elaborate ruse.

"Between using a tiny colored font and keeping the

contrast to a minimum it looks like they are regular tinted lenses." He smiled wickedly.

Now it was my turn to be indignant. "So you've been planning to cheat on your finals for months?"

"He who prepares wins the battle," he said trying to sound stately as he leaned back in his chair. My version of preparation included late night cram sessions. His included months of orchestrating a lie that was a sure fire way to cheat through the tests.

"So what does that have to do with the foot tapping" I asked trying to sound calm despite the hollow feeling in my chest that he had somehow made me party to another of his nefarious schemes.

"Well, I have gloves that let me type without a keyboard but I couldn't exactly use them, could I? So I put switches in my shoes that let me scroll through my notes," he gloated as he held up the thin wires. "See, the answer to the last question is still there," he said pointing to the Constitution. "Article 1 Section 8 of the Constitution states 'Congress shall have power to lay and collect taxes, duties, imposts... yada, yada, yada... and to coin money, regulate the value thereof, and of foreign coin, and fix the standard of weights and measures," he mono-toned. "So the answer to the last question was the legislative branch," he said matter-of-factly.

"Crap! Well, I guess it's fitting that I got the last question wrong on the last test of my life," I said.

"You're serious about not going to college?" he asked.

I nodded. His face scrunched in concern.

A wolf whistle erupted from the speakers around his desk. I jumped. He didn't move.

"What was that?" I asked.

"That is Vicki Johnson," Dillon replied. His hands drummed on the keyboard and the image of an attractive young woman appeared on the screen. She stood in an elevator wearing a professional looking pant suit. "Otherwise known as Miss 19b," he continued.

"What'd you do, tap into the building security cameras?" I asked, astonished at the image on the screen.

His mouth pulled back into a straight narrow line and he squinted at some unseen object in the distance the way he always did when he was concentrating. "Yeah," he said absently. "Why don't you play a game and I'll see if I can get the scanner to take your notes," he grabbed my backpack and left the room. The high speed scanner was in his father's office on the other side of the apartment. Dillon could have had his own, but we only used it a couple times a year.

I felt a little guilty, letting Dillon deal with the mess of wrinkled pages in my backpack, but I was frustrated with him and really wanted to try his new game. I fired it up and completely lost myself in the game world presented on his enormous TV.

My wizard was just about to destroy the dragon at the end of the final level when the wolf whistle pulled me back to reality. I paused the game and watched the video feed of the lobby on one of Dillon's screens. The woman I had seen in the elevator no longer looked professional. She walked through the lobby in heels that were too tall and a skirt and shirt that were too small. I chuckled as Ed the doorman's casual gaze turned into a gawking stare after she passed him.

"What's so funny?" Dillon asked.

Apparently he hadn't been watching. "Ed," I said motioning to the screen.

"Yeah, Ed and my father both agree that women are like meat. They class Miss 19b as a USDA Choice New York strip steak," he said without emotion as he continued with what he'd been doing. The comment made my stomach churn. I liked a beautiful woman as much as the next guy but being raised by my mom, who was pretty for her age, I never would've thought of women as meat.

"So what would Kari be?" I asked trying to gauge Dillon's perspective.

He smiled at me. "Definitely USDA Prime," he said, but then wrinkled his nose as if something smelled bad. "Actually, that doesn't quite fit," he corrected. His eyes narrowed again as he thought. A moment later, he nodded and said, "She seems like more than just a piece of meat."

"How profound," I said mockingly.

He snorted and turned back to his screens. I was surprised he didn't have some witty retort and stood to see what was absorbing his attention. The screen he looked at displayed the lobby to the Plaza Hotel. Panic swelled in my throat. I couldn't believe he'd hack the hotel's security just to ogle Kari again.

"What are you doing?" I asked tentatively.

"Well," he began, clearly annoyed at the distraction, "That screen shows the progress on the image search for these stupid coins," he pointed to a screen that showed an image of his three coins with a very large number underneath it that was growing by the thousands each second. One side of the coins had a depiction of a dragon being slain: the sword in the middle piercing the serpentine dragon that wound around the edge. The other side had an elaborately decorated zero and five. All three had little nicks and dings the way all coins do when they have been used for any period of time.

"That one shows the progress on deleting my back door programs in the school." This screen had one window that showed a live feed of the school entrance and another with text scrolling on it so fast I couldn't read it. I didn't have time to process the fact that he had hacked our school before he moved on.

"That is the security feed of the MegaBank branch in Dallas my dad is investigating," he pointed at an image that could have been any bank in America. Dillon's father, who was the head of security for MegaBank, looked like he was wrapping up a conversation with an extremely stressed bank manager.

"And that one shows the holograph insertion that is currently being streamed to the security system at MegaBank's west coast headquarters in San Francisco," he hissed through gritted teeth as he pointed to the image of a man swiping his card and walking into a room full of servers. "But if it doesn't hurry I can't sound the alarm and get my father diverted to San Francisco before he can come home," he said to the screen angrily. "Probably should have run the coin search on a different server," he mumbled to himself.

"You hacked MegaBank?" I said in disbelief.

"Oh yeah," he scowled. "My holographic thief has been mysteriously showing up at MegaBank's all over the country. He walks in with a valid security card, sits down at a computer and transfers money all over the place. No one ever sees him until they check the security tapes because that is the only place he exists."

"You're robbing your father's bank?" I almost screamed. Images of the FBI bursting through the door flashed through my mind.

"No!" he replied like he was surprised at the accusation. "I'm making sure I don't have to deal with my dad. Stealing would get him fired and I'd have to see him all the time. If I just bounce the money around some escrow accounts his boss makes him investigate it so they can keep it out of the press." The smile on his face was truly evil.

I relaxed a little at his explanation. "But why would you do that to your father?" I asked, confused at the hate he felt for him.

"Why do you think he spent all that money on this huge apartment?" He didn't give me time to answer. "So he could hide me on the other side of the apartment. He doesn't want me to hear him use his influence to keep my mom away. He doesn't want his mistresses to see me when he brings a different one home every other night. You have no idea what it's like when he's here."

My temper flared. "You're right. I don't know what it's like. My father died before I was born, remember?"

"Sorry, man," he responded quietly. "Sometimes I think it would be better to not have a father."

"For a guy who doesn't like your father you're well on your way to becoming like him," I said. He glared at me and I instantly knew I had hurt him, but it didn't stop me. "Dude, look at this," I said gesturing to the screens. "You're using your skills to keep your father away from you. You've got alarms set so you can watch

Miss 19b. And you've hacked into the Plaza Hotel to get a glimpse of a girl you've barely met."

"Yeah, the problem is I have no reliable way of tracking her." He turned back to the screen with the Plaza security feed on it, completely ignoring my rant. "I got a glimpse of her once but they don't have the same type of coverage or the sensors I have here." He began working the keyboard again and suddenly all six screens were filled with images from within the Plaza.

"So what if you could track her? What are you going to do, race down there and sweep her off her feet?" I said sarcastically.

He stopped typing and looked at me in horror.

"This is one you're gonna have to let go," I said.

The muscles in his jaw flexed from clenching his teeth, as he shook his head at me.

"Dude, I'm just trying to save you from yourself. I mean look at you," I said gesturing toward him.

"You know, you're right," he said shaking his finger like he was an old man scolding me. "I've gotta take a shower," he said. He got up and looked around the room as if trying to remember where to find clean clothes and a towel.

I couldn't believe how deluded he was. I looked around and noticed it was dark outside. "What time is it?" I asked to no one in particular as I pulled out my phone.

"10:23," Dillon answered from the closet.

"Crap!" I said as I headed for the door.

The first text message from my mom was two hours old. It read, "Which game was it this time?" The second was only a few minutes old and read, "meet you at home." I had totally missed our celebratory dinner.

"See ya dude," I yelled to Dillon as I bolted for the door. I didn't hear a reply. I hoped Dillon's obsession with Kari didn't get him in trouble.

"On my way" I texted my mom while in the elevator. I had lost my chance to tell her about college in a public place where she couldn't over react. I only worried about that until I reached the sidewalk.

My back contracted the way it always did when I watched horror movies. 84th Street was too quiet and too dark. I couldn't shake the feeling I was being watched. The bright bustling sidewalk of Lexington Ave beckoned to me like a warm fire on a cold day. My legs felt stiff and awkward as I walked. They were tense, waiting for the unseen watcher to pounce on me.

As I stepped onto the crowded sidewalk of Lexington Ave a calm relief seeped through my back and legs. I eased into a more casual pace.

I'd almost convinced myself I was imagining things when I saw a black SUV sitting at the light. A shiver shot through me and the tension in my legs returned. Two men got out as I started down the steps to the subway station. I didn't see the front of the SUV. I couldn't know if it was the same one.

I shook my head at my paranoia. There was no reason to worry.

I heard a downtown express 4 train pull into the lower station as I passed the turnstile. I vaulted down the steps and just made it through the closing doors. The men from the SUV rushed toward the train. They were too late. The doors had closed. One of them flashed a quick irritated look my way.

Now I was really freaking out. I wondered how

they found me and what they could possibly want. I needed to get home as quickly as possible. Dillon's tricks for navigating the city would be helpful at this point. I racked my brain, trying to remember his advice. I remembered Dillon bragging about which door opened at the foot of the stairs in Grand Central. I moved back a car to stand in front of that door.

I looked at every face on the train. No one paid any attention to me.

The train doors opened at the steps. I sprinted up them. At the top I turned and jogged toward the S train. Dillon was right again as I remembered which side of the tunnel was usually fastest. I wove through the crowds looking for anyone in a dark suit. I don't know what I was thinking. In Manhattan, every other middle aged man was in a dark suit, even this time of night.

The S train is really just a short shuttle that runs between Grand Central and Times Square subway stations. Even though you never have to wait long for a train, everyone still runs to catch the one that's there. My rush to catch it fit right in. No one took a second look as I threw myself through the closing door and into the crowded last car.

As the train pulled out of the station, I checked if there were any men in suits who looked disappointed. There were a lot of them. But they all looked like your typical New Yorker trying to get somewhere as quickly as possible. I took a deep breath, relieved that the transfer between trains had gone so quickly. Unfortunately, the mass of people packed into the last car kept me from moving up to Dillon's preferred door the way I had before.

My heart sank as the train pulled into the Times

Square station. Two men in suits stood by the red metal railings that keep people from crossing the tracks. They looked intently at my face through the windows of the train door. One was bald and almost as wide as he was tall. The other had close cropped hair and was a little bigger than me but not as wide as his friend. Both had neatly trimmed beards and intense brown eyes gleaming from their weathered faces.

I tried to convince myself that the tightness in my throat was from baseless paranoia.

Since I was in the last car I had to follow the rest of the crowd the full length of the train platform before heading into the rest of Times Square station. I tried not to stand out. I walked the same speed as everyone else. I kept the crowd between me and where the men had been standing. I took a deep breath. A quick glance through the crowd revealed that the men no longer stood at the railing. I let out a deep sigh of relief but stayed against the wall as I moved with the crowd into the station. The enormous woman I was following stepped away from the wall.

The shorter of the men who had been waiting for me leaned against the wall. "Where you goin' so fast?" he said in a very deep, gruff voice as he shrugged away from the wall and stepped in front of me. The taller one appeared from nowhere and stood threateningly close, cornering me against the wall. Why were they after me? I hadn't done anything wrong except maybe watch Dillon hack his way into anything he desired.

"Who are you?" I thought it was best not to reveal my knowledge of Dillon's activities if they were FBI.

The man in front of me hesitated slightly and glanced quickly at his partner. "We're a couple businessmen who want to make you a business proposition," he said.

I smirked. "What is this, a gangster movie?" They looked puzzled. "Come on, that's a little cliché don't you think? 'A business proposition?'" I mocked.

"Look kid, don't mess with us. We want that letter you found," the tall man said in an equally gruff voice.

My mind raced. I tried to make sense of what he was saying. "Wait, how do you know about the letter?" I said, trying to buy some time to gather my wits. They weren't FBI. If they ran in the same circle as Mr. Chan, I was in real trouble.

"Let's just say we know a few tricks to find what we want," said the short one.

I looked around hoping to find help but the crowd from my train was gone.

"I don't have it," I said, blurting out the first answer that came to mind.

"Who does?" asked the tall one.

"We delivered it."

"To where did you deliver it?" said the short one with a scowl.

I only hesitated a moment. I was trying to decide if answering them meant I had to face Chan again.

The short man reached inside his coat pocket. I imagined a sword flashing out and chopping off my head. Instead, he pulled out a gold money clip full of hundred dollar bills.

"Why don't you just tell us where that letter is and I'll make it worth your while?" he said in as smooth a tone as his growling voice would allow. His expression had changed to that of a concerned friend. I couldn't suppress my chuckle at the use of yet another cliché.

In the blink of an eye his hand flashed back to his coat. The money had disappeared and a small gun appeared in its place. My heart leapt in my throat. I closed my eyes. I should have taken the money when I had the chance. Now I was going to die.

"Hey, leave him alone." Nikki's tone was sharp but she sounded like an angel to me. In the moment it took to open my eyes the gun disappeared and the two men turned to face her. My heart skipped a beat. The thought of them killing Nikki filled me with panic. I don't think I have ever been happier to see a transit cop than I was to see the one standing beside her.

"What's going on here?" he said the way only a cop can.

"Just conducting some business," said the tall one.

"Yeah, give us a call if you're interested," said the short one as he stuffed a business card into my hand. I closed my eyes and shook my head in disbelief at their continued use of some of the worst clichés.

When I opened my eyes again Nikki stood in front of me with her multicolored eyes staring at me in concern. A wave of peace washed over me. The officer had stepped away and was talking to the two men with his pad open.

"Come on, let's get out of here," I said.

Nikki nodded and we scurried away.

When we reached the downtown 1 train Nikki asked, "Who were those guys?"

I explained everything that had happened from when we delivered the letter up until the time she saved me. Well, almost everything. I left out the part about grading women like meat. She didn't need another reason to hate Dillon.

Her eyes got wider with each part of the tale. It was so entertaining I started hamming up Dillon's obsession with Kari. By the time we got off the train at Canal Street we both suffered from a case of the giggles. I wondered when I had become more comfortable chatting with her than with Dillon.

"So, how did you come to save my life," I asked.

"I was coming home from 'Werewolves and Vampires' and saw you get off the S train acting all strange. When those guys cornered you I grabbed the closest cop and brought him over." she explained.

"Werewolves and Vampires?" I questioned.

"Yeah, you know, the vampire, werewolf thing is all the rage. It was only a matter of time before it hit Broadway." She shook her head in disgust as we came out of the subway station and turned to walk up Varick St. "But the costumes are SO cool." she said perking up.

I laughed as she started to explain her internship and how the actors spent several hours getting into their complicated make-up and costumes before the performance. It was nice to be distracted from the day's events.

"Wait," I interrupted her. Something had just occurred to me. "The S platform isn't on your way home. How did you see me there?"

"Well ... -" she hesitated. "What's a limo doing in front of your house?" she said pointing across the lanes of traffic entering the Holland tunnel.

Sure enough there was a black stretch Lincoln in front of my apartment building. The only time a limo touched Broome Street was for a wedding or funeral at the church and never this late on a Wednesday night. I imagined Chan or one of the suited men cornering my mom. My heart skipped a beat.

I darted across the street. Nikki followed. We blocked traffic. Drivers laid on their horns and cursed out their windows. Nikki apologized. I focused on getting to my apartment.

I slowed as we approached. The windows of my apartment were dark.

The back door of the limo opened and Kari stepped out.

3

"Excuse me. Do you live there?" Kari asked.

I wheeled around to face her and she stopped in her tracks. She looked confused. I could see why Dillon obsessed over her. She was beautiful. Beautiful, but dangerous. Not erotic danger. Danger like a tail twitching lion. You wonder when it might turn around and kill you just for fun. Nikki and I shared a quick glance. Without saying a word I knew she understood.

"Do we live where?" Nikki asked in the same caring tone she used with everyone except Dillon.

My mind raced, trying to think of any reason Kari would be here.

"In the ground floor flat of this building," Kari said pointing at the squalid apartment I called home.

Perhaps Dillon hadn't been far off on his assessment of Chan. Maybe he was an enthusiastic sword collector. My mom worked in an antique shop that sold all kinds of ancient weapons.

"I do. With my father," said Nikki without hesitation.

I wondered why they wouldn't just talk to her at the shop.

Kari smiled. It was devastatingly beautiful.

"Somehow I think you are neither Jane Jones nor Michael Jefferson Jones," she said. I involuntarily gasped. Her eyes instantly snapped to me. Why would they know my name? Kari stared at me wide eyed, while I shifted my weight from one foot to the other.

"You? But, you are just some kid who picked up an envelope on the street and thought to make some money," Kari said. I couldn't tell if she was asking a question or reiterating facts to herself.

"Is there something we can do for you?" Nikki asked. Her voice had that edge that meant her protective side was about to come out.

"I am sorry. I have been terribly rude," Kari said in a voice far too sweet to be real. "I am Kariai Tiesos, but everyone just calls me Kari." With her perfect British articulation she sounded like she was making a formal introduction to the queen. She extended her hand to Nikki. "And you are?"

Nikki didn't shake her hand. "Nicolette Kovatu but everyone just calls me Nikki," she replied, mocking Kari's tone. I suppressed a smirk. Kari might be dangerous but once Nikki got going she was unstoppable. I wished I had popcorn. This was going to be entertaining.

Kari stared at Nikki and said, "Nicolette Kovatu, Nikki, go home and forget all about this. It will be safer for you." The authority in her voice was palpable. It made the hairs on the back of my neck stand on end the same way they had with Mr. Morgan that morning. I pursed my lips to hold in my laughter at her attempt to dismiss Nikki.

"Oh, I don't think so," Nikki said wagging her head side to side the way only a New York woman can.

"I think it would be safer for YOU if I went home. Leave us alone, Miss Kariai Tiesos," she scolded.

Kari took a step back. She looked like she'd been kicked in the chest but quickly recovered. "And shall I call you Mike?" she asked in a casual, friendly tone as she reached forward to shake my hand.

Nikki stepped between us, and said, "Only if you want to sound like a fool," in a cutting voice. Kari had succeeded in drawing out the worst of Nikki, a skill I thought exclusive to Dillon

Kari looked confused. I felt a little sorry for her. She didn't stand a chance against Nikki.

A familiar motion caught my eye. Across the traffic, through the trees, carrying a bag from my favorite Chinese restaurant, my mother walked up Varick Street. She was only a block from our street. The seriousness of the situation hit me. I imagined Mr. Chan stepping out of the limo with his sword and demanding some artifact from her. Panic threatened to squeeze the breath from my chest. I had to get Kari, the limo, and whoever was in it, out of there before my mom arrived.

"Call me JJ," I said stepping around Nikki and shaking Kari's hand.

"We need to talk," she said in her most serious tone yet.

"This really isn't a good time for me," I said continuing to head toward the limo. I gestured politely and gently pushed on her waist, trying to guide her to the open door. "I'd be happy to meet with you tomorrow?"

Nikki sucked her teeth and made the same sound of disgust Kari had given Dillon. I looked over my shoulder. She stood, arms folded, with a look of rage I was sure could level the city.

Kari deftly spun away from me. I walked right past her and ended up standing next to the limo's open door by myself. Now Kari stood between me and Nikki. From the way Nikki glared at me I was glad Kari was there. She no longer looked like protective Nikki. She looked like mass murderer Nikki.

"I think you better give me some time now," Kari said. "Perhaps we could go inside where it is a little more private."

Nikki turned crimson. "You're not going inside," she snarled. I flinched. I'd never heard her be that rude. Not even to Dillon.

Kari turned to face her and said "I cannot leave until I have spoken to Michael...JJ privately. As I said, Nikki, you should go home." While she was saying this I mouthed the words "My mom!" at Nikki and pointed down the street. Nikki's eyes scanned the street and her expression instantly changed.

"Well then why don't we do both?" she said cheerfully. "If you want comfort and privacy you can't beat my place." I felt myself blush at this remark. Nikki lived in the penthouse of the Trump SoHo hotel that was only two blocks away and I lived in a hole of an apartment right next to the Holland Tunnel. She passed Kari and took my arm like I was escorting her to the prom. "It's just around the corner. We'll meet you in the lobby," she called.

I stole a quick look into the limo as we headed toward Nikki's. The weight on my chest lifted slightly at the sight of the vacant back seat but quickly returned when I saw my mom. She had crossed the street and was headed our way. If Nikki's ploy didn't work, Kari was going to meet her.

"I had hoped to meet your mother, JJ," Kari said. Not only had she not headed for her limo, it sounded like she knew the figure walking toward us was my mom. Nikki and I looked at each other and froze. Her horrified expression told me she was out of answers too.

"I am a friend JJ," Kari said. Her attempt to reassure me failed, " I am actually here to help you."

We stood in silence. I searched Nikki's enormous eyes hoping for answers but found only the sorrow she felt at not being able to help.

My mom's pleasant voice rang out as she approached. "Hi, Honey, if I'd known you were bringing Nikki I'd've gotten something for -" She saw Kari and froze. The smile disappeared from her face. "Take Nikki and go inside," she ordered coolly, holding out the bag of Chinese food for me to carry. I was too confused to move. If she knew Kari then they must have had business dealings before. But that didn't explain why Kari wanted to talk to me in private.

Nikki took the bag and spun me toward the apartment.

"It is indeed an honor," said Kari with a low graceful bow to my mother.

"He's not eighteen yet," my mom replied. "Come back on Monday."

My head was spinning. I tried to make sense of what she was saying.

"We cannot wait. There -" Kari began.

"Well you'll bloody well have to," my mom interrupted. I hadn't heard her use that tone since I was six and tested a small molotov cocktail in the bathtub. In fact, I had never heard her raise her voice with anyone but me. She usually overpowered others with her simple caring charm.

I unlocked the outside door to the apartment building and held it open for Nikki. My mom moved toward us without taking her eyes off Kari.

"You don't understand. We -" Kari pleaded, but she was interrupted again.

"I said come back on Monday. We won't even listen to you until then." The menace in my mom's voice sent a chill down my spine.

"JJ delivered the kamisan to us today," Kari called as my mom stepped through the open door and into the crowded hallway. My mom froze on the threshold and stared at me in horror, her eyes so wide they looked like they might pop out of her head. "There are complications we need to understand before Monday," Kari finished.

"Friends are always welcome in my home," my mom said without taking her eyes off me. I stared back in complete confusion.

"Thank you," Kari said. Her footsteps grew closer.

A smirk came across my mom's face. "Now JJ, I know I've taught you to be more of a gentleman than to leave Nikki waiting at the door," she said, only half teasing. I came to my senses, unlocked the door to our apartment and held it open for Nikki. Despite all her lectures on being a gentleman my mom insisted that I go in before her.

This left Kari trailing in behind her.

The sound of rushing wind filled the apartment as Kari tried to step through the door. She froze, mid stride, confused at what unseen force had stopped her progress. Whatever that unseen force was, it decided to not only stop her. It lifted her from her feet and flung her across the hallway. She slammed into the opposite wall with a loud thud. Kari slid down the wall until she was seated on the floor, gasping for breath.

Nikki's mouth fell open. She stared at me in shock. I realized my mouth was open and shut it. My mom, on the other hand, was practically dancing with joy as she approached the door,

"You said I could come in," Kari panted.

"No, I said friends are always welcome," my mom taunted.

"I am a friend," Kari said struggling to regain her breath.

"No, you tried to enter my home with weapons and a clear intention to use them or the enchantment would have had no effect," she corrected.

"Enchantment?" I mouthed to Nikki, unwilling to interrupt. She just shrugged her shoulders.

"I do have weapons, and I will use them to protect you and your son from any threat," Kari said. Her eyes fell on Nikki.

My mom followed her gaze before letting out a soft laugh. "Your prejudice is showing. Nikki is the least dwarvish person you'll ever meet. Either discard your weapons and come back as a true friend to everyone in my home or don't come back at all.

Kari slowly rolled to her knees and crawled out of the building.

"Mom, what just happened? How do you know Kari?" I demanded.

"I don't have to know her specifically to know

what she is," she replied in disgust.

"I feel the same way about Miss Kariai Tiesos," said Nikki, mimicking Kari as she said her name.

My mom smirked and gave Nikki an appreciative look before saying, "Nikki it is so nice to see you again." She sounded like nothing had happened

"Thank you Ms. Jones, it's been too long," Nikki responded cheerfully but her sidelong glance was telling. Her verbal jab made me momentarily forget about the bizarre last few minutes. Or maybe it was just more comfortable to think about normal teenage problems because I completely forgot about Kari.

Ever since I had attended a party at Nikki's posh penthouse our freshman year, I had worked diligently to keep her from seeing the squalid circumstances I lived in. I looked at the furniture in the living room and could feel my cheeks flush with embarrassment. The chipped and sagging bookcases full of disorganized volumes on ancient relics were the best part of the room. The threadbare cloth of the badly stained couch was only slightly less conspicuous than the ancient TV that was so small it fit on a TV dinner tray table.

"Nikki would you be a dear and set out the food?" Mom asked.

I turned in horror as Nikki happily began setting the food out on the card table in the dining area. She didn't seem to notice that none of the chairs matched or that they were all lawn furniture.

"JJ, listen to me," Mom said, placing a hand on each shoulder so I had to face her. For a moment I wondered what was so urgent. Then I remembered that Kari was still outside. "I was going to talk to you about this at dinner tonight but it looks like we won't have time for a leisurely discussion."

"Discuss what?" I asked, afraid of what possible revelation could explain our current situation.

"Do you remember all those times we talked about duty?" she asked.

I nodded. Of course I remembered. Whether it was cleaning my room, helping the old lady upstairs with her groceries, or helping Dillon with soccer so he wouldn't be teased, my mom was all about duty. It was the reason I dreaded the conversation about college.

"Well, let me be clear that your duty is to your family and friends." She stared at me intently. I shook my head. I wasn't getting her point.

She squeezed my shoulders tighter. Her breathing grew shallow. She was starting to panic. "You don't have any duty to these people. Your duty is to your friends and your family, the people you know and love, not to some organization that doesn't care about its members." We stared at each other for a moment. "You don't have to help these people. Do you understand?" she was pleading with me to agree with her.

I thought for a minute but I was way too confused. "I don't understand anything. What's going on mom?"

Kari knocked on the frame of the still open door. "May I come in?"

"Do you understand that you can say no?" my mom whispered to me urgently.

I nodded.

She turned to Kari and with false sincerity said, "Friends are always welcome in my home."

Kari's eyes narrowed and she tentatively stepped into our apartment. She looked like she was stepping into a very hot bath. She sighed with relief when nothing happened and quietly closed the door.

"Now will somebody please explain what's going on?" I asked.

"First, could you tell us how you got that letter?" Kari asked.

I wanted answers more than I wanted to share the details of my day so I went for the super short version. "A bike messenger hit me. His letter got mixed with my stuff so Dillon and I delivered it." Kari and my mom listened as if I was quoting Shakespeare.

"That's it?" my mom asked in relief. "See nothing complicated at all," she said to Kari. "You can come back when he's eighteen."

"Why did the messenger not retrieve the letter?" Kari asked, undeterred by my mom's dismissal.

"The FBI picked him up. Now tell me what's going on." I was really starting to lose my patience.

"Except they didn't follow protocol and ran over the messenger's bike," Nikki said from the far side of the room. She'd finished setting out the food and was walking around the apartment smiling at all the embarrassing pictures of me on the walls.

"Those would be goons," Kari said.

"Goons?" I asked.

"You know, goons," she said as if everyone knew what that meant. "The mercenaries of the Dragon?" she asked as if this clarified things. "Usually of dwarvish decent? Like your father?" She clearly thought this last question would link it all together.

I only knew two things about my father: he died before I was born, and my mom loved him very much. Whenever I had asked about him, her face had gone taught with grief and I always ended up changing the subject so I didn't have to see her cry.

My mother looked at me. The depth of her sorrow made my chest ache. "You'll be eighteen in a couple days," she began.

"Five days," Kari said.

I knew my mom's forced smile meant she was struggling to hold back her anger. "There's something your father wanted you to have when you turned eighteen," she said.

This made no sense. My father had left us with nothing. That was why we were barely scraping by in a hole of an apartment that was so close to the Holland tunnel I could tell time by the sound of the traffic.

She continued, "What Kari said is true. Your father was mostly dwarvish and -"

I interrupted her, "You mean he was short?"

She stifled a laugh. "Well, yes, he was short but that is not what I meant."

"Haven't you told him anything?" Kari asked indignantly.

"No. The deal was he'd open the kamisan when he was eighteen and that's it. Other than performing that one task I see no reason to involve him in that world," she responded defensively.

"Will someone PLEASE explain what my dad being short has to do with anything," I complained.

My mom looked at me. Sympathy filled her eyes. "Your father was mostly dwarvish and dwarves are historically employees of a dragon." I waited for her to get to the point. I expected her to tell some bad joke about the dragon being some Chinese crime boss who liked short henchmen. Instead she said, "Of course a pure blood dwarf is almost unheard of these days just like pure blood elves or pure blood humans. All the intermarriage has diluted the races," my mom rambled and I struggled to process what she was saying.

"Dwarves? Elves? Dragons?" Nikki interrupted. "You're kidding right? This is a joke?" She and I looked at each other, relieved that there was another sane person in the room.

"Oh no, not a joke at all," my mother said quite seriously. "I'm sure you have seen signs of the different races many times. When you see weightlifters they are usually mostly dwarf, while a ballet dancer is usually mostly elf."

Kari jumped in before my mom could take a breath. "You see dwarves have tremendous physical strength and endurance, but they are also slow and not very graceful, while elves are very graceful and quick without the brute strength."

My mother gave her a contemptuous look. "But elves only care about roaming the wild parts of the earth and having the freedom to express themselves. They really don't care when others suffer because they see it as just another part of life," she practically spat the words at Kari.

"At least they are not like the dwarves who are clever enough to build anything they want, but are so greedy and power hungry they let the dragon turn them into his personal slaves," Kari said raising her voice in protest.

"What about Napoleon?" my mother almost shouted. "He wasn't a dragon's puppet."

"Wait, wait, wait," I said holding up my hands to stop the argument. "Napoleon was a dwarf?" I said in disbelief.

Nikki choked on her laughter. Kari looked at her as if she had just blasphemed, but my mother smirked.

"Yes, Napoleon was mostly dwarf," my mom said.

"OK, I'll play along," said Nikki. "You've told us the virtues and vices of dwarfs and elves but what about humans?" Her playful tone and smile were infectious.

I realized my mom could be pulling some elaborate end of school prank.

"Humans have neither the strength of the dwarfs nor the grace of the elves," Kari said.

"But humans have one great trait that is more valuable than any other," mom said wistfully.

Kari rolled her eyes.

Mom smiled. "Compassion. Humans have a tremendous capacity to love."

"In the early days they were considered giant buffoons," Kari said condescendingly.

"Yes, the term 'gentle giant' comes from the way dwarves and elves preceived humans," mom replied, enamored with some image only she saw.

"So where are these secret civilizations of dwarfs and elves?" Nikki asked in a conspiratorial whisper. I nodded and tried to match her false interest in these fairytales.

Kari looked like she had just been given sour grapes but my mom smiled at Nikki again and said, "As I said before there are almost no purebreds left in the earth but the combination of the races has produced some remarkable people. Just look at the athletes today that are both powerful and graceful."

"So, what does this have to do with dad? And why is she here?" I said, pointing to Kari and playing up my eagerness to be part of the secret.

"This isn't a game JJ," my mom scolded. "When I met your father he worked for arguably the most dangerous dragon in the world."

"And a dragon is what, the leader of a dwarven tribe?" I interrupted.

"No a dragon is a dragon," Kari said angrily.

"Mom, have you totally lost it?"

She stared back at me without smiling. "This is not a joke," she replied sternly.

"Come on mom, dragons?" I asked, disbelieving.

Kari began speaking so quickly and earnestly I was barely able to understand her. "Dragons have been preying on elves and humans from the start of time. Their focus on hoarding riches and gaining power has been the root of most human tragedy. With dwarves as their foot soldiers they have done all sorts of damage. You don't really think humans would start world wars by themselves do you? Of course not, it has all been about the great dragons fighting for power. Every once in a while a young dragon strikes out and creates a new little empire by teaming up with the people he will eventually exploit. The creation of America was just such an example. He -"

"Whoa!" I interrupted waving my hands in front of me and shaking my head. "I'm not buying it. You're both nuts," I said.

"Let's keep it simple," mom said. "For now let's just say that your father worked in the banking industry as most ... people with his disposition do," she said. I was aware that she had been careful not to mention dwarves. "After I met him, his huma...other parts of his character began to take over. We dated for a while and fell in love. Before he proposed, he told me all about his work. This included certain ... plans ... that would ... be detrimental to ... those who were not in the banking industry. We talked about what could be done to prevent this plan from succeeding. Shortly after we were married he stole a ... ledger ... from the drag ... from the bank and hid it using mag...hid it so only certain people could get to it. I was pregnant with you at the time and we knew the goons ... security, would be coming for him so I went into hiding in a small town in Oklahoma. When the ... clergyman who was with me told me your father had disappeared I changed my name to Jane Jones so the ... security would have a harder time finding me. After you were born I moved back to New York with my new identity figuring the dra...the bank wouldn't look for me right under its nose."

"Wait," I said. My head was spinning. I couldn't focus so I asked the first question that popped into my head. "What was your name before?"

My mom hesitated. "You need to be very careful with names JJ," she warned in a solemn tone. "If you know someone's real name it gives you tremendous magical power over them. And the closer you get to their real name the more power you have. She looked at Kari carefully before saying, "Most of that world remembers me as Samantha Meikleham."

The name shocked me. Every once in a while, when my mother really wanted me to do something, she would call me Meikleham Jefferson Jones rather than Michael Jefferson Jones. I always felt compelled to obey when she did that.

I looked around the room, wondering if anything

in my life was real. My mom sat next to me, a stranger. I hadn't even known her name. The sofa hid the secret of its original color beneath its blotchy stains. The mass of unread books taunted me with the secrets they held behind their bindings. Even the smell of the Chinese food hid the normal dusty smell of the apartment. Was nothing real, as it should be? Finally, I found something that I recognized, something I knew was real -- Nikki's eyes.

And, she was worried about me.

"Where do you fit in?" Nikki asked Kari, quickly changing the subject.

"I am the squire of Chan Long, the current master dragon slayer of the Cyngor am Ryddid," she said in an official tone.

"The Council for Liberty," my mom explained.

"We are here to acquire the codex your father stole from the dragon because we believe it will provide us with key information necessary to slay the dragon that holds this country captive," Kari finished.

I smirked. She sounded like one of Dillon's random rants.

"So let me get this straight," Nikki said looking at my mom. "You married a dwarf who stole a codex from a dragon and magically hid it so only 'certain people'," she said this making quote marks in the air with her fingers and looking at me, "can find it. And now a dragon slayer wants JJ to get the codex for him?" she asked.

"Yes, that is the super simple version," my mom said.

"How could you keep that from JJ all this time?" Nikki asked before I got the chance.

"I told you, I was going to tell him tonight. I figured he could open his father's gift and never get near the danger the Cyngor am Ryddid will undoubtedly drag him into." She turned to Kari and said, "I see no reason for you to be here before he is eighteen"

"Chan is determined to kill the dragon this Saturday, his birthday. He pressured the librarian to reveal JJ's location and I came here tonight hoping to secure his services. It was only after I got here that I discovered he had delivered it himself," Kari replied. She and my mom looked at me as if they hoped to see something they hadn't before.

"So the guys in the subway were…what did you call them? Goons?" Nikki said.

Kari and my mom turned to look at her and I realized she was absolutely right. I wasn't sure I believed in dwarves, dragons, and elves but the goons had been real enough. Then I realized that since I hadn't told them where we had delivered the letter they might try asking Dillon.

I pulled my phone from my pocket and sent a text to Dillon as quickly as possible "r u ok". I wondered what would happen if a bunch of the goons who could track me in the subway tried to get through Dillon's security systems.

"JJ?" my mom said drawing my attention back to the conversation. I hadn't been listening.

"I'm sorry, what?" I said

"What's wrong honey?"

"I'm just a little worried about Dillon. He was with me when we delivered the letter and I want to make sure he's OK." She smiled and from the concern in her eyes I knew this was still my mom, regardless of her name. "I'm sure he's fine. His apartment is practically a fortress," I finished as I looked at my phone willing it to give me Dillon's reply.

"That filthy rapscallion that was with you at the hotel?" Kari asked.

"That filthy rapscallion happens to be my best friend," I shot back at her.

"We need you to focus on helping us find the codex," she said earnestly.

"And how exactly am I supposed to help you find this codex...ledger...whatever you call it?"

"Well, your father left a kamisan that could only be opened by you," she said very calmly as she handed me a re-sealable plastic bag. Within the wrinkled plastic was a credit card sized envelope, faded yellow with age. The only writing on it was some tidy script that read:

To: The Surviving Heir of Bewirken Managito

At that moment a text message arrived and I looked at it expectantly.

It was from Dillon and read, "I am quite well. Thank you for asking. I hope you are well too. I am busy at the moment but will call you when I am able."

Dillon was in trouble.

4

I bolted for the door, fumbling with my phone as I struggled to call 911.

Kari appeared in front of me, blocking the door. She had been on the far side of the table but somehow had gotten there before me. "Wait..." she said, holding up her hands.

"Get out of my way," I growled, "I have to help Dillon."

"How do you know he is in trouble?" she asked.

"Because it would be physically painful for him to write a text message like this," I said, holding up the phone.

"And how, precisely, do you intend to help?" she asked, taking my phone and reading the message.

I hesitated. I hadn't thought that far ahead. "If the goons are there I can call the police, just like we did in the subway." I said. But Kari had already pulled the battery from my phone and set the pieces on the bookshelf next to the door.

"What are you doing?" I objected.

"Goons have nearly unlimited resources. In another couple minutes that phone would be nothing more than a way for them to track you. Besides, that message means they control all communication around Dillon's building. You would not be able to call the police once you got there." Kari said.

"Not to mention that the right money in the right place can buy a lot of influence, even with the police," my mom added.

My heart pounded in my ears. I had to help Dillon. I had to move. I had to do something, anything. I couldn't fight. The police couldn't help. I started to panic. I searched the room for any feasible option. It was standing right in front of me. "Help me," I pleaded with Kari.

"I'm sorry. He is getting the just deserts of his greed and I see no reason to put anyone at risk to stop that. My duty is to defend liberty by defeating the dragon. That is your duty as well," she replied.

After working so hard to be our friend, Kari's callousness surprised me. I looked at my mom for help but she just gave me a look that said, "I told you so."

Nikki rolled her eyes. "You're not seeing the whole picture here Miss Kariai Tiesos," she said.

Kari cringed when Nikki used her full name and I wondered if Nikki had used it intentionally. "His friend is a dwarvish swine," Kari responded without trying to hide her disgust.

"Oh, I agree," replied Nikki. "But that dwarvish swine happens to know where he and JJ delivered that letter. If I understand you correctly a dwarf would happily surrender that information for the right amount of money."

Kari's eyes went wide. She shifted her weight uncomfortably.

"Seems to me that you have as much reason to

worry about goons getting to Dillon as JJ does," Nikki added.

"My orders are to protect JJ and recover whatever may be useful for our assault on the dragon. I will warn Chan of the danger but cannot abandon my duty," Kari replied.

"If you think I'm going to do anything for you until Dillon is safe you're crazy," I said. "So either help me make sure he's safe or get out of my way." She looked at me as if daring me to try to get around her. "If you want to stop me you'll have to hurt me. I don't understand the enchantment that kept you out of here, but I'm pretty sure if you hurt me you will no longer be considered a friend."

Kari hesitated. She looked me up and down and then across the room at my mom.

"No, JJ," my mom said. "You are not plunging into a den of goons. I don't care who's in trouble."

I stared at her in disbelief. What happened to her plea about duty to my friends?

"I'd rather see you help them get the codex and be done with it than let this world ruin your life like it has mine." Her final words stung.

"Really, mom, it ruined your life? I mean, I know we don't have much, but if you'd never met Dad and never gotten involved in 'this' world," I pointed at Kari, "then I wouldn't've been born."

"I can't lose you too," she whispered shaking her head. "They already killed your father. I can't lose you too." Her plea hung in the air and threatened to overthrow my resolve.

"I have to make sure Dillon is ok," I whispered back.

"Alright," Kari said. "I will help you on one condition." I nodded. "That you promise you will help me find the codex after we make sure Dillon is in his normal condition." She seemed to recall Dillon's normal condition quite clearly as she wrinkled her nose and failed to suppress a shudder.

"Deal," I said already heading for the door.

"NO!" cried my mom.

"Let me be clear, my duty is to my family *and* friends," I replied, echoing her earlier instructions.

Her shoulders dropped in defeat at my response. She looked at Kari and said, "Kariai Tiesos you keep him safe or I swear that you and the Cyngor am Ryddid will suffer more than you can possibly imagine." Every hair on my body stood on end and I realized that was my reaction to magic. I didn't know what type of magic she had just performed, but the power in it scared me.

"That was not necessary Sam," Kari replied. "I know the pain of losing loved ones to a dragon and promise to do everything in my power to return JJ to you unharmed." They stared at each other for a long silent moment.

I worried about the time we had already lost. "We need to go," I said timidly.

Kari nodded and turned toward the door.

"I'm coming too," said Nikki as she grabbed her purse and headed for the door.

"NO!" my mom, Kari and I screeched in unison before looking at each other in surprise. I was trying to get one friend out of danger there was no way I was going to put another one into danger.

"You cannot come," Kari said as she motioned me

toward the door.

"If he's going with you so am I," Nikki said. We didn't have time for any further delays and I knew if Nikki got started again it would get ugly.

I took her gently by the arm and was surprised at how easily she let me pull her away from Kari and into the front room. I leaned closer to her and whispered, "Nikki, I don't have time for you and Kari to battle this out." She scowled at me. "I don't want you in danger and I think it would help my mom if someone kept her mind off all this."

Her expression softened. "I don't want you in trouble either," she replied and immediately blushed. We pulled away from each other, suddenly uncomfortable with the closeness.

Nikki looked at my mom and compassion washed over her face. "OK, but promise me nothing will happen to you," she said, jabbing her finger in my chest.

"You heard Kari, she'll keep me safe," I said as I bolted for the door.

"Where does your friend live?" asked Kari as we dove into the back of the limo.

I gave her the address and closest cross street as she opened her cell phone. "To that address Joe," she said to the driver who eased the limo away from the curb as carefully as Kari had stepped into my apartment.

"What are you doing? Let's go." I prodded.

"There's a lot of traffic," he said with a southern drawl that was, if possible, even slower than his driving.

"Broome St has no traffic. It's not even a through

street," I pleaded.

"Do you mind?" Kari said covering the phone with her hand and glaring at me. I stared in disbelief before realizing she was asking someone on the other end to send a couple guys to check out Dillon's building.

The limo stopped at the light. Joe signaled to turn right. Not only was that the opposite direction from Dillon's apartment but the traffic for the Holland Tunnel was so backed up we'd be stuck there for ages.

"Are you crazy? You don't turn into traffic you cut across it," I said indignantly mimicking instructions I had heard Dillon give in the past. He looked at Kari.

"Do as he says. He lives here, and the faster we get this over with the better," she said.

Joe did a little better once I explained that in Manhattan the lines on the road were only suggestions for where you should drive, and right-of-way when merging was less about the law and more about who cared least about their car. Kari chuckled at these statements but didn't contradict me.

No matter how urgent I tried to sound Joe would not be rushed. He commenced an agonizingly painful explanation of how he came from a long line of distinguished members of the Cyngor am Ryddid. I kept interrupting him, doing my best to remember all the tips and tricks I'd heard Dillon tell cabbies. I felt bad but if I hadn't given him directions we'd probably still be stuck in traffic.

By the time we reached 3rd Ave. traffic was as clear as it gets. I'd given him every piece of advice I knew and thought my head would explode if I had to listen to anymore of his slow drawl. I slumped back in my seat exhausted from the effort of maintaining my patience with him before realizing I was still holding the plastic bag Kari had given me. I opened it and reached in to grab the tiny envelope. As my fingers touched it, the writing twisted and curled around itself until the once generic address read:

To: Meikleham Emmanuel Jefferson Jones.

A warm feeling came over me as I came to the surprising realization that this was my real name. Sure, Michael Jefferson Jones was the legal name that appeared on my New York State ID and Social Security Card but I knew it wasn't the magical name my mom had talked about.

"Don't open the kamisan here." Kari said watching me closely. "Wait until you have some private time to sit at a table in a quiet place."

I thought it odd that she wouldn't want to have her precious information right now but replaced the envelope in the bag.

"Why do you call it a kamisan?" I asked as I stuffed it in the front pocket of my jeans before she could see my name on it.

Her face twisted as she carefully considered her reply. "Just think of it as the name for a magical package," she said.

"Obviously, I'm new to this whole magic thing. Why don't you tell me how it works so I don't have to watch Joe drive anymore?"

She paused again as if gauging how much to tell me. "There are all kinds of magic but they all work on the same principle. You simply command something to do what you want."

"So I could magically make Joe drive faster by

commanding him to?" I asked.

She smiled. "You could, but the key to magic is the contest of wills that takes place when the command is issued. You must overcome the will of what you are commanding." I must have looked as confused as I felt because she paused to think before continuing. "For example, I made a mistake with your friend Nikki. I gave her my name so I could get hers and command her to go home. Unfortunately, I underestimated her. I was unable to overcome her will and unwittingly gave her my name. It was careless."

"So that's why moms use their child's full name when they are trying to get them to do something," I said as the realization hit me.

"Precisely, some do it without even understanding the magic behind it. Knowing someone's full name gives you tremendous power."

"So how'd you get to the door so fast when I tried to leave the apartment? Was that magic too?"

She smiled her heartbreaking smile and said, "No, I am mostly elf, which means I am very quick. It is why I was made Chan's squire at such a young age." There was an undertone of pride in her voice.

"You guys gotta get out of the dark ages and use some modern terms," I said, suppressing a laugh. Kari's head cocked sideways in confusion. "Goons? Squire?" I asked.

Kari was clearly bothered that I had made light of her title. "Goon comes from the French word dragoon which is what Napoleon called his troops who fought with muskets. The dragon bought the allegiance of his troops and they turned on him at Waterloo. Since then all mercenaries of a dragon have been called 'goons.' It is a derogatory term. I know others have used it to mean any hired thug but the original definition has a much more specific meaning."

I felt like I was back in school again and regretted making my comments.

"As for being Chan's squire it is a high honor. I make sure he has what he needs for combat and fulfill his most critical assignments; such as retrieving you. In battle I protect his flank, replace his weapons as necessary, and tend to his wounds if needed." She said this last part like it was the rehearsed answer of a politician.

"Ok, I get it," I said trying to cut off the lecture. "You sound like Mr. Morgan," I muttered under my breath.

"Who?" she asked.

"Mr. Morgan was my crazy government teacher who was always rambling about conspiracies," I said dismissively.

Kari smirked in an odd way I hadn't seen before. "You do know that we live in a world of conspiracy right?" she asked.

"Oh sure, now you're going to tell me I need to wear foil on my head to keep the government from using mind control on me right?"

"No," she responded calmly. "But, how would you define a conspiracy?"

"I don't know," I felt like I was being quizzed and didn't like it. "A secret plot I guess." This conversation had taken a turn for the worse and Joe's driving meant I was stuck with it.

"A conspiracy is when people secretly plan to do something illegal, usually to enhance themselves," she explained. I nodded and tried to find anything else I could pay attention to. "So you just finished high school right?" she asked. I nodded again. "Did you ever know anyone who cheated on their homework or on a test?"

I instantly thought of Dillon before realizing that I had seen a lot of kids cheat. "Yeah," I responded hoping to discourage her.

"And did you grass them up?" she asked.

I had no idea what she meant. Gratefully, Joe was good for something. "She means did you tell on them," he said.

"I keep forgetting I need to speak American," Kari said shaking her head. "Have you ever informed on them?" Kari asked.

"Of course not," I replied.

"So you see you are complicit in their conspiracy to break school rules," she said.

"Yeah, but that's high school. That's not like a real conspiracy," I complained.

"Really? And when the kids who successfully cheated in high school get to university do you think they cheat?" she asked.

"I guess. I mean, everyone cheats at some point in school."

"Have you?" she asked

Her question reminded me of why I hadn't had many friends in high school. Dillon and Nikki seemed to be the only people who didn't care that I didn't join in with the crowd. I shook my head.

"What do you think happens when these cheaters become leaders in companies?" she asked,

"Or politicians?" asked Joe.

"Or the head of a bank?" Kari added.

I looked at her in disbelief. It actually made sense to me that people who were successful by breaking the rules when they were young would continue to break the rules when they were in a position with more power.

Kari nodded. She could see that I understood. "You see now, I'm not talking about aliens or mind control. I'm talking about stuff you have seen every day. Secret plots to break the rules."

"Here we are," Joe said as he pulled on to 84th and parked next to a fire hydrant.

I was glad the conspiracy lesson was over but any joy I may have felt vanished when I saw two black SUVs double parked outside the front door to Dillon's building.

"Stay here," Kari said.

"What is it with all you guys and the clichés? There is no way I am staying in the car. You don't even know what floor he lives on," I said.

We both looked up at the building. Every window on the fourth floor was broken. My heart sank.

"Looks like the third floor to me." Kari sprang from the limo and danced silently across the glass strewn sidewalk. She paused and cocked her head to one side. I didn't hear anything. She looked at me the way Mr. Morgan always did and said "Stay."

I opened my mouth to argue that she hadn't even gotten the right floor, but I never got the chance. A woman's scream echoed through the street. The petite figure fell from the broken windows. Her cry of terror ended with a sickening crunch as she landed on the sidewalk in front of Kari.

I cringed, closing my eyes in a failed attempt to forget the scene. My stomach threatened to expel its contents.

"Sati!" Kari screamed. The agony in her voice pulled my gaze back to where she knelt beside the crumpled body.

I stumbled toward her without realizing it. I wanted to say I was sorry, but the words stuck in my throat. She stared at the broken windows as she slowly stood and drew two eighteen inch blades from under her coat. When she turned to look at me, I knew the lioness was out. Someone was going to die.

She dashed into the building. I regained control of my legs. I had to catch her and tell her it was the fourth floor.

I was still a car length from the first SUV when a goon stepped from the back of it. He had olive skin. His black hair was immaculately styled. His suit was at least as nice as those I had seen in the Plaza. He pulled a gun with a silencer from his jacket and pointed it through the doorway. I knew he was aiming for Kari. I veered into him, doing my best impression of a football player. We slammed into the open door of the SUV. The crack of the gun was louder than I thought a silenced gun should be.

Before I could clear my head I was sent sprawling onto the sidewalk as Joe threw me aside. The long sword in Joe's other hand glistened silver in the streetlights. It flashed toward the gun. The clang of metal echoed through the street as his sword sent the gun flying. It skipped across the street and slid under a parked car.

The goon rolled under the open SUV door. He

sprang to his feet, a sword of his own in hand. I watched in a daze as the surreal duel began. I remembered that Dillon was in danger. Kari was headed to the wrong floor.

I ran into the lobby. Ed, the doorman, lay on the floor in his own blood. I flinched at the sight and raced to the open elevator doors. There was only an open pit where the elevator should be. The stairwell door had been ripped off its hinges. I sprinted up the stairs, determined to find Kari.

The third floor door was firmly shut. I was confused. How could Kari have gotten through the locked door? Thud, thud, thud came from the fourth floor. A shiver ran down my spine. It was the same sound I had heard outside; silenced gun fire.

I rushed up the steps to the fourth floor, dropped to my knees before reaching the open door, and crawled forward to peek around the corner. I should have seen the brightly lit security alcove between the elevator and the door to Dillon's apartment. It was dark. A large section of the alcove wall was now a smoldering hole big enough to drive a truck through. The flickering light from small burning clumps of debris mixed with the streetlights from outside like some bad horror film. The luxurious open living space of the apartment was strewn with splintered wood and fragments of furniture. My eyes adjusted to the darkness. The body of a man dressed in a suit lay on the floor. Three more goons came into view, holding their guns in front of them. They moved toward the island in the middle of what remained of the gourmet kitchen. Kari crouched behind the island with her blades drawn. Beside her, Mr. Morgan clutched his cane.

The shock at seeing him forced a gasp from my lips.

The goon saw me. I flopped to the floor. Bullets whistled over my head. Kari moved like lightning. She sprang to the nearest goon. Her blades moved so fast I couldn't see them. The goon dropped to the floor like a puppet whose strings had been cut.

Mr. Morgan was slower than Kari. He was still quick enough. He knocked the arms of the goon toward the ceiling, jabbed him between the eyes with the tip of his cane, and sent him crashing to the floor.

The third goon leveled his gun at Kari. A sickening crunch echoed through the apartment. He swayed slightly, then fell forward on his face. Dillon stood over him. He gripped the smashed laptop like a baseball bat.

"Oh man! That was my favorite laptop too," he said, examining it.

I was elated to see Dillon alive and ran into the demolished apartment.

"Dillon, are you OK?" I cried.

"I don't know," he said shaking his head as part of the laptop fell to the floor. "I really liked that one."

"You were supposed to stay in the car," Kari barked.

"You said you were going to the third floor so I had to correct you," I replied.

"I am on the third floor," she said.

"In America this is called the fourth floor," Mr. Morgan said to her and she scowled at him.

"Stupid Americans, bunging up a perfectly good language," she mumbled under her breath.

"Mr. Morgan, what are you doing here?" I asked in

disbelief.

"The better questions are 'What are you doing here?' and 'Why were goons attacking Mr. Gottschalk?" he replied in his condescending teacher tone.

"No time for a lecture now, professor," Kari said. Now I understood her look in the car when I mentioned Mr. Morgan. She already knew him.

The choppy sound of a barking dog floated through the broken windows before someone yelled, "Hey, I'm callin' the cops!"

I had totally forgotten about Joe and the goon. "Joe!" I said, racing toward the window.

Even after taking a moment to register what I said, Kari beat me to the window. She looked through the window for only a moment. "No, Joe, you fool!" she screamed and darted toward the stairs.

It took me longer to understand what was happening. A body lay on the sidewalk next to Kari's friend Sati. For a moment I thought it was Joe but then realized it was the lifeless remains of a goon. Joe stood by the front of the limo, his sword held at arm's length so the point was just under the chin of the goon I had tackled. The goon lay on his back. His fingers twitched but were still several feet from the sword he'd lost.

The barking came from a French poodle farther up the street. It strained against its leash, intent on reaching Joe. A slender man wrestled with the leash as he fumbled with his phone.

I wondered what made Kari so upset. It looked like Joe had everything under control.

The goon clenched his fist and the trunk of the limo exploded. The poodle yelped. Its master fell to the ground. The huge fireball boiled through the branches of the scrawny trees. Joe's momentary astonishment was all the goon needed. He grabbed his sword and thrust it through Joe's belly.

Joe doubled over on the sidewalk, dropping his sword. The goon stood, looked up at me, and smiled. He touched the top of his head as if he were tipping an invisible hat and stepped into an SUV. I watched in stunned disbelief as he pulled away. Kari sprinted after him, screaming in rage.

The faint sound of sirens whispered in the distance.

5

Dillon's cell phone rang.

"Looks like cell phones work again," he said without answering it.

"We need to go," said Mr. Morgan, turning from the window. I hadn't realized he was standing next to me.

I was frozen in disbelief. The smoke from the burning limo stung my nostrils. I stared at the bodies of Joe and Sati as they lay on the sidewalk.

"Mr. Jones," Mr. Morgan called, "we need to go."

I turned back to the carnage filled apartment. Dillon stood rooted to the spot, mourning the loss of his laptop. Mr. Morgan limped past a pool of blood that surrounded the bodies of two goons I hadn't noticed before.

My knees wobbled and I fought the urge to throw up.

"Mr. Gottschalk, we need to go, NOW" Mr. Morgan ordered. The normally agile teacher leaned heavily on his cane as he labored toward the stairs.

"No offense, Mr. Morgan but I'd rather not go anywhere with you," Dillon replied without taking his eyes from the mangled laptop as he gingerly set it on the remains of the kitchen counter.

"Then precisely what do you intend to do, wait for the police?" Mr. Morgan asked in a tone that clearly indicated that was a bad idea.

"Why not? I've got enough evidence on this hard drive to prove they attacked Ed and hacked the school and MegaBank," Dillon said.

"And precisely how did you come by this information?" Mr. Morgan asked with a smirk. Dillon looked up at him unwilling to answer. "I suppose you were changing grades again when you crossed their electronic path?" Mr. Morgan had nailed it. The proof was on Dillon's face.

"You're a smart kid Mr. Gottschalk. Perhaps you should come with us and get all the facts before you decide to do something foolish," Mr. Morgan said.

"And who exactly is 'us'?" asked Dillon.

My adrenaline surged as the sound of sirens wafted through the windows helping me find my voice and steady my wobbly legs. "Us would include Kari," I said.

Dillon looked at me for the first time and hope shown in his face. He turned and disappeared into the safe room where he'd been hiding.

"Interesting motivation," said Mr. Morgan still smirking as he turned toward the stairs. He nearly fell but caught himself with his cane.

"Are you OK?" I asked testing my own legs. I was surprised at how my confidence grew with each step.

"Just a minor wound," he said dismissively as he leaned against the doorway. His blood soaked pant leg belied his words.

I walked briskly to Mr. Morgan, focusing only on

reaching him. I knew if I looked at the bodies I would vomit. "Let me give you a hand," I said pulling his arm around me to support his weight.

"What about Dillon?" he said.

"Don't worry, he's coming," I said. I looked over my shoulder at the empty doorway where Dillon had been and called to him, "Come on Dillon!"

He emerged from the safe room, struggling under the weight of a large duffel bag. "I'm coming," he said as he waddled toward the stairs.

Mr. Morgan grimaced with each step as I helped him down the smoky stairs. It took longer than I wanted but we were still quicker than Dillon, who huffed and puffed between each footstep.

"Mr. Morgan, what are you doing here?" I asked.

"I was the closest ryder when the call went out," he said, struggling from his pain.

"You were the closest what?" I asked.

"Ryder," he replied. "Foot soldier of the Cyngor am Ryddid is a very long name so we shorten it to ryders, with a y," he panted. "Sati asked for my help because I was closest to Mr. Gottschalk's apartment."

I nodded. Despite what I had seen, I still had a hard time picturing my least favorite teacher as a comrade in arms with Kari.

When we reached the sidewalk Kari was kneeling next to Joe. I tried to look away but couldn't. His blood stained shirt had been ripped open. I expected to see a deep gash. Kari lifted her hand, revealing only a thin scar.

"He lost a lot of blood," she said tenderly caressing the scar. "I closed the wound but cannot create blood for him," she mused. "Which vehicle did you bring?"

she asked Mr. Morgan with fresh fervor in her voice.

"The van," he said, struggling to speak. He leaned on me more heavily. "Sati drove," he rasped nodding toward her twisted corpse. The image and sound of her hitting the sidewalk flashed through my mind and a fresh urge to puke washed over me. I choked it back.

"Joe will need your help getting into the van," she said to me as she sprang to Sati's twisted remains. She pulled a set of keys from the pocket of her dead friend and dashed across the street.

The growing whine of the sirens rang in my ears as I helped Mr. Morgan to the curb and between the parked cars. Kari backed a white van down the street to us.

"I thought I told you to help Joe!" Kari shrieked at me as I tried to helped Mr. Morgan into the front seat.

"In case you haven't noticed, he's hurt too," I fired back at her.

With a startled look on her face she noticed Mr. Morgan's leg and gasped. "Oh professor, I'm sorry," she said. "Go help Joe!" she barked at me as she dashed around the van to help Mr. Morgan.

I rushed to Joe. Dillon staggered out of the building, sweating under the weight of his bag.

Joe was pale and his eyes did not focus on me as I pulled him to a seated position.

"You sure know how to show a guy a good time on his first trip to New York," he mumbled.

"Yeah, how about you get up now and I'll take you to see a Broadway show," I said struggling to get him to his feet.

Dillon gently lowered his bag to the sidewalk before hurrying over to help.

"Big dude," he said as we heaved Joe to his feet and walked him toward the van.

"He saved my life," I replied.

"And you saved Kari's," Joe said.

At this comment, Kari turned from Mr. Morgan's blood soaked leg that she had just healed and looked at us in wonder. I felt my cheeks flush in embarrassment. "What was that Joe?" she asked as we set him in the open side door of the van.

"He tackled Inicma when he was about to shoot you." He nodded toward me as we helped him into his seat. I wasn't used to people acknowledging me. I couldn't decide if Joe's praise made me want to hide under a rock or stand on top of the van and take a bow.

"Help me with my stuff?" Dillon asked heading back to his bag. I was happy to have a reason to avoid Kari's piercing gaze.

"What is all that?" she called over the wail of the approaching sirens as she closed the side door.

"I can't leave without bringing the proper tools," Dillon said smiling. Kari rolled her eyes as she headed for the driver's seat. I smirked. Apparently, Nikki wasn't the only one who reacted to him that way.

We had barely loaded Dillon's ridiculously heavy bag into the back of the van before Kari began to pull away. "Hang on, Joe," she said as Dillon and I clambered into the back of the moving van.

"Hang on Joe?!" Dillon said indignantly. Kari tapped the brakes and the back doors slammed shut behind us.

"No offense, but I am trying to keep the cost of saving your life down to just one of my friends," she said. My stomach twisted. Dillon looked like she had just kicked him in the gut but her comment wasn't laced with as much contempt as I would have expected. I wondered how I would ever find a way to say I was sorry for ignoring the risks she'd told me were inherent in saving Dillon.

I took one last glance over my shoulder. Dillon's street had been deadly that night. The light from the burning limo cast a sad shadow across the buildings. The black smoke hung over the street like a shroud. Lights from a fire engine flashed through the din as our van careened onto Second Avenue.

"Call Ops and have them notify the medical team at NYU," Kari said to Mr. Morgan.

"Presbyterian Hospital is closer," Dillon offered as he climbed over and into the back seat.

"Yes, but we do not have a medical team there," chided Kari while Mr. Morgan dialed his cell phone.

The gyrations of the car sent me sprawling to the floor as Kari swerved around a bus, ran the yellow light at 80th and skidded to a stop at the red light on 79th.

"If you have people at NYU and are worried about time you could go down the FDR, stop on the on ramp from 30th and hand him over the wall to Bellevue, they're right next to each other," Dillon suggested.

Both Kari and Mr. Morgan turned around in their seats to stare at Dillon. I smiled at their awed expressions.

"The way you're driving it would take about two minutes and you'd avoid the lights as well as the worst bridge and tunnel traffic," he explained sheepishly.

"He knows the city better than anyone," I said as I pushed past Joe and sat behind Kari. She looked at Mr. Morgan, who shrugged as if to say, "Don't ask me."

"OK, where from here?" Kari asked checking the cross traffic.

"Left," said Dillon.

Kari floored it through the red light, making the left turn from the right lane without cutting anyone off. I looked for cops but all I saw were normal Manhattan drivers. None of them honked at us.

"Send the NYU team to Bellevue and tell them we'll be stopping on FDR Drive in two minutes," Mr. Morgan said into his phone. "We'll need blood and may need some internals," he said after a pause and hung up.

Joe let out a sigh and slumped against the side door.

"No! No! No! Stay with me Joe," Kari cried turning to look at him as we careened down 79th.

"Watch out!" cried Mr. Morgan just in time. Kari narrowly avoided slamming into a yellow cab.

"I love you," mumbled Joe when I pulled him upright.

"Ah Joe, we just met," I said jokingly, trying to hold him in place. He smiled slightly.

"I think he means he loves Kari," Mr. Morgan instructed.

"Keep him talking" Kari said as she swerved around a town car and up the ramp to FDR Drive. My mind went blank.

"So who is it that's after that letter?" Dillon asked Joe leaning forward in his seat.

"Dragon," mumbled Joe.

Dillon looked at me as if to ask what Joe was talking about. I was too busy watching Kari drive to answer. She wove through traffic on the FDR at speeds

I had only fantasized about. Dillon turned back to Joe and asked, "Is that the name of the guy who did this to you?"

Joe smiled before slurring out, "No, that was Inicma."

"Enigma?" Dillon questioned.

Joe perked up. "Not enigma, Inicma," Joe corrected in a slow clear drawl.

"He's the dragon's right hand man," Mr. Morgan added as if he were commenting on a film in his class.

"He's the head goon?" I asked picturing the smug grin on Inicma's face as he'd stepped into the SUV.

"He leads the goons but I would not classify him as a goon," Mr. Morgan replied. Kari cut across two lanes of traffic and through a gap I would have thought too small for the van. Joe was too weak to sit up and fell on top of me as the van pitched violently.

"He's like the dragon's chief of staff. Goons are just mercenaries," Joe mumbled as I pushed him upright.

"That means all of the dragon's nearly limitless resources are at his command," Mr. Morgan said, grabbing the dashboard as Kari slammed on the brakes to avoid hitting the taxi that cut her off.

"Dragons. Goons. Right," Dillon stated while nodding his head in disbelief. "Is that why you guys are using swords and canes instead of guns, you didn't want to ruin the medieval motif?" he asked sarcastically.

"I use a cane because I prefer to disable people rather than kill them," Mr. Morgan said.

"I can use a gun but prefer the precision of a blade," Kari added.

"I don't suppose you've ever heard the phrase,

'don't bring a knife to a gun fight'?" Dillon taunted.

"We use blades because shooting a gun at a dragon is like shooting a spit ball at a teacher," Joe said. He smiled and pointed at Mr. Morgan. "All it does it make them angry."

"A gun would have worked just fine on those goons," I said, thinking of how casually Inicma had taken aim at Kari.

"Stop just up here on the right," Dillon directed. Kari veered over a low curb and onto the narrow end of the onramp from 30th, bringing the van to a screeching halt. I was glad to be alive after a ride like that.

Three men that looked like doctors stood on the road between us and the hospital, six feet above where the van had stopped. The retaining wall looked like an insurmountable plateau, but Mr. Morgan hobbled toward it like it was a pool on a hot summer day. Kari flew around the van to open the door for Joe.

By the time we'd helped Joe to the wall the doctors had lifted Mr. Morgan over it, placed him on a stretcher, and started a transfusion of blood. Kari and I helped them lift Joe over the wall. Relief washed over Kari's face as they laid him on a stretcher.

"Hey JJ?" Mr. Morgan called.

"Yes Mr. Morgan?" I asked, wondering what could be so important.

"Tell your mom I said 'Hi'," he said. The implications of his request made me queasier than the dead bodies had.

A horn blared behind us and we both jumped at the sound. The aggravated motorists who were trying to get onto FDR Drive were stuck behind the parked van. Kari and I smiled at each other as we walked back to the van under a constant barrage of profanity and horns from the growing line of cars. After what I had just been through a few angry cabbies was nothing.

"Will someone please tell me what's going on?" Dillon asked as we drove away at a casual pace.

"We're going to JJ's house," Kari said politely.

"No, I mean why are people trying to kill us over that letter, who are they, why are you helping us if you already have it, and what's the deal with you and Joe?"

I smiled at the last question and leaned my head against the window, completely exhausted. Kari began to explain about my father and the dragon. Dillon allowed Kari to drone on about the elegance of elves and the depravity of dwarves much longer than I thought necessary. My mind wandered over the agreement I'd made with Kari. Kari had kept her end of the deal. It had cost the life of one of her friends. I knew it was my turn to keep my end of the deal.

I closed my eyes, wondering what could possibly be in such a little envelope that was so important.

I'd almost fallen asleep when we turned onto Broome St. Nikki sat on the steps of Our Lady of Vilnius Church, a few doors down from my apartment building. The dark haired deacon, who had lived there for as long as I could remember, patted her back as if consoling her.

My heart leapt into my throat. Why wasn't she with my mom?

Deacon Peter looked at me with pity as I got out of the van. Nikki looked up at me with tear stained cheeks and immediately burst into tears again.

"What's going on?" I asked steeling myself against the answer I knew I wouldn't like.

"Th-th-they t-t-t-took your m-m-m-m-mom," Nikki managed to squeak out through her sobs.

My heart dropped from my throat right into the pit of my stomach. I looked at Deacon Peter, then at Kari, then sprinted for home. I told myself it couldn't be true. She had enchantments on the apartment to protect against enemies. I convinced myself that I would walk through the front door and she would be standing there happy that I was safely home.

The door to our apartment was open. Reality began to sink in. I rushed through the door and immediately knew I wasn't going to find her there. I knew I was in our apartment, but I hardly recognized it.

I turned in disbelief, taking in the disarray. The couch was splayed across the floor like a botched dissection experiment. The books that had lined the shelves now covered the floor. Every possible hiding place for a letter had been completely overturned. A broken picture frame lay at my feet. I gently picked it up and turned it over. It was a picture of me and my mom on the steps of the public library when she had chaperoned a field trip.

A hollow, cold emptiness grew in my chest, swallowing all other emotions. Grief, dark and deep, like the heartless bottom of the sea. Grief that robbed me of control. My eyes filled with tears.

I stood in the middle of the front room, where I had last seen her, and closed my eyes. Her plea for me to understand that my duty was to my friends and family rang in my ears, but the warmth of her presence was gone. Her voice was like a distant echo. I clung to the memory until the sound of footsteps outside the door intruded and Nikki's sobs washed the image away.

Kari, Dillon, Nikki, and Deacon Peter were standing in the little hall outside the apartment's front door in awe of the mess.

Anger erupted inside, filling the chasm of my grief. "What happened? How could you let them take my mother?" I growled at Nikki. My heart ached at the disbelieving look of pain on her face.

"I'm so sorry," she said in a squeaky voice as she dropped her head into her hands, "I should have been there but she gave me some strange tasting tea and then did that magic thing to send me home." She looked up with pleading eyes. "Please forgive me. I didn't even realize I was on my way home until a black SUV almost hit me when I crossed the street. I ran after it as fast as I could but Deacon Pete stopped me," she sobbed. My heart went out to her. She was as distraught as I was.

My anger shifted to the old deacon as I moved toward Nikki to comfort her. "Why would you do that?" I spat at Deacon Peter as I put my arm around Nikki.

"Because it was Inicma who took your mother," he said in that slow, calm, all knowing tone and cadence that all old people seem to have mastered. "I knew it would be more valuable for me to keep Nikki safe and to let Kari know who had her than for us to get killed trying to stop him."

"Did they hurt her?" I asked as the image of Inicma slashing Joe flashed through my mind.

"I don't think so," said Nikki in a remarkably calm voice as she leaned against my shoulder. "It looked like she was in some type of trance."

"She was under a spell. Which means she probably

told them anything they wanted," the deacon said. He and Kari shared a knowing look.

I looked at Kari. I would need her help more than ever and I wanted to make sure she understood where I was coming from. "This whole ledger, or codex thing, doesn't mean anything to me unless we find my mom," I said to her.

"We will get her back," Kari said. "I promise."

I looked around the chaos that used to be our apartment wondering what to do next. A tiny pink sticky note caught my eye. It was stuck to the door jam. Above a phone number and Inicma's signature it read, "Call me when you have the codex." The simplicity of the note was ominous.

As I lifted the tiny ransom note from the door jam, the entire apartment burst into brilliant pink flames. Kari grabbed the front of my shirt and jerked me and Nikki out of the apartment. We stumbled out of the building and into the street fleeing the heat of the inferno.

I collapsed in disbelief in the middle of the street as I watched the flames devour the only home I had ever known.

6

I smelled bacon and eggs the next morning. I was so relieved that the horrible nightmare about goons and dragons was only a dream. Mom was in the kitchen making my favorite breakfast. The only problem was I couldn't hear the traffic in the Holland Tunnel so I didn't know what time it was. Then I heard two women arguing.

"Your actions were foolish," the first woman chastised.

"Yes Master," said the second submissively. I thought I recognized the voice.

"Clearly I was mistaken to have chosen someone so young for such an important position," said the first voice in disgust.

"What would you have had me do?" asked the second voice and I began to realize who was talking.

"I would have had you protect the boy and his mother and ensure we could obtain the Codex," said the first. My heart sank at these words. I knew who the second voice was before she responded.

"He would not listen. His will is too strong," Kari said.

"You should have found a way to make him listen

and fulfill his destiny to deliver the codex," the second voice said acidly. I definitely had not heard this voice before.

"I thought I had. I had no way of knowing the danger," Kari explained.

"None the less, you have failed in your duty. I hereby relieve you of your... " but I couldn't make out the remaining words as the woman's voice became distant and muffled.

It hadn't been a dream. Kari was being punished for what happened last night. I wasn't sure if the pain in my stomach was from hunger or from the realization that people really had died, my home really had been razed and my mother really had been taken.

The low morning sun streamed through tall windows, glistening off the gold leaf on the ornate raised pattern that covered the high ceiling. I was in what looked like an antique bed with an ornately carved headboard and footboard. In fact, the whole room was full of furniture of the same style. It matched perfectly. If it hadn't been for the large flat screen TV mounted opposite my bed, I would have wondered if I had been transported back in time to the Renaissance.

A squat metal cylinder sat on a little wooden stand next to my bed. From a distant memory of some movie I recognized it as a room service tray. My hunger drew me to it in hopes of finding the source of the smell that was making my mouth water.

Sure enough the plate was full of bacon and eggs. I shoveled the perfectly cooked bacon and moist eggs into my mouth as quickly as I could swallow it.

Next to the plate sat a menu for the Plaza hotel and a newspaper. I stopped eating and stared at the front page. Pictures of me and Dillon stared back from under the headline "Teen Rampage Kills 7".

I grabbed the paper and read:

Two teens, identified as Michael Jefferson Jones and Dillon Gottschalk went on a city wide rampage last night leaving seven dead and at least five seriously injured. According to authorities the rampage started at Gottschalk's apartment on East 84th Street when the two teens began riotously celebrating the end of school and began attacking the computer systems of an undisclosed major US bank.

Police, responding to complaints from neighbors, fell under semi-automatic gun fire. The ferocious attacks, that included the use of explosives, claimed the lives of five officers whose names have not yet been released.

The doorman of the building, Edward Yori, and two undisclosed bystanders were also murdered by the teens as they escaped police on the Upper East Side and fled Jones' home in SoHo.

Officials said that Jones' mother, Jane Jones, helped the two teens flee the city after setting off incendiary devices in their SoHo apartment, presumably in an effort to destroy evidence..."

This last statement was too much. I threw the paper across the room. The food no longer held any appeal.

I racked my brain trying to make sense of what had happened. I could only vaguely recall what happened after the fire started. I remembered sitting in the back of the van between Dillon and Nikki. I remembered sitting outside my house as it burned. And then I remembered Kari's promise. "We will get her back, I promine," she'd said. I needed to see Kari and find out what was happening.

There were three doors in the room and I found the bathroom and the closet before finding the exit. As I stepped into the hallway of the luxurious suite, a door to the right opened and Kari stepped out with a black duffel bag over her shoulder. She had changed into a tan summer cover up that was open in the front to reveal a form fitting tank top and jeans. Even in the casual attire I had no doubt she would turn every head in the lobby again.

"Where are you going?" I asked.

"I have been dismissed for failure to perform my duties and must return home," she said as she turned and slowly walked away.

"Wait, you can't go. We haven't found my mom and you don't have the codex yet." I said following her down the short hall.

"This is no longer my place. I am sure the new squire will be more than adequate," she said, opening the door to the suite.

"I don't want to work with the new squire," I said pushing the door closed before she could step through it.

With her head hung low she whispered, "Please do not embarrass me any further."

I looked past her into the living area. Everyone was looking at us. Nikki and Deacon Peter sat on a couch. Dillon stood in front of it with his heavy black duffle bag over his shoulder. I hardly recognized him. He wore clean and neatly pressed clothes and his hair was freshly washed and brushed. Nikki wore a tee shirt that said "I'm not me. I'm my evil twin." On the far side of the room Mr. Chan and two other men, I assumed they were what Mr. Morgan would call ryders, leaned over a table strewn with papers. I had clearly interrupted some important conversations.

Mr. Chan said, "She has been dismissed. Stand aside." I recognized his squeaky woman's voice as that of the person Kari had argued with earlier that morning. It was so incongruent with the imposing image of Chan that all fear of him melted away and I burst out laughing. Everyone in the room looked at me as if I were crazy. The twisted tension in their faces should have scared me but the overwhelming emotions from the previous day and the incredible emotional release of laughter pushed me to laugh even harder. Mr. Chan looked incensed but Dillon started to chuckle as well.

"What is so funny!?" Chan's squeaky demand sounded like an angry old lady. My emotional control was exhausted and the laughing fit overwhelmed me. Tears filled my eyes from laughing so hard. I held the growing stitch in my side and leaned against the door for support. Dillon laughed out loud. Nikki and Deacon Peter chuckled. Kari and the ryders were horror stuck.

"Stop that laughing at once!" Mr. Chan screeched. Nikki and Deacon Peter burst out laughing and Dillon doubled over. Kari's face went taught with the strain of suppressing her laughter.

"I said stop laughing this instant!!" screamed Mr. Chan and even the two ryders chuckled. Everyone else in the room was now laughing uncontrollably. Tears poured down our faces.

"You will stop this insanity at once!" he screamed in the voice of a high soprano as he drew his sword. In a flash Kari had pulled her two long knives from under her cover up and stood defensively between me and Mr. Chan.

Everyone fell silent.

"You dare challenge me?" said Chan. His voice was menacing despite the high pitch.

I swallowed the last of my laughter. Chan's voice may have been funny compared with his huge body but the ease with which he wielded his massive sword was terrifying.

"You dare to draw your sword on the only hope we have of obtaining the codex?" she retorted.

Mr. Chan looked down at his sword for a moment and then sheathed it.

"You have been dismissed. Away with you." he said to Kari, dismissively waving his hand.

"He wants me to stay," she said.

"That doesn't matter. The boy is no longer your responsibility," Mr. Chan squeaked.

"Oh yes it does matter," I said. Kari had promised that we would get my mom back. She had kept her end of the deal. She had shown that she cared about Joe and Sati. If I had to trust anyone in this bizarre new world it was going to be her. "I made a deal with her not with you," I said. "I will not give you the codex when I have promised it to her."

"You say that as if you already have it," Chan replied. From the hungry look in his eyes I knew if I had it he would do anything to take it from me.

"No, but I have the kamisan," I said double checking that the plastic bag was still in my pocket.

"The codex may be in the kamisan or it may not," he replied smoothly. I wondered how a codex could fit in such a tiny envelope. My expression must have changed because his wicked smirk gave me chills. "We all certainly hope it is there, but after Inicma's actions, it appears more likely the kamisan only contains information about how to obtain the codex."

I realized my adventure might only have just begun. Panic threatened to squeeze the air from my chest. "If getting the codex involves more than just opening the kamisan, I most definitely am not going to help you without Kari," I said.

"Oh yes you will Meikleham Jefferson Jones," he replied. Deacon Peter snapped his head to look at Chan. I felt like someone had knocked the wind out of me. An overwhelming desire to help Chan find the Codex washed over me. I knew he had just used magic on me. He was trying to force me to act against my will and I hated him for it.

"Step away from the door Meikleham" he said. My heartbeat pounded in my ears. Anger rose within me, as I involuntarily shifted my weight away from the door. My eyes locked on the depthless dark pools of Chan's eyes. Fear, hate, and anger bubbled in the back of my mind like a cauldron ready to overflow.

"That's right. You will be better off letting that foolish little girl leave. You must let her go, JJ" he said in a more soothing voice. The bubbling cauldron of emotion erupted, dissolving the spell.

"No," I spat. "I will not let her go." Courage welled up inside me, dispelling the panic in my chest. Chan took a step back and shook his head like he was shaking off a punch.

"I warned him your will was too strong," Kari muttered under her breath.

"I will not get the Codex without Kari," I said, Warmth washed through me. I felt confident. I felt powerful. I pushed my luck.

"Chan Long, you will never use magic against me again," I said and poured all my energy into willing him to agree. Everyone stared at me, then at Chan. The power flowed from me towards Chan and splashed against an invisible wall between us. I pushed harder with my mind trying to push through the invisible force that was Chan's will. The invisible barrier trembled against the force I exerted but did not give way. It shuddered again and began to move towards me as a smirk appeared on Chan's face. I knew if the wall reached me it would crush me and I would relent to whatever Chan wanted. The wall began to move faster. I couldn't hold it. I focused all my desire, all my hopes of saving my mother on just one of Chan's eyes searching for a bottom to the black void at the center. Immediately, the wall of his will shattered and my magical command slammed into him.

"Be it as you wish," Chan relented and everyone but Kari looked surprised. I'd won.

"I will not use magic to compel you to action

again," he said. Some strange magic rippled through the room that assured my victory but made it somehow less sweet.

"However, Babat is now my squire and will take the lead on searching for the codex," he said nodding toward one of the ryders.

Everything about Babat was so completely ordinary that he was nearly impossible to describe. His medium build, medium brown hair, featureless face, and ordinary suit would allow him to go anywhere without being noticed. In fact, the only distinguishing characteristic was his nervousness. He wrung his hands and rubbed his fingers as if he was trying to knead some invisible piece of clay out of existence. He didn't look capable of saving my mom.

"I don't know who he is," I said nodding toward Babat, "but Kari and I have a deal. I promised her I would help her find the codex and she promised we'd get my mom back. I trust her. So if you want my help then Kari leads," I replied.

"Kari has given homage to me so whatever deal you think you might have with her is subject to my whim," he replied with a sly smile.

"Actually, you released me from that vow just a few minutes ago when you relieved me of my office, service, and obligations as squire," Kari replied.

Chan blanched at the retort. "And precisely how do propose to help him without the support of the Cyngor am Ryddid?"

Kari's face turned red with fury. "You would do well to remember that you are the master dragon slayer and not the Cyngor am Ryddid. The Cyngor am Ryddid is full of members who fight for liberty, not for you. I may not be your squire but I am still a member of the Cyngor am Ryddid and can do as I please," she said through clenched teeth.

"Precisely, as a member of the Cyngor am Ryddid you are obligated to not interfere with this operation. You are no longer assigned here and have no resources with which to help the boy if you remain. Thus, regardless of your desires, or his, there is no place for you here," he said dismissively.

" Actually, I'm pretty sure Kari has sworn to protect JJ," Nikki said. The whole room turned to look at her. "I don't know what twisted rules you have in this group of yours, but it seems if you want JJ's help, then his sworn protector, who happens to be a member of your group, would have a right to stay." She smirked and gave a little nod toward Deacon Peter indicating the comments had been his idea.

"Is this true Kari?" Chan asked in disbelief.

"It is true," Kari said smiling at Nikki. "I am sworn on the fate of the Cyngor am Ryddid to protect the boy and return him safely to his mother."

Chan's shoulders sagged in defeat. "Very well, you may attend to the boy as you see fit but you will not have access to any of my resources," Chan relented. Dillon sat down in a chair and began rummaging through his bag. I briefly wondered if he had intended to try to follow Kari if she left.

"Agreed," said Kari turning to smile at me.

I was relieved that she was staying but still worried about my mom. I was not ready to smile yet.

"But Babat will still lead the search for the codex," Chan called over Kari's shoulder.

"And what about saving my mom?" I pressed.

"The dragon is usually very discreet and only uses Inicma when the utmost discretion and cunning are required. Considering the public scene they have created, the contents of that codex must be of paramount importance. Since Inicma has offered to trade your mother for the codex I would say that obtaining the codex should be your first priority. Once we have it we can determine why it is so important and how it can be best used to bring about the demise of the dragon," he replied so smoothly he sounded like a used car salesman.

"I didn't hear how that would save my mom." I said, distrusting this answer.

"Understand this," Chan said. I gritted my teeth at his condescending tone. "The only way they will let her live is if I've defeated the dragon. I'm the chosen one and I need that codex to finish planning my assault on the dragon's lair. If you get me the critical information that codex contains I promise I will do my best to free her as I fulfill my destiny to slay the dragon."

The way he proclaimed himself as the only hope to save my mom made me seethe. I wished I was bigger so I could beat some sense into him. He made no pretense of willingness to trade the codex for my mom. He was so wrapped up in pursuing his destiny I knew I couldn't trust him to worry about my mom's safety. I'd seen Inicma kill without thought and knew he would not hesitate to kill my mom. I considered arguing with him but figured I might need his resources to get the codex. I had once heard it said "the enemy of my enemy is my friend" so for the time being Chan and Babat were my friends.

"Alright," I said nodding to Chan. There was a

strange sensation, like an unseen connection had just been established between me and Chan. Kari sighed and I remembered how seriously she and Chan had taken her promise to my mom and realized I had just entered into some sort of magical contract. Chan grinned at me, pleased that he had exploited my naivety.

"So let's get started," Babat said cheerfully. His rich deep voice rolled from him like thunder. It was so completely contrary to his nondescript appearance it startled me. I didn't know how to respond, or what getting started involved.

"I think we would all be more comfortable if JJ showered and changed first," said Kari shying away from me as if I was a rancid piece of meat. It had been too long since I showered and changed my clothes. Even Dillon looked better than I did. "And he may need a little personal time to sort out how to best go after the codex," she said. She winked at me so Babat couldn't see, then glanced quickly at Deacon Peter.

Babat's mouth opened and closed like he wanted to say something but couldn't think what it was. He wrung his hands more vigorously as if he was trying to squeeze the words from them.

"I quite agree" said Deacon Peter. "I will show you where some clothes are" he said, heading for the room I had slept in.

"And I think we need to find a way to disguise JJ since there is a city wide man hunt on for him. So I'll go down to the theater to pick up some things to help with that," said Nikki.

"And I am checking the police and news reports to make sure we are not only safe here but will also know how to avoid them when we set out," Dillon added, typing away on his laptop.

"And I think I will go with Nikki, just in case." said Kari.

Babat's mouth opened and closed a few more times. Nikki and Kari were half way out the door and I was already at the door to the bedroom when his rich voice rolled down the hall. "Yes, of course. JJ, you clean up. Nikki and Kari go get supplies and you...do whatever it was you said," he said as if he was actually giving directions. I chuckled as Deacon Peter closed the door behind me.

"That was a terrible risk you took challenging Chan like that," he said as he moved toward the walk-in closet.

"Was it?" Of all the things that had just happened I thought that was one of the least significant.

"Certainly, commanding another person to do something when you have no right to do so is a devilishly tricky business," he said as he pulled some khakis off the hook that looked too big even for Chan. "If you fail to command someone you become less likely to succeed in the future and more susceptible to any magic they may direct at you. I suspect that is why you were able to beat him, because he had failed to control you." he continued while selecting an enormous blue button up shirt, and a very small tweed jacket.

"But Kari said people use that type of magic all the time even when they don't know they are using it." I countered.

"It's very common, but I have found that compelling people to do something is always fraught with danger. It is better to teach what is right and true." he said as he pulled out a pair of clown sized loafers and a tiny bundle of socks. "Once they understand the truth, most people will decide to take the right course of action. So you don't need to demand anything of them, you can simply ask them to do what they already know and want to do. Of course there are those who still make the mistake of choosing poorly," he said as he laid the clothes out on the bed.

"You're kidding right?" I said looking at the clothes. "Even if those would fit I'm not going to dress like some adventure movie archeology professor."

"If you were looking for a crazed criminal teenager in Manhattan would you expect him to be wearing a nice shirt and jacket?" he asked.

"Probably not, but that doesn't change the fact that they won't fit me."

"These are enchanted clothes the same way Kari and Chan's are enchanted. They always fit the wearer perfectly and never show any bulges or bumps of items concealed beneath them."

"You mean like a sword," I said filling in the information he was implying.

"Yes, like a sword, or small book," he said raising his eyebrow.

It took a moment before I realized he was talking about hiding the codex under the jacket. "Alright," I agreed.

"See, I just taught you the truth and you made the right decision without me having to use any compulsory magic," he said cheerfully. Then he leaned forward and in a whisper said, "And I am the only person on earth who could really try it because I am the only one who knows your real name."

"I doubt that very highly," I said remembering the text on the kamisan.

He smiled at me and then whispered, "When I recorded your name at your birth I added another name no one else knows; not even your mother. It's time I told you that your true name is Meikleham Emmanuel Jefferson Jones." He smiled as if he had just given me a great gift.

"I know," I replied.

He blinked in disbelief. "How could you possibly know that?"

"Because that is the name on the kamisan," I said pulling it from my front pocket and showing it to him.

"Your father truly was a cleverer sorcerer than I had imagined possible. To me it appears only as 'private'," he said.

I looked at the curious envelope. "Really?" I said pointing to the name on the envelope. "You don't see Meik...."

"Don't say it," he cut me off quickly. "Never say it again. I know of no way your father could have known what I was going to name you but if anyone finds out your true name you will be in even more danger." He glanced at the door. "We have been in here too long. Take your shower. But after you have finished leave the water running and open the kamisan. I would recommend sitting on the bed or at the desk."

I tried to ask him another question but he raised his hand and said, "We have no more time for questions. They'll start to get suspicious." I wrinkled my forehead in confusion. He noticed and said, "I'm not exactly their favorite person. We can talk later."

"Thanks Deacon Peter" I said as he headed for the door. I was surprised at how much I trusted and liked the man I had always thought so odd.

"Please call me Pete," he said, quickly stepping out of the room.

I did as I was instructed. I always did my best thinking in the shower. The warm rhythmic flow of the water was like a lullaby that drowned out my confused, unorganized thoughts. I leaned against the shower wall with my eyes closed and thought of my mom in some squalid prison suffering in ways I didn't want to consider. I set myself to saving her. No matter the cost I would save her. I would save her, or I would die trying. I tore myself away from the serenity of the shower and left the water running with its inviting drone.

Wrapped in a towel, I sat on the bed, and opened the kamisan.

7

The moment I grasped the flap of the envelope the color vanished from the room. I dropped the kamisan in horror. The room looked like a gray newspaper picture that was going out of focus. It faded until the picture became a solid hazy gray around the edge of the bed. As the rest of the room faded, the bed grew in clarity. It now looked like someone had drawn it with a black pen on a brilliant white piece of paper.

I looked for the envelope but it was no longer there. Instead there was a wide rectangle that looked like someone had drawn a very clever three dimensional picture of the top of a foot locker using the same black pen and white paper that had been used to draw the bed. The room beyond the bed became a depthless black abyss.

I tentatively touched the three dimensional cover. It lifted opened like a normal foot locker. The lid lay back on the bed in front of me revealing a great variety of unusual items stored within it, again, drawn in the same black pen. In fact the only thing that was not a black line drawing was me.

"How marvelous," a cheery voice said.

A man stood on the open lid of the foot locker. It

was only a line drawing but his eyes gleamed as they peered through the space between his long hair and the bushy beard that clearly hid a smile. He wasn't very tall but was broad shouldered with a generous belly. The suit and tie he wore would have made me think he was a goon if he weren't a drawing.

"I had rather hoped your mother would be clever enough to keep you safe," he continued. "Apparently, I was not clever enough to keep myself alive," he said with a sad edge. "But, at least I was able to keep that codex out of their hands."

"Who are you?" I asked, but the man just kept talking and I realized this was just a recorded message that I was not meant to interact with.

"All the same, I am thrilled that I had a son and that he lived to get this message."

My heart thumped in my chest. My mom had never shown me any pictures of him, or had even been willing to talk about him before last night. Now he was talking to me.

"So, let me answer your question about what's going on with this funky letter." He stooped down, winked at me and said "bet that was your most burning question huh?" Actually, my most burning questions were about how I could get my hands on the codex and trade it for my mom but the recorded message continued.

"Well this is a device of my own creation," He said spread his hands like he was modeling the kamisan. "Well, alright it is an improved modification of a kamisan device that is sometimes used in magical circles for communication," he said, waving his hands dismissively.

"These," he said gesturing to the items in the bottom of the foot locker, "are items I thought you might find useful. To take one, simply lift it out of the chest. You can always put something back in the chest later, but make sure you always take at least one item with you."

The image flickered like someone had changed the channel. He was no longer cheerful but looked bored as he monotoned, "To leave the kamisan, simply close the chest. To get back in, touch the kamisan with an item previously removed from it."

The image flickered again. This time he was intensely serious. "I encourage you to hide the items you take from here carefully to prevent someone else from accessing the treasures I have left for you. Since this is your first time opening the kamisan I will point out the items that will help you retrieve the codex. This is the only time I can give this message because it is the only time I will know for certain that only you are receiving it." He stooped to point to one of several keys hanging on hooks on the side of the chest. "This key will clear the bull so you can retrieve the codex and that key" he said pointing to another, "will open the codex. Since there are so many goons and tourists around the codex during the day I would recommend retrieving it at night...probably a weeknight. You should wear some protection when you do, so, I left you the best armor possible," he pointed to what looked like pajamas for an action figure. "And a few weapons," he gestured to the back of the chest where tiny doll sized swords of varying sizes, an axe, and bow and quiver hung neatly. "The rest are assorted books you should find useful in learning magic, a few rare potion ingredients, and a few family heirlooms and keepsakes that may prove useful." he said gesturing broadly to the piles of assorted items in the bottom of the chest. "Oh yeah, if that rascal Pete has done his job, tell him to take a cold shower with that," he said with a wide smile pointing to a scrub brush in the bottom of the foot looker.

The image flickered again and he looked sad. "Remember that the heart of any beast, man, dwarf, or dragon is the key to its undoing. Those with enough love in their hearts to fight for the life, liberty, and happiness of others will have the courage to bring about the eventual downfall of the dragon. That is how it has always been and how it will always be." He paused. His bushy beard shook as if his chin were quivering. He looked down as if ashamed. Then he looked back up and said, "Please tell Sam that is why I did this...because I love her." and the image was gone.

My chest was tight and my eyes watered. I held back the tears. I wished I could have talked with him. He had all the attributes of a goon except for the fact that he loved my mom. I tried to imagine the life I would have had if it weren't for the dragon? I would have grown up in the suburbs with my parents. He would have taught me how to be a man. I wouldn't have had to try to figure out so many things by watching strangers. We could have traveled around the country on family vacations instead of being stuck in one place. I yearned for the family I hadn't known.

I don't know how long I sat staring absently at the contents of the chest thinking about what might have been, but eventually the commitment I made to rescue my mother overcame my self-pity.

I reached into the chest to grab the first key, but

paused as the color drain drained from hand until only an outline remained. I saw my hand touch the image of the key, but felt nothing. As I lifted it from the chest, the key's black edges faded into shadow. The center dissolved from white to a rich brown until the cool weight of the brass key rested in my hand, which had returned to its normal appearance. I set the key on the bed and it kept its color.

Taking my father's advice, I next reached for the largest sword in the box. Once again, my hand turned into a black line drawing and I had to concentrate on grabbing the tiny sword without being able to feel it. When I lifted it out of the chest, the sword not only began regained its color but also began to grow. The hilt was quickly larger than the original image of the sword. I reached as high as I could but from my seated position on the bed my arm was not long enough to maneuver the sword from the chest. I decided there was no way someone who had never touched a sword could handle such weapon and replaced it on its hooks.

I expected the armor to be some type of metal but was surprised when the material was thinner and lighter than newspaper, and smoother than satin. I was so excited that I stood on the bed and put it on without closing the kamisan. The cloth instantly stretched and shrunk so that it conformed to my body like a perfectly tailored custom wet suit. The tan tones shimmered until they matched my skin tone so perfectly it was almost impossible to see the edge of the armor at my ankles and wrists. It stretched so perfectly as I moved, it was almost as though it wasn't there. I wondered how anything so thin and light could provide any protection. As I ran my hands over the smooth surface of the armor my fingers found a small hidden pocket at the waist. I checked the rest of the armor and found a scabbard inside the left calf.

I pulled the smallest dagger from the kamisan. It fit the scabbard perfectly.

I reached for another sword and thought the ax next to it shuddered. I wondered if I had been in this strange black and white drawing for too long. The sharp contrast between the black lines and white paper was uncomfortable and I was sure Chan would be wondering why I had spent so much time in the shower. I needed one more item that would let me get back into the kamisan without pulling out a weapon so I grabbed the first normal looking item I saw. What looked like an unassuming watch, turned out to be a beautiful stainless steel diver's watch with a forest green face. The time looked right but the second hand was broken and stuck on the ten. Still, it had been my fathers and would easily let me back into the kamisan if needed.

I closed the lid of the chest and watched as it slowly shrank and yellowed ever so slightly. The room reappeared beyond the edge of the bed; gray shapes appearing first and then slowly filling with color. I felt like Dorothy opening the door to the Land of Oz after a life in Kansas. The colors seemed brilliant and rich. Even the dark shadows under the furniture seemed brighter compared to the harsh edges of the line art world I had just left. I felt a little dizzy and it took several minutes before I could get up and turn off the shower.

I put the kamisan back in its plastic bag, tucked it into the small pocket in the armor and changed into my new clothes, which really did fit perfectly.

Anxious to share what I had learned with my friends I rushed to the living area where Pete was watching Dillon perform what looked like open heart surgery on a laptop.

Babat stood by the table Chan had previously used. "I was beginning to think you'd drowned in the shower." His low booming laugh rolled through the room. The five ryders at the table laughed courteously.

"I've always found the shower a wonderful place to think," said Pete.

"Me too," I said dropping into an arm chair with a smile.

"So, let's open the kamisan and see what we can do to get the codex," Babat said as he crossed the room, completely oblivious to our comments.

My stomach churned at the thought of this stranger hearing my father profess his love for my mom and rummaging through the items he'd left for me. I looked at Pete hoping for some help. He seemed to see my unspoken fears.

"Now, Babat," Pete began in a patronizing tone, "it seems to me the last time someone tried to get around one of Barry's protective enchantments we found him so covered in dried chocolate pudding that he was stuck to the ground and we were barely able to save him from the colony of army ants growing between his legs."

Dillon and I smiled when Babat stopped with a horrified look on his face. "I thought Liz did that," he said with a confused look on his face. I turned away from Babat and put a hand to my mouth to keep from bursting out in laughter as I imagined Babat in such a predicament.

"Certainly not, Barry set that up for her," said Pete.

Babat's face turned red. He rubbed his hands as if the rubbing could erase the memory. His mouth opened and shut without a sound leaving his lips.

Just then, the door to the suite opened. Babat and the ryders reached for their weapons. Kari and Nikki awkwardly pulled a large crate into the room laughing as if they had just overheard our conversation. They froze in the entryway when they noticed everyone staring at them.

"What's going on?" Nikki asked hesitantly.

After a moment's silence, Pete gave an impressively diplomatic answer, "Babat, was just inquiring about the kamisan."

"Great, so where should we start looking?" Kari asked me over her shoulder as she and Nikki dragged the crate out of the doorway.

I took a deep breath. "Well I'm not—"

"We haven't opened the kamisan yet so we don't know," Babat interrupted as he claimed the other arm chair.

Pete reached across the coffee table and patted him on the knee. "Given that JJ was about to tell us where the codex is I think maybe he has already opened the kamisan?" he said the way a kindergarten teacher would to an upset student.

Babat's mouth started to soundlessly move again and Pete sat back on the couch.

"Sometimes I think this guy could use a good voice over artist," Dillon said and I couldn't help but chuckle.

"Look here ..." Babat rumbled, wagging his finger at Dillon. But he couldn't come up with anything else to say.

"I can wag my finger," Dillon finished the sentence in his best Babat impression and in time with the opening and closing of Babat's mouth.

Even the men standing by the table chuckled until Babat silenced them with a steely gaze.

"Listen," Kari said, "Chan has given this assignment to Babat so you need to be nice." She fixed Dillon with a penetrating stare that quickly silenced us all. "JJ, you were about to explain?" she said smiling at me.

I turned to Babat and tried to explain, "I opened it but the codex wasn't there." He looked disappointed. "But I did get this key," I said pulling it out of my pocket and holding it up for them to see.

"Is it safe to say that you had to be the person to retrieve that key?" asked Pete before Babat could get any words to come out of his mouth.

I choose my words carefully so Babat wouldn't get upset. "Yes, the message could only have been received by me and could be delivered only once."

Babat stopped looking like he was about to scold me and returned to wringing his hands.

"Can you repeat for us exactly what the message was?" Kari asked.

I knew I wouldn't get it word for word so shook my head. "It said we should retrieve it on a weeknight because there are lots of goons and tourists around it in the day and it said this key would clear things up."

They all looked at each other searching for answers.

"Well that's not particularly helpful," said Babat. "Virtually all of downtown Manhattan is full of goons and tourists on any given day."

"Did the message say anything else," asked Kari.

I wracked my brain trying to remember what the strange line drawing of my father had said. After dwelling on the love he expressed for my mom and wondering if one of the unexplored books held the critical clues, I remembered more details.

"It said we should bring weapons and armor," I added.

"Well that's even less helpful," said Babat tossing his hands in the air in frustration. He stood up and started to pace back and forth across the room.

"I'm curious about that key." said Pete. "Did he really say it would clear things up?"

"Actually, I believe he said it would clear the bull." I said.

Pete and Kari looked at each other.

"You don't think he would...?" said Pete.

"I understand he was very unpredictable," said Kari.

"What?" Babat, Nikki, and I said at the same time.

"On October 19th 1987," began Pete and I felt like I was sitting in history class again, "the global stock markets crashed. It was the largest single day loss in history so they call it Black Monday. The dragon added many corporations to his hoard that day and many people were ruined. Some blamed the crash on automated trading but no reason for the international crash was ever officially determined. Many-"

"Please just tell us what this has to do with codex," interrupted Nikki as she came over and sat on the arm of my chair. "I had enough history in High School to last me until history is what I reminisce about." I smiled. Once again Nikki was coming to my rescue.

Pete smiled at her. "As I was about to say, many believe Black Monday was orchestrated by none other than Bewirken Managito." The name stung in my ears. Pete smiled. "That's right, your father."

I tried to wrap my brain around the fun loving image of my father in the kamisan causing such mayhem. "My father caused a global stock market crash?"

"Yep, before good old Barry met your mother he was the dragon's prized inventor and magician. Some say his orchestration of Black Monday was what catapulted him to the top of the dragon's organization."

"I thought Inicma was the top of the dragon's organization," Dillon said.

"He is now," replied Pete.

The muscles in my arms and back tensed as I rejected the thought of my father acting like Inicma. I leaned forward, about to defend him, but Nikki's hand on my shoulder caused me to pause. "I still don't understand how that helps us find the codex," she said. A calm confidence seemed to radiate through me from her gentle touch and I quickly relaxed.

Pete forced a smile at her, "Well, a couple years after Black Monday an artist spent a great deal of his own money creating a piece that celebrated the strength of the American people in recovering from the crash. Without permission, he installed this rather large sculpture right outside the stock exchange. It rather infuriated the dragon so he had the city remove it. Of course by that time Barry had met and was quite taken with your mother," Pete said looking at me. "She was quite fond of the statue and as a gift to her, your father asked that the dragon restore the sculpture. Of course Barry positioned it as a monument to his success on Black Monday. The Dragon agreed but had it installed a couple blocks from Wall Street in Bowling Green Park."

"The Wall Street Bull is a monument to his father?" Dillon exclaimed in disbelief. He quickly massaged the keyboard next to the dissected laptop with violent key strokes.

The full weight of this news still hadn't hit me until Pete said, "No, that was the lie Barry told the dragon. The bull remains a tribute to the strength and resilience of the American people. Bringing back the bull was a gift to show JJ's mother he was willing to shift his allegiance from the dragon to the fight for freedom.

"It wasn't a gift to show her his allegiance," I said as I remembered the emotion in my father's voice. "It was a gift to show her his love." How powerful would an emotion have to be for someone like Inicma to give up his near limitless power? There could be no doubt. My father loved my mom.

"So he hid the codex where? Under the bull? Near the bull?" asked Nikki.

A long awkward silence fell across the room while everyone looked at each other for answers. "I think you should take the key to the bull and find out," Pete finally said to me.

"So when do we leave?" said Nikki and Dillon simultaneously.

Babat was confused. He looked between Nikki and Dillon. "It doesn't matter when we leave because you two aren't coming." Nikki and Dillon looked at each other like they had been scandalized. "You're transferring to a safe house within the hour," finished Babat.

"Look man, these guys trashed my home and busted up my gear; including one of my favorite laptops." Dillon said, standing to face Babat.

"Technically, you destroyed your laptop," Kari said. Dillon reeled around to face her, but she just smiled at him. "And thank you," she continued. Dillon blushed and quickly sat down to continue pummeling his keyboard.

"I have selected my team," Babat said gesturing to the sullen group of men he had been talking with. "We will take the key to the bull and see what happens."

Kari shifted her weight uneasily. "And who is going to run ops and communications for you?" she asked hesitantly.

"I am using Chan's team as is my right as Squire. You can wait at the safe house with JJ and his friends," he replied.

Dillon hit a key on his keyboard with a particularly loud pop and the TV in the room clicked on. A map of the roads in the financial district appeared in the center of the screen. Live feeds from traffic and security cameras filled the edges of the screen and lines connected them to their location on the central map. "With the way traffic is down there, if things go wrong it'll be a bit like a fish caught in a fiendishly grand net," he said.

I shook my head. Dillon had gone from random outbursts to waxing rhapsodic. His fingers flew over the keyboard again and the map grew until a three dimensional rendering of the subway and service tunnels under that part of Manhattan crowded out the video feeds. " 'Twill require a feat of pure genius if you ask me," he said, imitating Kari's accent.

Babat's mouth fell open and he stopped rubbing his hands. The mousey looking man who had been working with Babat whistled in appreciation. "Where did you get that?" he asked in wonder.

Dillon didn't get a chance to answer.

"Very well, you may help my team prepare. However, after that is finished you will have to go to the safe house with JJ," Babat said to Dillon

"Congratulations," Kari said, extending her hand toward Dillon. His jaw dropped and his eyes went wide as he gave her his hand. She gave it a firm shake and quickly released it.

"Given the protections Barry has used before," Pete mused, "JJ may be the only one who can use the key." Babat looked at him with a start. "I wonder if the dragon would notice if a full team examined the bull." Pete paused for a moment. Babat resumed rubbing his hands and I wondered if there was any part of them that wasn't heavily calloused. "Oh well, I'm sure you've thought through how a second trip would work if JJ is needed," he said to Babat. I smiled at the way Pete had introduced Babat to truths he hadn't previously considered.

Babat kneaded his knuckles while looking around the room as if searching for an acceptable answer. "Perhaps you are right, we will have to bring JJ with us," he admitted. He turned to look at Kari, "but I am under strict orders that you are to be given no resources. In fact, you will need to remove your things from my room. I am already bending my orders by allowing you to accompany Nikki to the safe house." I tensed at Chan's orders to exclude Kari. Nikki patted my shoulder reassuringly.

"Actually, since I have been relieved of my duties as Squire I made a few calls and have decided to claim my rightful place on the board of the Cyngor am Ryddid." There was an audible gasp from Babat and the ryders as they stared at her in wonder. "Since I have inducted Nikki into the order you will not need to look after her. I will be back before you leave this evening to—"

"I never said we were going tonight," Babat interrupted at the same time I said, "You did what to her?"

"We'll talk about it later," Nikki said to me like she didn't want anyone else to hear her.

"Of course you are going tonight," Kari said to Babat, ignoring me and Nikki. "The message said to go on a weeknight. Since today is Thursday and I know Chan will not wait until Monday you must be going tonight. Shall I assume you will be taking a small and discrete team at around 11:30?" Kari replied in an authoritative but friendly tone.

Babat stopped rubbing his hands and squeezed them together so tightly I thought he might crush them. He was dumbfounded by the way she had not only taken control of the conversation but had also framed their plans. Dazed, he nodded his agreement.

"Very well, I will collect my things and be out of your way. I will be back at ten to make sure all necessary arrangments have been made for JJ's safety." She paused and looked at Dillon like she was sizing up a new car. "And you can cancel your safe house. I believe Dillon will prove useful in the work Nikki and I will be doing."

Dillon looked like the cheshire cat.

"Yes, I will collect Dillon at that time as well. Good luck planning your escape from the fiendishly grand net?" Kari said.

She and Nikki swept from the room leaving us all speechless. Only the sound of Dillon's keyboard disturbed the silence.

8

It was just after midnight. I sat in the back seat of a Lincoln Town Car heading down Broadway toward the Wall Street Bull. Babat sat next to me in the back of the car that looked just like any other used for executive car services in New York. Brad, one of Babat's men who appeared far too dwarvish for my tastes, was living up to Kari's praise as a driver. He navigated the traffic as skillfully as any New York cabbie.

As promised, Kari and Nikki had come to pick up Dillon at ten. Despite my objections they'd wasted no time applying makeup and hair coloring that made me appear old enough to not look ridiculous in my tweed jacket and khaki pants. It had been impossible to tell if Nikki was trying to make me feel better or was just making fun of me when she pretended to swoon at my new appearance.

Dillon had replaced the communications earpiece Babat had given me with one he said Kari had slipped him during their brief hand shake. I wasn't sure if it was how awkward the earpiece felt or the effects of listening to Dillon argue with Babat's team all afternoon that had caused my pounding headache. Dillon had laid out what felt like every possible detail of the streets around the bull; the one way streets, what their traffic patterns were, and how the most obvious escape routes were both easily surveilled and shut down. After much shouting and arguing he and Brad had convinced Babat that five cars would both clog the escape routes and make us more likely to be spotted. In the end they decided to send just one other car; the yellow cab with two passengers that was currently following us.

"Look to your left," Dillon startled me as his voice rang in my earpiece, I snapped my head to look out the window and caught a glimpse of Nikki smiling at me from the passenger seat of the white van that sped past us and cut off Brad's intended lane change. I felt a little guilty that Dillon and Nikki were riding into danger but the increasing unease I had been feeling as we approached the bull melted away as I realized Kari was nearby and ready to help.

"What's wrong?" Babat asked at my sudden movement. Brad grumbled about stupid New York drivers as he cut off the next car.

"I just realized that we had reached Liberty Street. Dillon said that was the point of no return?" I quickly lied as I noticed the street sign.

"Actually, I believe he said 'Broadway becomes a veritable gauntlet of death' south of here," Brad said, quoting Dillon exactly.

My muscles tensed and the pounding of my head echoed in my ears as we slowly drove into the heart of the financial district. I looked out the window at the slender streets that had been converted to pedestrian walkways. The enormous buildings formed man made canyons so deep and narrow that sunlight only touched the streets for a few minutes at mid-day. This time of night on a Thursday those canyons, which would be bustling with businessmen, financiers, and goons during the day, were completely empty.

"Is it true that everyone on Wall Street is a goon?" I asked Babat, hoping for an answer that would ease my fears.

"Not in the sense that they know they are working for the dragon," he replied. "Most are just trying to live a comfortable life and are completely oblivious to the fact that they are cogs of a machine that is slowly bleeding this country dry," he said in a distant, contemplative voice.

"We're here," said Brad. I suddenly had butterflies in my stomach. It was worse than having to give an oral report in class.

Whitehall street forks to the east from Broadway, forming a narrow wedge between the two streets. Bowling Green Park covers the entire wedge with a broad fountain filling the middle of the park and the bull standing on the narrow northern point.

Brad pulled to the curb on Broadway in a loading zone immediately across from the bull. Babat got out of the car on the curb side. I got out on the road side, searching the street for the white van. It was parked four cars in front of Brad.

Some people feel claustrophobic in a city and pine for wide open spaces. Until that moment, I had never experienced that feeling in New York. The tall stone building that hid the canyons of Wall Street loomed like an enormous tidal wave over the statue of the bull. I felt as if it would come crashing down upon us at any moment, destroying us in a cloud of dust.

I looked around to see if anyone was watching us

or might be a threat but only found the yellow taxi stopped on the far side of the street before reaching the intersection. That was the main purpose of the second car; it provided us with an option to use Broadway or Whitehall to escape.

"Well," said Babat, who had appeared at my elbow. "Clear the bull," he directed with a slightly condescending tone.

I had seen the bull many times in my visits around the city and even had a picture in front of it when I was on a seventh grade field trip. It is taller than a basketball hoop and half again as long as it is tall. It was only as I approached the bull that it occur to me that I had never seen or heard of there being a keyhole in it. I pulled the key from my pocket and walked around the statue looking for any opening that might fit the key.

"Well?" Babat said in an annoyed tone as he walked around the bull. His head jerked from side to side like he was at a tennis match. His paranoia was contagious.

"I don't see any key holes," I replied as I ran my hand over the side of the bull hoping to feel some invisible opening.

"Of course there aren't any key holes. Just start sticking the key anywhere you think it might fit," Babat replied.

The only place that was remotely close to a hole in the bull was the mouth. I figured if it was magic maybe I should just feed it the key. So I walked to the front of the bull and slipped the key into its mouth. As the key touched the bull, a faint click echoed from the belly of the beast but nothing else happened. I withdrew the key and heard the same faint click. Then I remembered something else my father had said, "Remember that the heart of any beast, man, dwarf, or dragon is the key to its undoing."

I quickly crawled under the bull.

"What are you doing?" Babat hissed. "People are staring at you."

"The heart is the key" I replied, touching the key to the bull where I guessed its heart would be. A small slot clicked open just a few inches from the key. I slid the key along the bull and into the slot. It fit perfectly.

As the key slid to a stop it vanished and the bottom of the bull faded until it was as clear as glass. A stainless steel briefcase hovered in the middle of the bull's chest. The perfectly polished handle, hinges and a protruding lock gleamed compared to the dull gray texture of the rest of the case.

I tested the stomach of the bull. My hand passed through it like it was air. I grabbed the case and pulled it toward me. It floated downward like a leaf on the breeze. The transparent portions of the bull regained their color as the case passed until the bull was back to normal and the case dropped on my chest. It was heavier than I'd expected.

"Goons incoming," Dillon's voice rang in my earpiece.

"Get off this frequency," Babat barked. A minivan jumped the curb. Babat dove away, narrowly avoiding being crushed.

The van screeched to a stop. It blocked my exit from under the bull in that direction. The bull deftly shifted its stance from charging left to charging right. The motion was quick and silent, until it smashed the side of the mini-van. Glass tinkled across the sidewalk.

The bull's chest heaved. It snorted. The quick burst echoed through the streets like a kettle drum.

I thought it would crush me, and tried to roll from under it. The case was too heavy. I ended up lying on top of it next to the bull.

"On my way," a new voice said in my earpiece. A ryder opened the back door of the yellow cab. The hair on my arms reacted to the magic a moment before the cab exploded. The blast hurled the ryder through the open door into the street.

The fireball clambered up the sides of the stone building, a column of roiling light. The black square of an SUV burst through the curtain of smoke that cloaked the street. It headed straight toward me without regard for the ryder sprawled in front of it.

"Come on kid!" Brad yelled. He flailed his arms, urging me into the back of the town car. His gravelly voice echoed as I heard it in my ear piece again.

I struggled to find my feet. My hands slipped on the smooth metal surface of the case. It fell heavily on my knee. I fell to the ground. I wasn't fast enough. The SUV was going to plow me into the pavement. "JJ!" Nikki's horrified scream rang in my earpiece.

I reflexively held the case in front of me and cringed in anticipation of the pain. The bull shifted his stance and lunged forward. The ringing of its hooves vanished in the earsplitting crunch of rending metal as the SUV slammed into it. The back of the SUV came off the ground. It stood on its front bumper, driving the bull's head to the ground. The bull's knees buckled. It staggered toward me, each step ringing like a bell as it struggled to regain its balance.

"Get out of there JJ," Kari calmly ordered in my earpiece. I found my feet and scrambled away from the bull. I threw myself toward the safety of Brad's waiting car, clutching the case to my chest. As I dove into the back seat of the town car I looked over my shoulder. The SUV fell back to the ground with a deafening crunch.

Brad slammed the door behind me and jumped into the front seat. I sat up to peer at the scene. The bull tossed its head from side to side trying to free its horns. It shook the SUV like a rag doll. Babat rounded the back of the bull, sprinting for the car. His enormous sword didn't hinder him, despite occupying both his hands. He was only a few feet from us when Brad locked the doors.

"What are you doing? Let him in!" I screamed. The car peeled away from the curb, clipping the car we had parked behind.

"Brad?!" exclaimed Babat. He effortlessly thrust his sword through the trunk of the car. He clung to the hilt as we sped down the street, dragging him behind us.

I turned from Babat's horrified face, intent on doing what I could to stop Brad. I didn't get the chance. Kari slammed the van into the side of the Town Car, sending me sprawling across the back seat. The car and van careened through the base of a light pole. The windows shattered. Glass rained down on my head as we slammed into the wrought iron fence around Bowling Green Park.

By the time I pulled myself off the floor of the back seat, Babat stood at Brad's door, his sword against Brad's throat. "Why?" he bellowed at Brad over the sound of the thrashing bull and SUV.

"Inicma took my wife and daughter. He said he'd kill 'em if I didn't do what they said," Brad groaned.

Babat began opening and closing his mouth without making a sound. I shook my head in disbelief. Given what I was doing to save my mom, I couldn't blame him.

"Then you are a traitor," Kari said as she calmly walked to Brad and roughly jerked out his earpiece. "And you know what happens to traitors?" She leaned so close to Brad's face that Babat had to withdraw his sword.

"Yes," Brad said and he seemed relieved.

"Good." she said, withdrawing from his face and plunging one of her blades into his chest. I turned my head in disgust only to see the point of her blade protruding through the back of Brad's seat.

I felt nauseous and wondered if I had misplaced my trust in Kari.

An earsplitting crunch came from the bull and all fell silent.

"Guys we gotta move if we want to get out of here alive. We've got police, fire, and swat on their way," I heard Dillon say in my ear piece.

"Which way?" Kari asked as I climbed out of the car, case in hand.

"Better go east or we'll be spotted." Dillon replied and this time I heard him without my ear piece as he trotted across the street, Nikki right behind him. All the color had drained from her face. She was nearly as pale as Kari.

I looked in the direction Dillon pointed. Across Bowling Green Park was the entrance to Beaver Street, and the canyons of Wall Street. I shivered. That was the maze of narrow streets Babat said the dragon controlled and Dillon said offered no easy escape.

The bull walked toward us, its horns bent at odd angles. The SUV and mini-van lay in crumpled heaps behind it, completely blocking the street. An even bigger shiver ran down my spine at the thought of trying to explain this mess to the police.

"We should use the subway," Babat said, pointing to the Bowling Green station entrance at the south end of the park. No one listened to him. We followed Dillon in the other direction, around the wrought iron fence that ringed Bowling Green Park and stood between us and Beaver Street.

We paused in front of the bull, which stared at us intently.

"Thank you," Nikki said with a surprisingly reverent tone of gratitude, nodding her head toward it.

"Yes, thank you," I said. Somehow the words were inadequate. The same words from me sounded hollow compared to Nikki.

It bent its front leg and lowered its head in a graceful bow. The horns no longer looked disfigured.

A strange shadow from the flickering flames of the cars flashed against one of the buildings. A human sized black bird with the head neck and shoulders of a woman burst through the smoke. The creature's face was calm, cold, and calculating; like the vice principal at school. Its penetrating stare sent a chill through me so startling that I could only watch as one claw shredded the bull's back like tissue paper. The other claw snatched the case from my grasp.

Kari moved so fast I didn't realize she had pounced on the wing of the creature until they were spinning through the air together. They landed in the fountain at the center of Bowling Green Park as we watched in horror.

"It's a harpy. Get out of here," Babat ordered as he ran to help Kari.

Dillon and Nikki stood in shock as Kari and the creature emerged from the fountain's waters. Kari's twin blades were almost invisible. She blocked the harpy's talons with blinding speed before spinning to attack. But the creature deftly dodged the attack and slashed at her again.

Nikki stood frozen, horror on her face as she stared at the creature.

Dillon took a hesitant step toward them. Even if Dillon had a stack of laptops in his funny looking backpack, I didn't think they would be effective weapons against this thing.

I grabbed his arm. "You can't help her that way. Take Nikki," I said. "We'll catch up."

He looked at me like I had just woken him from a dream. The resolve to act washed across his face. He nodded once, grabbed Nikki by the arm, and pulled toward Beaver Street. She stumbled after him without complaint, transfixed by the battle.

I could only watch Kari retreat from the fury of the harpy while I fumbled with my pant leg, trying to extract my dagger from its sheath. It certainly was not an easily accessible place to keep my weapon. I resolved to fix that in the future.

Behind me, the bull scraped across the cobblestones. The open gash in the wounded beast twisting as it dragged itself toward its original place, away from the battle.

By the time I started toward the fight, dagger in hand, Babat had joined the fight. The difference was amazing. Kari was a whirling dervish, always spinning and slashing with her dual blades. Babat stood like a statue as he wielded the enormous sword with two hands. You could hardly tell he was moving. He hovered around the harpy quickly flicking his wrists to block or strike at the creature.

"JJ, grab the codex and go," he yelled pointing into the water with one hand as I approached.

"He will not live long enough to touch it," hissed the creature. She lunged in my direction. Kari and Babat skillfully shifted to block its way. The creature took advantage of the change in position. She stepped back, opened her wings and quickly took flight. Kari's twirling slash narrowly missed. The harpy blocked Babat's slash with its talons as it soared over them.

I could see the codex in the water. I sprang over the edge of the fountain but the creature was right on top of me. I held up my dagger and instinctively lifted my left hand to guard my face. My father's watch sprang into a beautiful round weightless shield as the harpy slashed at my head.

The harpy roared in frustration as its talons thrashed against the shield. The force drove me to one knee. The creature wheeled in the air and screamed as her talons slashed across the back of my shoulder, hurling me face first into the fountain.

The corner of the codex pressed hard into my chest. I wrapped my arms around it, barely realizing that the shield had disappeared as quickly as it had appeared.

When I surfaced, Kari and Babat stood over me, fending off the creature's attacks. Through the wrought iron fence, I saw Dillon and Nikki sheltering in the shadows of Beaver St. Nikki rooted through her backpack. Dillon waved a long piece of metal beckoning us toward him with one hand and spoke frantically into a mouth piece held to his lips with the other. I didn't hear anything in my ear piece.

"Ready?" said Babat.

I rolled over in the water about to ask what I was supposed to be ready for.

"Now!" said Kari. She and Babat dove to either side, leaving me face to face with the creature. I was about to die.

The creature pounced. The crack of gun fire split the air and the harpy stopped in mid-air. Blood sprang from its chest as it took flight in retreat. More gun fire, and the creature faltered as it fled. I searched for the source and found Nikki firing the type of gun I had only seen in movies. She looked as comfortable with it as any action hero.

I clutched the codex to my chest as Kari and Babat lifted me from the water and ran toward Nikki. My feet hardly touched the ground. As they vaulted over the wrought iron fence at the edge of the park I looked up the street toward where the creature had fled. The bull had resumed its original pose. The street lights glistened off the strip of shiny new metal that replaced the open gash, a battle scar from the harpy.

A man in a black suit staggered around the back of the bull. It was Inicma. He leveled his pistol at us.

"Watch out" I yelled, pulling Kari and Babat together so we tumbled to the ground as Inicma opened fire. The bullets whistled over our heads.

Nikki leaned around the corner and took aim. She

didn't get a chance to fire. The familiar clang of the bull rang once more. Inicma sailed into the air, propelled by the bull's kick.

We scrambled over to Dillon and Nikki, unconcerned with Inicma's fate.

"This way!" Dillon said. He turned and ran down the street. His fingers flicked the air as if he were popping keys on his keyboard. Moments later he turned right into the tiniest alley I had ever seen and stopped.

"Um, Dillon?" I asked as he slowly scanned the pavement around him.

Dillon put the piece of metal he held into a manhole cover, turned to Babat and said, "Would you do the honors."

Babat quickly lifted the heavy round cover from the manhole and we disappeared into the labyrinth beneath Manhattan.

9

Kari was incredulous. "How is it that you are still alive," she asked me as Babat slid the manhole cover in place with a clang.

"I'm sorry, would you prefer I was dead like Brad?" I barked back at her.

"Shhh," Dillon hissed in the dark as he clicked on a tiny flashlight that was taped to the back of his forearm. It's glow barely cut through the dark. His fingers immediately began stroked the air like it was an invisible keyboard. The light danced around the dingy tunnel, revealing pipes, rats and bugs that matched the putrid smell.

"Brad will be fine, I had to make the wound impressive enough that they would not kill his family," she whispered. As soon as she said this, I remembered Brad's relieved reply to her and realized that was his agreement to be wounded to keep his family safe. "And no, I do not wish you were dead. I just do not know how that harpy did not tear you in two."

"First of all, learn to use contractions so you don't sound like such a stiff and secondly Shhh," Dillon whispered in annoyance. I smiled at how comfortable Dillon was becoming around Kari.

"I'm wearing some armor my father—" I began to whisper my explanation, but Dillon interrupted again.

"Look, everyone in the city is looking for us and I'm trying to find a way to get us all out of here alive. So if you wouldn't mind closing your yap for a while, I'd appreciate it," he scolded me. The irritation and stress in his voice hadn't finished echoing about the miserable tunnel before the wail of a siren surrounded us. We stood motionless until it faded in the distance.

Kari's gesture to Dillon to lead the way was almost indiscernible in the dim light of the flashlight.

We followed Dillon for the next two hours. After he reamed Nikki and Babat for asking questions we went most of the way in silence. He took us through storm drains, service tunnels, and one sewer tunnel. We crawled through the foulest muck on earth on our hands and knees. The stench overwhelmed us all. Even Babat threw up. The slop clung to our clothes and skin. With no clean place to wipe our hands, climbing ladders and forcing open rusted hatches became all the more difficult. When we passed close enough to a surface grate we welcomed the fresh air but cowered at the sounds of sirens and anxious discussions that inevitably filtered through the openings. Three times we hit dead ends which Dillon explained as old pipes or features that were no longer in the cities records. Everyone except Dillon was hopelessly lost when he had Kari pick the lock on an unusually normal looking door and we filed into an enormous, smooth concrete tunnel with a curved roof.

My legs felt like lead and my arms ached from carrying the codex but at the moment I was grateful to be in a dry, well lit tunnel that was tall enough to stand in and only smelled of car exhaust. It only took a few feet heading down hill for me to realize we must be in the Brooklyn Battery Tunnel that connects Southern Manhattan with the Carroll Gardens section of Brooklyn. With Dillon seeming in better spirits and the low rumble of cars beneath us I risked testing my voice. "Dillon, are we going to walk all the way to Brooklyn?" I asked sheepishly.

"Actually," he said cheerfully, "I figured we would stop at Governor's Island. I could use the fresh air and expect that even the harbor water is cleaner than we are. Maybe we can figure a way to get cleaned up enough to ride the 10:30 ferry."

"I thought that only ran on weekends," I replied.

"And today is Friday," he said smugly.

"I do not think we will get clean enough to avoid attention," Kari said, stamping her feet in an unsuccessful attempt to shake the muck from her pants.

"The earlier we stop the better as far as I'm concerned," moaned Nikki, who was shuffling through the tunnel next to me.

"That reminds me," I said. "What's up with you? First you become Kari's best friend and the next thing I know you're whipping out a gun?"

"Kari and I got to know each other this morning and have come to an agreement," Nikki said, as if that explained everything.

"Yes, I have become quite fond of Nikki," Kari chimed in.

"And Kari turned you into a sniper in an afternoon?" I asked in disbelief.

"Look, are you complaining that I saved your life?" she snapped at me. I hesitated a moment slowing my pace. Nikki never talked to anyone but Dillon that way. Well, except when she first met Kari.

"No, I'm not complaining at all." I tried to sound penitent. "It was amazing. Thank you," I added, realizing I had never properly thanked her. "It was just a surprise," I mumbled at my feet. I wanted to ask her where she got it and how she knew how to use it but didn't want to upset her again.

She looked at her feet. "I didn't want you to know," she said so softly I barely heard it over the hum of the cars.

"You didn't want me to know what?" I asked, trying to use the tender tone my mother used to show concern when I was in trouble.

"That my Dad is a criminal," she said to her shoes.

At first I didn't understand the last word. I had expected her to say "gun enthusiast." Her father being a criminal didn't mesh with the guy I knew. He was the one who had lined up the construction job for me over the summer. Then it hit me. How many construction owners made enough money to buy a penthouse?

I looked at her shirt and briefly wondered if she really was Nikki's evil twin. She searched my face with her big eyes. "Really, what type of crime?" I asked as if she had said her father was a doctor and I was asking what type of medicine he practiced. I didn't want to sound like I was passing judgment. After all, my father had caused a global economic crisis.

She smiled at me in a way that said "Thank you" and then looked back at her feet. "He's Ukrainian" she said hesitantly.

I stumbled over my feet.

I had always assumed the stories of a ruthless

Ukrainian crime syndicate in New York were only urban legend. From the way she talked, the stories were not only true but her father was a pretty high ranking member of the organization.

I realized she still hadn't answered my question. "So ... what?" I hesitated trying to find the right words. "Your father gave you your own gun or something?"

Nikki actually laughed but her eyes showed only sorrow as she switched from looking at the floor to looking at the ceiling, "Actually, he did. When I was twelve he gave me a little .22 Saturday night special and taught me how to shoot." She shook her head and I saw her eyes start to tear up. "He said he wanted me to be able to protect myself in case someone tried to hurt me to get to him."

"I'd say you've moved up from the little Saturday night special," I said, trying to make light of the situation.

"You don't understand" she bellowed. Tears streamed down her face. "I don't want any part of the criminal underworld. I want a nice, quiet life," she turned from me like she was looking at the far side of the tunnel. "With a nice guy" — she sniffed — "and a family"

"You will Nikki," I said, tucking the codex under one arm so I could pat her back in consolation. "We'll get you home and you won't have to deal with this madness anymore."

Kari glanced at Nikki with a look I couldn't decipher.

"Yeah, we better get her home or we'll have the whole Ukrainian mob after us too," Dillon joked.

"No," scolded Nikki. "Dad said he had to go to a

conference in Florida, which actually means he is getting a shipment tonight and won't be back until tomorrow afternoon." She looked at her watch. "Actually I guess I should say *this* afternoon. Anyway, I left a note saying I'd be at the beach with JJ all day so he'd only worry if I'm not home until tonight."

"Um, Nikki, my face is all over the news as part of a crime spree across New York. I don't think he is going to be too happy about you spending the day with me," I replied.

"Oh no!" she exclaimed, putting her hands over her mouth. "See, he likes you so I use you as an excuse every time I go do something normal."

"Why would he like me? I mean he even got me a construction job so I wouldn't have to go to college." My voice squeaked. I felt like I had just been given a death sentence for no particular reason.

Her jaw flexed and her face flushed. "I'll kill him for trying to get you into the family business," she snarled.

I thought of her taking aim at the harpy and wondered if she was serious about the death threat. "But, that doesn't answer my question. Why me?" I pressed

Her anger vanished. "Well, he has all my friends checked out and you came up squeaky clean." She looked like there might be more, but left it at that.

I figured her father would probably be less thrilled with me if he knew I'd gotten her involved in a battle with harpies, goons and an enchanted bull. And her answer didn't explain why he had arranged a job for me, particularly if it was actually a position in what Nikki called the family business. I didn't get to ask any more questions.

"Here we are" Dillon said as he motioned to a metal gate in the side of the tunnel. It was an elevator. I smiled. Any form of transportation that got me out of slogging through smelly tunnels was welcome.

"Our chariot awaits," said Dillon bowing and splaying his hands toward the door when it opened. The elevator brought us to an enormous building that was full of ducting and the whirr of fans.

"What is this place" I asked to no one in particular

"This is the ventilation building for the tunnel. We're just off Governor's Island." Dillon led us through the giant machines and out the solitary door. The cool fresh night air rushed across my face as I stepped through the door. I breathed deeply, clearing the chalky feeling the exhaust caused in my throat and dulling the sharp memory of the sewer.

The Manhattan skyline reflected in the water of New York harbor and was so bright it illuminated the entire scene. A concrete walkway stretched from the ventilation building to Governor's Island. Trees swayed in the cool breeze, beckoning us to come rest on the lawns they sheltered from the cloudless sky.

"I'll get us some transport," said Babat, reaching for his phone as we moved through the gate and on to the walkway.

"Don't call anyone." Dillon swatted the phone from Babat's hand. It bounced down the manmade pile of rocks the walkway had been built on; the cover and battery flying in different directions.

"What do you think you're doing you worthless piece of ..." Babat said grabbing the front of Dillon's shirt and lifting him halfway over the walkway railing.

Kari grabbed Babat's wrist and said, "Put him down Babat. He is the reason we escaped as cleanly as we did."

"Well, not exactly cleanly." Nikki held her hands out as if showing off her muck caked clothes.

Babat glared at Kari without putting Dillon down.

"And he's right. We can't call anyone." she said.

Babat let go of Dillon and turned to stand toe to toe with Kari. "And how do you propose we get off this rock if we don't call for transport? Wait for the tourist boat in the morning?" he sneered.

"Look, if Brad was a traitor then all phone numbers and safe houses are known to the dragon," she replied without backing down. Babat blinked and shook his head like he was trying to shake her words from his head. "A call to anyone or a retreat to any of our strongholds will bring them down upon us," she explained.

"Exactly." Dillon beamed at Kari.

"Are you saying we can't make any calls?" Babat asked.

"Oh no, we can make calls with the Internet phone on my computer. We just can't call anyone we know because Inicma will be watching those phones." Dillon replied.

"So we call the front desk at the Plaza and get a message to them that way," said Babat.

Dillon winced. "Um..." he hesitated, flicking his fingers in the air.

"That might work if we can make it cryptic enough that anyone watching wouldn't understand it," said Kari.

"No it wouldn't." Dillon grimaced. "News reports

indicate there was a big raid on terrorists staying at the Plaza. Sounds like it got just as messy as our little adventure downtown," he said sheepishly.

Kari stared at Dillon. Babat's mouth opened and closed without making any sound and he began kneading his hands again. My knees wobbled. That meant we couldn't get help from Chan. We were on our own.

"They've shut down just about all mid-town trying to catch the leader. I assume that means Chan escaped," Dillon said, a hopeful tone in his voice.

"Is there anything else we should know?" Kari asked.

Dillon hesitated. "Well … they are accusing JJ's mom of stealing some rare book from the library."

My strength gave out. I dropped the codex, turned my back to the others, and practically collapsed. I sat on the edge of the walkway, numb to reality. After the accusations against my mom, I didn't think anything would surprise me. Even if I did trade the codex for her, she would be thrown in jail the first time she went out in public. I wracked my brain for options, but they all seemed hopeless. I realized that everyone else had fallen silent too and glanced over my shoulder to see them looking blankly into space. Only Nikki was looking at me.

"We will have to go back down and walk to Brooklyn," said Kari absently.

I turned away from them and rubbed my right shoulder. I'm not sure if I winced at the soreness as I rotated it or at the thought of carrying the codex any farther.

"I have an idea," said Nikki and she instantly had

everyone's attention. "Until tonight, the dragon really didn't know about me. I could call one of my father's … associates to help us."

Everyone looked at each other, not daring to be the first to respond.

"I think that is a great idea," Kari said with false optimism. "I am sure that would be a safe call."

"Would they take your call, I mean it *is* 2am?" asked Dillon.

"She wouldn't have suggested it if that was a problem," replied Kari.

Dillon beckoned Nikki to come closer to him as he took out the earpiece that was attached to his glasses. My muscles flexed at the sight of Nikki puting her face next to Dillon's so she could talk and listen while he worked the unseen screen in his glasses. She gave Dillon the number. He wiggled his fingers like he was a wizard casting a spell.

There was a pause.

"Hi Vlad, it's Nikki. Are you running perimeter tonight?" she said in a bubbly tone I had never heard from her before.

Another pause.

"I'm in a little trouble and don't want daddy to know. Any chance I could get you to help me out?" she asked. Her face twisted with the strain of keeping up the charade of a bubbly teenager but her voice did not betray her.

A longer pause.

"Oh, nothing that urgent." she said dismissively. "I'm on Governor's Island with some friends and we could use a lift." She made it sound like some harmless prank had gone a little wrong.

The longest pause yet.

"Oh, thank you Vlad. Don't worry, it will be our secret."

I felt a lurch in my chest as she said this.

"Oh, I'll let one of my friends tell you." She handed the ear piece to Dillon, turned toward Babat and said, "He should be here within the hour."

I listened to Dillon describe where we were and sighed in relief. We didn't have to walk any further.

Babat sauntered over and stood next to me, looking at the codex with eager eyes. "So, let's see what all the fuss is about," he said picking up the codex.

A knot twisted in my stomach. He tried to twist the lock with no success and I took some small comfort in the knowledge that the key was safe in my kamisan. Babat had no claim on the codex. It was my ticket to saving my mom and I didn't like him to touching it.

"Kari, come pick this lock." he said. The hair on the back of my neck bristled that he would try to use his magic on her.

"That case is unlike anything I have ever seen. There is no way to pick that lock," she replied dismissively as she took a seat next to Nikki on the other side of the walkway.

I smirked that his weak magical attempt had failed.

Babat studied the case for a moment while Nikki and Kari chatted in voices too low to hear. Dillon came and sat next to me.

"Dude, I could really go for a Mountain Dew and some Reese's right about now." he said.

"Fine, then I'll break it open," Babat said as if everyone hadn't moved on to other conversations. He dropped the case to concrete and whipped out his sword.

"NO!" shouted Kari as Babat swung his sword at the case. The clunk from the impact shook the walkway as the blade wedged itself in the nearly invisible crack around the outside of the lock. Babat's sword turned from polished chrome to dull tan and a hiss filled the air. Kari vaulted across the catwalk and tackled Babat. Babat's sword dissolved into a line of dust that blew away in the evening breeze before he and Kari hit the walkway.

"Get off me," Babat barked, pushing Kari off him.

"I just saved you from becoming a pile of sand," Kari glowered at him.

"And, how did you know that was going to happen?" asked Babat.

"I did not know what would happen. I only know that trying to force a magically protected case usually results in a miserable death," she replied.

"How could you possibly have known it was magically sealed." His voice was laced with accusation.

"It just came out of an enchanted bull and was not even scratched by harpy talons. How could it not be magically protected." she said indignantly.

"Then how are we supposed to open it?" Babat asked as if his actions had been the obvious solution.

"JJ?" Kari asked, turning toward me. Babat once again began moving his mouth without saying anything.

"Yeah, there's another key in my kamisan that will open it," I said, too exhausted to worry about the response to such a blunt revelation.

"AUGGGH! Why are all of you trying to undermine me?" Babat bellowed. My anger grew inside me. I was too tired to try to suppress it.

"Because you're an idiot," said Dillon standing to face him. "Keep your voice down or you'll wake up the whole city."

Babat's face turned purple and he reached to the top of his empty scabbard but grasped only air.

Kari stepped between them. "I did not know about the second key either," she said to Babat. "At least not until I saw the case."

Babat turned to me and said, "Who's side are you on boy? I am the leader of this team and need to know everything if we are going to be successful. Your insubordination just destroyed one of the greatest dragon slaying swords of all time."

My adrenaline fueled rage propelled me back to my feet. "Insubordination!?" I screamed. "I am not subordinate to you. Whatever team you thought you were leading died in Manhattan and it took this team to save you. If you think you're going to lead us then Dillon's right, you *are* an idiot."

"Chan made me squire that makes me leader," he hissed through clenched teeth.

"If anyone is the leader of this team its Kari. You're just Chan's talking head," I spat with as much venom as possible.

"And sometimes not even a *talking* head," Dillon said under his breath. He opened and closed his hand as if it were a silent puppet. I couldn't suppress my smirk.

Babat's eyes reflected the city lights as he looked first at Dillon then to Nikki, and then to Kari. He took a deep breath and sighed, his shoulders slumping in defeat.

"I have only tried to do what is right," he said softly to Kari. Then he turned to me and dejectedly said, "Slaying the dragon is the only hope for dealing with the Fed. That may not be the best thing for you but it is the best thing for the rest of the world."

"What are you talking about!?" I screamed. His statement made absolutely no sense.

"Don't you know anything?" Babat chided. "Chan wants to kill the dragon and destroy the Fed," he said as if that was common knowledge.

I was dumbfounded. His outrageous statement forced me to let the anger go and think more rationally. "You're crazy. Not only have you bought into Mr. Morgan's crazy conspiracy theories, you want to attack our government."

"It's not part of our government. It –"

Babat lecturing me like Mr. Morgan was more than I could take and I cut him off. "Look, I don't care about your ridiculous conspiracy theories, or some stupid council, or Chan's narcissistic crusade to slay a dragon. All I care about is saving my mom," I said calm and unyielding.

"You may only care about yourself and your little circle of friends but like it or not you're in the middle of the battle with the dragon. Some of us care about more than ourselves. Some of us care enough to try to save the country. To save the world," he replied, equally as calm and committed.

"Good causes don't have to be mutually exclusive. Maybe we can find a way to save both your mom and the country," Kari said patting each of us on the shoulder.

Light filled the upper window of the nearest house.

We scattered like cockroaches. I grabbed the codex and scrambled toward the water. The rocks were more slippery than they looked. I lost my footing, bounced off a couple rocks, and splashed into the water.

10

I swim well, but not well enough to swim quietly and hang on to the codex. I flailed my way into a small gap between two rocks. The water was just shallow enough for me to sit and keep my head above water.

I stayed as still as the stone that surrounded me and listened for any sign we had been discovered. Only the gentle lap of the harbor waves disturbed the silence.

The cold water sucked the warmth from my body. It was a small price to pay to have most of the muck washed away.

Just when I thought it might be safe to come out, the faint sound of voices drifted on the wind. They were too faint to understand but our argument had wakened someone on the island.

The sound of a motor boat echoed across the water drowning out the voices. My muscles froze and my mind raced. It was too early for it to be Vlad. I was certain someone on the island had called for a boat to check the walkway, but the harbor patrol boat just continued up the east river. I stayed huddled in the rocks until my legs ached from the cold. Every boat that passed made my heart jump.

"Nikki?" the soft call came from the far side of the walkway. I hadn't heard Vlad arrive and even though his call was soft, I jumped at the sound.

Babat appeared from nowhere and lifted me from my little hole. We clambered over the rocks and followed Nikki onto Vlad's motor boat. I dropped into one of the seats in the middle of the boat and tried to rub the pain from my legs.

"I take you home," said Vlad looking suspiciously at the rest of us

"Actually," said Nikki, playing the coy teenager again. "I was wondering if you would take us to the store?" She swayed back and forth looking up at Vlad with her head leaning to one side.

I decided I didn't like Vlad.

"You not allowed to the store," scolded Vlad.

"Yeah, well we have the book we stole from the library," she said pointing to the codex. She hadn't wasted her time waiting for Vlad. Her story would match what he heard on the news.

"And if we take it home the cops might catch us with it and will start investigating daddy," she said as she sashayed the short distance between them and took his arm. I wanted to punch Vlad for no reason in particular. Vlad stared at her and she stared back. "Please," she said in such a sticky sweet voice that I involuntarily rolled my eyes.

"OK," said Vlad. "I take you. But you be out tomorrow and not tell father."

"Thank you Vlad," she said and gave him a quick hug. My face suddenly felt hot.

"What store are we going to?" I whispered as she passed me on her way to sit by Kari on the bench seat across the back of the boat.

"Not a store, a stolen goods warehouse in Brooklyn," she huffed.

As Vlad urged the boat across the water, the cool night air rushed over my wet clothes and multiplied my frustration with Vlad. I hugged my chest to stay warm and tried not to scowl at him. It only took a couple minutes to reach Brooklyn, but it seemed much longer. As we approached what looked like an abandoned dock, Nikki came to stand by him.

"Who's minding the store tonight?" she asked.

"Igor" said Vlad.

"Ugh, Igor is such a pain," Nikki whined, playing up the role of the spoiled teen. "He probably won't even let me in."

"Yes, I call him," said Vlad as he brought the boat alongside the dock.

I hopped out and held the boat to the dock for the others while Vlad talked into his phone in what I figured was Ukrainian.

"No problem," said Vlad, looking longingly at Nikki. What was that? He had to be at least ten years older than her. "Igor come with me. You hide over there." He pointed to a nearby abandoned shipping container.

"But I'm not sure which one it is," pouted Nikki. "How will I get in?"

I felt my face flush again.

Vlad looked surprised and concerned at the same time. "4457. Security code 1204," he said slowly, almost as if he was questioning her.

"Thanks Vlad," she said and quickly gave him a peck on the cheek. I watched the concerned look on his face disappear and realized that my hand was grasping for my dagger. It wasn't there. I had lost it in the fountain.

Vlad said, "You have key right?" as Nikki stepped off the boat and I saw the momentary flash of panic in her face.

"Of course," she said to Vlad in her sticky sweet voice. She grabbed my arm and we trotted toward the storage container.

"Remember, I only cover for you tonight," called Vlad. I wanted to turn around and stick my tongue out at him but didn't.

"You don't have the key do you?" I whispered to her as we reached the others huddled behind the storage container.

"Shhh," she hissed at me. She let go of my arm and peeked around the corner. I realized my reaction to Vlad was similar to the disappointment I felt at her letting go of my arm. It made no sense that I would feel that way about Nikki. She was just a friend.

Igor strode to the boat, and exchanged some words with Vlad in Ukrainian before boarding. Vlad took one last look over his shoulder before they disappeared into the night.

"So what do we do now?" whispered Babat.

"We need to find warehouse 4457," said Nikki in a commanding tone.

Dillon's fingers started wiggling and Kari closed her eyes like she was meditating.

"How are the gloves working," I asked Dillon.

"Like a dream," he replied. He turned to Nikki and asked, "Any idea what street that warehouse was on?"

Nikki shook her head.

"Follow me," said Kari. She walked forward staring at the ground as if she were looking at spots of invisible treasure buried below the surface. We followed her through a maze of storage containers, across an empty parking lot and over some railroad tracks. I felt oddly exposed under the bright cones of light in the parking lot and couldn't help looking up to see if a harpy was circling overhead. The darkness of the shadows between parked freight trains was comforting in an equally odd way.

"Well this doesn't make any sense," said Kari stopping at a barbed wire topped chain link fence at the edge of the rail yard. On the other side of the fence was an empty street, the other side lined with warehouses. The street lights were spaced the perfect distance to ensure a cone of light covered every part of the sidewalk. A chill ran down my back but I wasn't sure if it was because I was afraid or just cold.

"What doesn't make sense?" asked Babat.

"Igor's tracks go right through the fence," said Kari now looking at it in confusion.

"We're at a gate," said Dillon, but it looked like a solid fence to me. Everyone else was looking at him like he had lost his mind.

"The hinge is over there," he said pointing to the left. "If we can get brain boy here to lift it a little it should swing open," he nodded at Babat.

There was a slight click as Babat grabbed the fence and easily lifted the section of fence between the two poles. It pushed open just as Dillon had predicted.

"Only a dwarf would so easily recognize such a device," Kari mumbled under her breath.

Dillon smiled at her happily.

With Kari leading the way we crossed the street to number 4457. It was a nondescript warehouse that blended in with every other warehouse on the street and had the standard rolling metal covers over the doors. Kari quickly picked the locks and we stepped inside the warehouse office. There was a single desk, some filing cabinets and a cot that looked much more inviting that it should. Nikki punched in 1204 to disarm the alarm.

"At least you know your dad thinks about you." I said.

"What makes you say that," she replied in a cold tone.

"Your birthday," I said. "The code is your birthday."

She half smiled as she opened the door between the office and the warehouse waving us into the large space. Rows of box laden shelves reached to the ceiling.

"It's not the Plaza but it's better than nothing," Nikki said.

"Looks perfect to me," I said dropping onto a ratty old couch between the door and water cooler. I closed my eyes basking in the relaxing softness of the seat and immediately fell asleep.

📖 📖 📖

The noon day sun filtered through the windows at the top of the warehouse when I woke to the sound of Babat snoring. He was splayed on a mattress that had been pulled in front of the large metal door used for driving trucks into the warehouse. Dillon was asleep in a chair. Open boxes cluttered the floor around him like he was a child who had just finished opening

Christmas presents. I lay on the couch with a light blanket over me. Babat let out a mighty snort that was so loud it rattled the metal door and Dillon's eyes snapped open.

We looked at each other and I smiled.

"Why are you doing this Dillon?" I asked quietly to keep from waking Babat.

"What do you mean? I'm doing this to rain vengeance on the villainy that threatens our country," he said in a presidential tone.

"I don't think so," I smirked. "You've always been about what's best for Dillon."

Dillon glanced at the floor and then back at me. "Thou doubtest the virtue of my valor?" he said.

"Yes."

He smiled. "The truth is, it's her," he said looking down in embarrassment.

"Kari?" I barely kept my voice low. "Dude, there is no way. She's like a super ninja magical freedom fighter goddess and you're a teenage mega-hacking geek."

"And what have I been doing the last 36 hours?" his voice went up an octave and he narrowed his gaze at me. "I suppose none of that counts?"

"I'm sorry. I'm really grateful for all you've done. We never would have made it out of there without you." I said penitently. "It's just ... this is some serious stuff and I don't want you to get hurt."

"Yeah, well..." he trailed off.

"Even if we don't all get killed trying to save my mom there is no guarantee Kari would ever give you the time of day," I said.

He looked at me for a moment and mumbled something under his breath.

"What?"

"I said, 'I have to at least try to become the type of guy she deserves,'" he said.

I stared at him in shock as his face turned a bright crimson. "If you tell anyone I said that I promise I will hunt you down and destroy your credit," he threatened.

I didn't know what to say. To hear the same person who considered women pieces of meat talking about becoming a better person for a woman he'd met two days ago was startling.

From the corner of my eye I saw a shadow move across the floor. I jerked my gaze upward expecting to see a harpy crashing in on us. Instead, a shiny silver "get well soon" balloon floated past the windows at the top of the warehouse. It dipped beneath a window that had been propped open and floated into the warehouse.

"Check that out," I said to Dillon. He turned in his chair to watch it gently drop until it bumped against the office door just above my head. I stood to grab it but the balloon shot up and out of my reach as if a gust of wind had come through the warehouse and carried it off. Perplexed at the strange behavior I looked at Dillon who just shrugged his shoulders. As soon as I backed away from the door the balloon dropped and bumpede against the door again. I made several attempts to grab it, including jumping off the arm of the couch to see if I could reach it, but every time it danced away so I couldn't even touch it, much less grab it.

I figured Kari would know what to do so I opened the door and peeked into the office. The balloon hovered above me. It took a moment for my eyes to adjust.

"What are you doing! Get out!" Nikki yelled. She was sitting on the cot holding a thin blanket to her shoulders. Her eyes were puffy and her hair looked like a bird's nest that had been run over by a truck.

Kari sprang to her feet from a small mattress in the middle of the office and landed in front of me, blades drawn. She looked like she had just stepped off the pages of a fashion magazine.

"Whoa!" I said holding my hands up in front of me. "I think you have a visitor."

"Get out!" shouted Nikki and I backed out the door into the warehouse to avoid Kari's advance.

"What's going on?" said Babat looking in wonder at Kari holding her blades in my direction.

"We're experiencing yet another unfathomable branch of the female psyche," said Dillon.

Kari glared at him. "Sorry about that, reflex reaction," she said as she sheathed her blades. "What do you mean a visitor?"

I pointed up at the balloon that dropped until it landed in her outstretched hands. The instant her hands touched the balloon it popped. A wooden pole with a small piece of paper tied to it appeared in her hands.

"It is from Chan," said Kari quickly scanning the piece of paper.

"Would it kill you to say 'It's from Chan'?" Dillon asked under his breath.

Kari rolled her eyes. From the corner of my eye I saw Dillon give a little fist pump. I smiled at his small celebration.

"He says *they're* safe," she said with extra emphasis on the contraction. Dillon beamed like he'd just won the lottery. "He says to reply if we are safe and he will let us know when he has arranged a safe rendezvous."

"What's the pole?" I asked.

"It is a staff," she corrected. "And it was included in case we needed a weapon when the balloon found us," she said dismissively. She turned to go back into the office. I started to follow but she turned and said, "You will have to wait out here for a few minutes while we get ready."

I didn't understand what they had to get ready for. I must have looked confused because she smiled and whispered, "To pass the time, why don't you ask Babat to teach you a few things?"

After that comment I'm sure I looked even more confused.

"He may be an idiot when it comes to leadership, planning, and personal relationships but there is no one who knows more about sword lore and swordsmanship," she whispered so only I could hear. Then she shut the door in my face.

I turned to look at Dillon and Babat but they just shrugged their shoulders. Dillon launched into an excited explanation of how he had raided the warehouse and had hacked the cell phone company to create five new, untraceable phones for us. Babat looked impressed and helped as we cleaned up the mess around Dillon's chair. I figured a self-deprecating approach would be best if I was going to take Kari's suggestion and make amends with Babat. As we dropped the last of the empty boxes in the garbage I hesitantly remarked, "So, I didn't do so well against the harpy last night."

He smiled. "Yeah, that was pretty stupid. Even the best swordsmen struggle against harpies," he said dismissively.

Kari was right. His personal skills needed some work. "Any pointers would be appreciated," I replied with more of an edge than I had intended.

"Ok," he smiled again. "My first pointer would be, don't drop your weapon"

I stared at him in shock. "I didn't realize anyone had noticed," I said in awe.

"I'm not as quick as Kari but I have studied and worked harder than anyone. So, when someone whips out a missing artifact of Horvorath I pay attention," he said pulling my dagger from his belt. "And from your miraculous escape from the harpy I'm guessing you have his armor as well?" he said twirling my dagger in his hand.

In my shock at seeing my dagger again I answered without thinking, "I have no idea who Horvorath is or whose armor I have."

"And, I'm the idiot?" he replied. He handed me the dagger and turned to walk away.

I was surprised at how grateful I was for the return of the dagger. Even though I'd had it for less than a day, its weight in my hand felt overwhelmingly reassuring. "I'm sorry about that," I said to Babat. "Thank you for saving my dagger."

Babat stopped with his back to me, looked at the roof and sighed before turning to face me. "Horvorath not only slew the dragon of Rome but legends say he was the last pure blood dwarf and the only dwarf to ever slay a dragon. He was one who truly cared more for others than he did for himself. The tales of his weapons and armor are so astonishing that most dismiss them as impossible myths."

Astonished by this revelation I cradled the dagger in my hands like it was a delicate museum peace and examined the intricate engravings in the hilt.

"Oh for heaven's sake, if you're going to have a mythical weapon at least hold it properly," he said in disgust as he came back to put the dagger in my hand properly.

"Maybe you could show me how to use it?" I asked.

He stared at me for a moment, as if he was trying to decide if I was worth the effort. "Alright, on two conditions?" I nodded. "First, claiming the honor of wielding Horvorath's arms includes taking on the duty to serve others." He held his hand up to silence my objection. "I understand that you want to save your mom. My requirement is that you give some consideration to everything else that is happening in this world."

"Is this one of those magical contract things?" I asked.

He chuckled. "You bested Chan. My limited magic can't touch you. I'm just asking for some consideration."

I paused, unsure if I believed him. "Ok" I said and was relieved that I felt no magic. "What's your second condition?"

"Show me your armor."

I rolled the edge of the armor at my wrist so there was enough of it to grab then gently stretched it away from my wrist.

"As I suspected," Babat said. I couldn't tell if it was admiration or concern in his voice.

"What?" I prodded.

"This is Horvorath's armor. You must be very careful with it," he said.

"I thought by definition armor was tough," I replied.

"This is the finest dragon armor ever created. It is made of spider silk," he said.

"Dude, that's awesome, some spider silk is stronger than steel," Dillon interjected. He had just come back from the warehouse with another box.

"By weight that is true. However this material is a single layer of the finest spider silk. Normally, more easily broken than a cobweb," Babat replied.

"No way," Dillon replied. "If it was that easy to break you couldn't even weave it, much less wear it."

"Legend has it that Horvorath enchanted the spiders to weave the armor themselves. There are no seams in it. And as I said before, it is dragon armor. Its strength comes from its enchantment rather than the material. That is why you must be careful with it," Babat said.

"OK, how do I 'be careful' with it?" I asked, expecting some instructions for washing and caring for it.

"Of course it has enchantments that make the material stronger and to magically fit the wearer. Those are relatively simple enchantments that change the will of the material. However, to protect the wearer from a dragon the enchantment requires a much stronger and renewable will so it uses the strongest will possible. The will to live," he said as if that explained everything.

I gave a confused nod and prompted him for more, "And?"

"Look, the harpy screamed when it attacked you not because it was mad but because your armor sucked some of its will to live. A harpy slash will kill almost anything, imagine how much of the harpy's will to live your armor had to drain from it in order to protect you." he said.

"But that's good right?" I asked.

"That's a very good thing if you are fighting a harpy or a dragon. If someone shoots you or attacks you with a sword the armor can't draw on anyone elses will to live. So, it will feed on your will to live until it kills you."

"That's not so good," I said a little disheartened at this new revelation.

"Legend has it that Horvorath took so much damage from the dragon's goons that when he finally faced the dragon he rushed head long into it wanting to die. When the dragon blocked Horvorath the armor drained the dragon of its will to live. It plunged itself onto Horvorath's sword killing itself and crushing Horvorath in the process," he mused as if it was a well known story.

Now I understood why I was so tired the night before and why I had so easily lost my temper. When the corner of the codex pressed into my chest the armor took some of my will to live.

"Well, let's get you some basic understanding of how to use that marvelous dagger," Babat said as if the previous conversation was inconsequential.

For the next hour I felt like I'd been thrown into an honors high school class that combined gym with physics as Babat showed me how to hold a blade, how to stand, how to move my feet, how to parry, and how to use the short reach of a dagger against opponent's with longer weapons. Dillon wanted no part of it and busied himself with the non-descript metal box he had found.

Babat tried to spar with me using a sword length board but every time I parried the dagger sliced off the end of the board. He had just gotten the same result with a pipe when Kari and Nikki emerged from the office.

Kari looked the same as when I first met her but Nikki was striking. She wore her hair down. It fell over her shoulders accentuating the curve of her face. I had never noticed how long her hair was because she always wore it up at school. She wore a long black blazer that ended almost half way down her thigh but was open in the front to reveal a form fitting red blouse and black jeans that actually fit her. She had a much more attractive figure than I would have guessed from her normal attire.

Dillon pushed my mouth closed. I hadn't realized it was open. Nikki smiled at me. Her enormous eyes shined a bright rusty color today. I felt flushed and figured the practice with Babat must have been harder than I thought.

"Can we finally take a look at the codex?" Babat asked. His voice startled me. I had forgotten that anyone but Nikki was there.

"Yeah, sure, the key's in the kamisan," I said pulling it from the small pocket in the armor.

"Not here," Kari said with a knowing look. "Go into the office and never open it when others are present."

I went to the office, intent on quickly retrieving the second key and returning to the warehouse. I touched the watch to the kamisan and the office began to dissolve. I didn't understand why it was taking so long. I wanted to get back to the warehouse. The footlocker appeared and I quickly opened it. I grabbed the key and tried to shut the lid. The image of my father appeared, preventing me from quickly closing the chest. He monotoned, lo leave the kamisan, simply close the chest. To get back in, touch the kamisan with an item previously removed from it." The abbreviation of the message startled me. "Remember that the heart of any beast, man, dwarf, or dragon is the key to its undoing. Those with enough love in their hearts to fight for the life, liberty, and happiness of others will have the courage to bring about the eventual downfall of the dragon. That is how it has always been and how it will always be." I grew impatient. This was taking too long. I wanted to be back with my friends. "Please tell Sam that is why I did this...because I love her." My frustration with the delay evaporated with this last comment. The image of my father disappeared. I closed the chest and the darkness vanished.

"That was quick," said Kari as I stepped out of the office with the key. I felt relief wash over me as Nikki stepped to my side. The others circled as if they were waiting for me to reveal the cure for cancer. I set the case on the floor of the warehouse and gently turned the key.

11

The case snapped open. Everyone jumped. Dillon was a half-step behind Kari, who had drawn her blades. Babat was grasping for the hilt of his missing sword and Nikki had her hand under the back of her jacket.

The book inside the case was not what I expected. Rather than a large worn tome with dog eared and irregular bunches of parchment protruding at odd angles, this was pristine. Two polished metal posts held a three inch stack of perfectly aligned legal sized pages between thick leather covers front and back. The front cover was perfectly smooth with the exception of some strange script beautifully embossed in gold. It looked brand new. I couldn't believe it was old enough to be called a codex. My heart sank as I realized this might be just another clue to finding the real codex.

"Bugger!" exclaimed Kari.

"This isn't the codex is it?" I said.

"No, it is the codex, but we lack the skill to read it," she said opening the codex and letting the pages fall from her fingers one at a time. Every page had the same strange script as the embossed cover. Some had patterns I recognized as tables. Some had pictures that danced on the page hinting that they were maps. The others were full of text. Sometimes they looked like a novel, and sometimes they looked like a recipe book. I couldn't read any of it.

"So, it's no good to us," I said thrilled that we could get on with trading it for my mom. "Let's call Inicma and get my mom back," I said. The part of me the magic touched when I agreed to help Chan twisted uncomfortably inside.

Babat began moving his mouth without speaking "We must know what it is before we trade it," Kari said. Her expression seemed something like sorrow as she looked at Nikki then back to me.

"But you just said we can't read it," I countered. I regretted ever agreeing to help Chan. If we couldn't read it then I couldn't keep my part of the agreement. I didn't want to think about what would happen if I broke a magical agreement with Chan.

"There are only two, maybe three, people not in the dragon's employ who can read this," she pondered aloud.

"You can't go there," said Babat in an ominous tone.

"Well his mother is not exactly in a position to help is she?" snapped Kari.

"What about my mother?" I asked.

"Your father willed his skills to your mother. She inherited his ability to read the ancient dragon language. I imagine that is how she was able to make a living selling antiquities," said Kari. She starred off into space as if searching for an alternative.

"The only other person who could read this is the librarian, and you don't want to go there," said Babat. He shuddered as some distant memory stole the courage from his face.

"You said there might be a third?" I prodded. I wondered what type of monster the librarian must be to scare Babat.

"The adjunct librarian may also have the skill," Kari said as if she were in a far off place.

"Yeah but going to the adjunct puts you too close to the librarian. Either is suicide," Babat argued.

"I have no other choice," Kari said, coming back to herself. Her words echoed my own thoughts. A choice between putting myself at Chan's mercy or facing this mysterious librarian was no choice at all. I would have to face this horrifying creature.

"Chan won't be happy if we're stuck in Hicksville when he wants to rendezvous," Babat argued. I shuddered at the thought of anyone being stuck in the Long Island town of Hicksville.

"Then I will leave at once," Kari said.

I slammed the case shut and everyone stared at me like I had six heads.

"I am staying with the codex," I said.

"JJ, you don't want to do this," Babat pleaded. I don't think he realized what he was saying but the hair on my neck stood on end as the dull flow of his spell washed against me. I pressed back with my will and the flow evaporated.

"I made that stupid deal to help Chan learn what was in the codex so we have to get the librarian to read it. But understand this, the codex is the only thing I have that will get my mother back. It is not leaving my sight." I glared at Kari and Babat. This was not something I was going to give in on.

"Actually, I believe you agreed to get him the

critical information the codex contains," Kari said.

"What?" I asked. I didn't understand why she was correcting me.

"The exact wording is important in magical agreements," she replied.

"Why don't we just go to a copy shop and copy it," Dillon asked. "Then we can give Chan the whole thing and get on with saving JJ's mom." I was giddy. Dillon's solution was so simple. I could get my mom back now and still meet my obligation to Chan.

"Because dragon script is magical writing," Kari said. My excitement evaporated. "The mechanical copy would not be magic and would therefore be unreadable. We must go to the librarian," she explained.

"Then you and JJ can go by yourself," said Babat. "I'd rather face two dragons than the librarian," he shuddered.

"That is only because you have never faced two dragons," Kari replied with a knowing smirk.

"JJ?" Nikki asked quietly. I was surprised at how close she was to me and equally surprised that I was comfortable with the closeness. She looked worried about me and I knew she was going to ask me not to go. "I want to come with you," she said so softly I almost couldn't hear it. Not only was she not trying to keep me from danger, she was actually asking my permission to come along. It made no sense. She looked like she was waiting for me to punch her for asking. Then I realized she thought last night's revelations about her family had changed my opinion of her.

"Nikki, you've been amazing," I said and realized too late that this was still a type of magic. I felt the power flow from me into her and her face lit up. "This is going to be really dangerous. I don't want you to get hurt." I almost recommended that she go home to the safety of her father, but knew that would hurt her. I wondered if her father was strong enough to hold off a bunch of goons and realized I would be less worried about her if she was with me and Kari.

"It makes no sense for either of you to go," said Kari. "I have visited the librarian before and can safely do so again if I am alone." Babat stared at Kari in disbelief.

Nikki forced a thin grin and said to me, "I don't want you to get hurt either. I know I can't stop you. So I'm coming with you."

"You're all nuts!" shouted Babat.

"OK," I said to Nikki, completely ignoring Babat. I felt some invisible knot in my stomach disappear as I gave Nikki my agreement. I remembered what Kari had just said about the words being important and realized I hadn't just agreed to let her come to see the librarian. I had agreed to let her come with me and I knew that meant she would be with me to the end.

"I really should do this alone," Kari said. Her shoulders sagged in defeat. Babat nodded his head.

"We're coming," Nikki, Dillon, and I said together.

Everyone looked at Dillon.

"Faint heart never won fair lady," said Dillon winking at Kari. Both Nikki and Kari rolled their eyes. "As much as I appreciate the double eye roll, you are *not* leaving me alone here with the swordless wonder," he said motioning to Babat who looked abashed.

"I guess we're all going then," I said, glad we were staying together.

"I don't want to go," said Babat. "I'm perfectly content to stay here."

"And wait for the Ukrainian mob to find you lounging in their secret stash of stolen goods without a weapon. That sounds like a good idea." Dillon said sarcastically. Nikki punched him in the arm. I swallowed my laughter.

"We'll figure something out," Kari said to Babat and then asked generally, "Does anyone have any cash?"

We all checked our pockets and came up with a grand total of sixteen dollars.

"Just enough for a subway ride," Kari said.

"Or a small breakfast," I said as my stomach grumbled.

"There's some cold pizza in the fridge," Nikki said.

"I still have these," said Dillon holding up the three gold coins Chan had given him. "But I have no idea what they are."

"Those are the currency of the Cyngor am Ryddid," Kari said dismissing him. "We will have to visit Tony's. And perhaps you," she nodded to Babat, "can work out a deal to stay with him." Babat wrinkled his nose like something smelled bad. Kari turned from us and headed toward the office as if the plan had been decided.

"The currency of the Cyngor am Ryddid?" Dillon said looking at Babat with a confused look on his face.

"I guess you don't know everything," said Babat smirking. He pointed to the coins in Dillon's hand and said, "That, is hard currency. The Cyngor am Ryddid does everything it can to avoid the influence of the dragon so they pay their debts and accept payments only in hard currency."

"You mean this is real gold?" Dillon asked. .

"Yep, half a troy ounce each," Babat replied. Dillon's face lit up.

Kari stepped out of the office with Nikki's theatrical makeup kit in hand and said, "

"Come on, we need to get moving if we are going to make it to Hicksville in time. Disguises are required for Dillon and JJ and I will not be subject to your stench if I can avoid it." she said looking at me, Dillon, and Babat. That ended the conversation. We still smelled like the sewer.

📖 📖 📖

The sun was well on its downward journey when we walked out of the warehouse and onto the streets of Brooklyn. The heat of the sunny June day shimmered off the pavement and brick walls.

Sweat trickled down my back beneath the dress shirt and jacket. Dillon and I looked like ordinary middle aged business men thanks to Nikki's costume and makeup expertise. When I'd asked where the seemingly endless supply of disguises had come from she had almost choked on the reply, until Kari admitted that she had a kamisan of her own.

Although the walk to the subway was only four blocks, we were all wet with perspiration by the time we walked down the steps into the station. The air conditioning on the train brought a refreshing chill to the dampness that had seeped through my shirt.

Nikki scowled at Babat as he stepped in front of her to take the seat next to me.

"So you still weren't stepping forward enough in

your block. You have to get closer with a dagger so ..."
Babat began as if our training session had never ended.

"Be a gentleman and give your seat to a lady," Kari
interrupted pulling him from his seat so Nikki could sit
next to me. I tried to give my seat to Kari but she
declined. The obvious attempt to push Nikki and me
together made me uncomfortably tense. We sat in
silence the rest of the trip.

Dillon continued to demonstrate near ominpotent
knowledge of the city as we followed him. He never
looked at the subway maps and never wiggled his
fingers to look something up on his computer. We
changed trains twice, and when the doors of the G train
opened at the Church Ave station, we couldn't have
been closer to the steps.

After walking three blocks I loosened my tie. After
another three blocks I took off my suit jacket. A deep V
of sweat had soaked through the shirt. Dillon even
reluctantly removed his special gloves by the time we
reached Tony's.

A tiny green awning hung from the side of the four
story brick building. Its small white letters read,
"Tony's Pawn Shop." The unassuming doorway was
wedged between the large front windows of a barber
shop and a dry cleaner. Kari led the way through the
door and up a narrow stairway to the second floor.

Tony's shop occupied the entire second floor. At
first glance it looked just like any other pawn shop. It
was dirty, the lighting was terrible and it was cluttered
with a wide variety of used stuff. But, when I looked
more carefully I realize this was far from an ordinary
pawn shop. Instead of a bag full of golf clubs there was
a barrel of staves. Instead of shelves full of comic books,

DVDs, and video games they were filled with tiny leather bound books and scraps of paper. I stopped at a shelf I would have expected to hold stereos. Instead, it contained a polished steel shield for $1200. Dillon was looking at a glass cabinet that contained gauntlets and leather bags rather than the customary cell phones and cameras.

Like other pawn shops this one had a glass counter that separated the back of the store from the front. Beneath the glass were watches, coins and every type of jewelry. Babat looked longingly at the rows of swords hanging behind the counter where guitars should have been.

A man stepped from the office behind the counter. He was tall and much too heavy for his slight frame. His hair and beard were ragged and speckled with gray. His eyes flitted over us as he waddled to a stool behind the counter.

"What do you want Kari?" he said in a tone that sounded suspiciously like "go away."

"Nice to you see you too, Tony," said Kari as she pulled a small leather pouch from inside her jacket. "We need some cash," she said jingling the pouch of coins and dropping it on the counter.

"Not interested," said Tony, but his eyes flickered greedily when they glanced at the pouch.

"Really?" she said, smirking at his obvious lie. "Alright, my mistake everyone," she announced to us. "We need to go to the Church Avenue Pawn Shop; Tony's not interested." She took her pouch and headed toward the stairs we had just climbed. I smiled and played along with her act.

"But ..." Babat began eyeing the swords. He

stopped when Kari fixed him with a stare and continued to walk away.

Kari had reached the first step when Tony said, "Wait." He failed in his attempt to hide his desperation. Kari stopped on the first step but did not turn around. "You and I both know you don't want to answer the types of questions Church Ave will ask," Tony said.

"Oh, but I thought you were not interested," said Kari patronizingly as she turned to smile at him.

"I'm not interested in your coins," he said. "But I will give you five hundred dollars for that watch," he said to me staring at my wrist.

I pulled my sleeve over the watch. "Not if you're charging twelve hundred for a regular shield. This must be worth at least ten times that," I said. There was no way I was going to sell the watch so I tried to set a price that was higher than he would want to pay.

Tony's smile didn't touch his eyes as he feigned penitence, "Of course. I'm sorry. I didn't realize it was also a shield." For a pawn broker, he wasn't a very good liar. He'd known it was a shield. "I'll give you twelve grand for a trinket like that," he said turning toward his office like the matter was settled. The greedy look in his eyes told me it was worth much more.

"We are not here to sell artifacts," said Kari stepping to the counter. Tony looked disappointed and sat back on his stool. "We need to trade some gold for cash. Or are you not in that business anymore?"

"No one believes those coins are gold. They only buy bullion bars with a stamp and serial number from a reputable refiner. Do you have any idea how expensive that is?" he complained.

Kari smiled and said, "And yet I am sure you made a nice profit. The price of gold has gone up thirty percent since our last exchange and I see you still have two ten ounce bars left."

Tony looked down the counter where the bars were on display and frowned. "Like you said, I still have twenty ounces left that haven't sold."

Kari leaned on the counter and lowered her voice. "Chan is going after the dragon so he can pull the plug on the Fed." Tony's eyes widened. "Let's say he's successful. What do you think the Fed's member banks will do when he tries to take away their control of the money supply?"

"That would make the current financial crisis look like a picnic," Tony replied, his eyes wide with horror.

"And what will happen to the price of gold?" Kari prompted.

"It'll go through the roof," Tony practically chuckled. He looked longingly at the bars of gold at the other end of the counter.

"Wait, if Chan wins the economy gets worse?" I asked, even more horrified that I had agreed to help him.

"Temporarily, yes but in the long run it gets much more stable," Babat answered.

Tony had regained his composure. "I know you think Chan will win, but what if he doesn't?" he asked.

"You tell me. What would the dragon do to the people of this country as repayment for attacking him?" Kari replied.

Tony smiled. "He'll punish them for even thinking about supplanting him."

"Either way the price of gold is going to go

nowhere but up in the near future," Kari said.

I felt sick. I kept finding reasons to not trust Kari. It seemed like no matter who won a lot of innocent people were going to suffer as a result of Chan's assault on the dragon.

"It'd have to be at least a hundred coins to make it worth my while," said Tony. "And I'll not pay you a penny more than I did last time."

"I have seven, but I believe Dillon has three he might be willing to part with as well," she said looking at Dillon.

"Another new client huh?" said Tony his face lighting up. "You got some coins you want to sell there, son?" he said to Dillon.

"Only if the price is right," Dillon replied. His eyes glowed with excitement at the invitation to haggle.

"I'll give you the same I gave her, four hundred each," Tony offered. I was amazed. After all of Dillon's complaining about Chan's payment, he was about to get twelve hundred dollars for delivering that letter.

"Ya know Kari," Dillon said. "I think I could hack into SB refiners and allocate some serial numbers so we could forge our own stamps." He paused and watched Tony's eyes grow wide with wonder. "I'm not sure we even need this guy," Dillon finished.

"Alright, six hundred, three hundred in cash and three hundred in trade," Tony said to Dillon as he reached in to the glass case and pulled out a pewter casting of a dragon the size of a stapler. "You could have yourself a nice pet," he said as he set it on the counter. When he let go the pewter figure came to life, climbed his arm and perched on his shoulder. Dillon shook his head.

"You'll give us six hundred each and Babat gets to stay here through tomorrow," Kari countered.

"Actually," interrupted Babat and Kari glared at him. "You'll give them seven hundred each and I'll give you ten more coins for that sword." He pointed to one hanging on the wall behind Tony. I squinted to see the tiny tag. The price was ten thousand dollars.

Tony looked at the sword and laughed. Babat reached across the counter grabbed Tony by the throat and lifted him out of his seat with one hand; something I would have thought impossible. "And we'll have you sworn to silence the next time you do business with harpies," Babat snarled at him. Kari looked startled and drew her blades.

"I...I don't do business with harpies." stuttered Tony.

"I can smell 'em you lyin' rat," said Babat. His fingers squeezed Tony's throat as he pulled him half way over the counter so they were nose to nose.

The pewter dragon bit Babat's hand. He yelped and loosened his grip.

Tony fell to the floor, knocking over his stool. "You can't rob me in my own store. I have the protection of the Cyngor am Ryddid," he choked.

"And I am Chan's squire. I revoke that protection as punishment for dealing with the enemy," said Babat. "Now take the deal," he scowled leaning over the counter and glaring at Tony.

"Alright, I'll give you seven thousand and the sword for twenty coins," he panted.

"And you will take an oath of silence Tony," said Kari. I felt the magical charge in the room.

"I can't," said Tony

"Yes, you can," she pushed. I had never seen Kari look more frightening.

"I can't" shrilled Tony raising his arm in defense as he started to weep.

I hadn't noticed but Nikki had gone around the counter. Kari froze at the sight of Nikki kneeling next to Tony. "Tell us why you can't, Tony," she said in a soft voice as she rubbed his shoulder. The magical energy that flowed through the room was like none I had felt before. There was no attacking surge of power or clashing of wills. It was peaceful and as deep and powerful as the Hudson River flowing into the sea. His sobbing stopped immediately. He lowered his arm and stared into her eyes. The horror in his face melted away and was replaced with reverence for Nikki.

"I was forced to take an oath upon pain of death that I would notify Inicma of any contact with the Cyngor am Ryddid. To take a contradictory oath would be death," he said bowing his head in shame. Kari and Babat went rigid.

Nikki smiled at him and then turned to Kari and said, "If we don't tell him we are going to Poughkeepsie do we really need to put him under oath."

The flicker of a smirk flashed across Kari's face before she yelled at Nikki, "You idiot! Now he knows and we have to kill him." She vaulted over the counter making a flourish of her blades. Even with the brief training Babat had given me, I recognized her motions as all show. If she had wanted Tony dead he would be.

"Wait!" Nikki screamed putting herself between Kari and Tony. Kari stopped short. Nikki suppressed a smile. Dillon pulled on his gloves and started wiggling his fingers in the air.

"Let's finish the deal. Then you can call Chan and tell him to meet us somewhere else," said Nikki.

"Yeah," said Tony, some hope flickering in his face as he got to his feet. "I'll give you the sword." He lifted the sword and scabbard from the wall and placed it on the counter. "and the seven grand," he said going to a small cabinet by the office door.

"Nikki?" said Kari nodding at her.

Nikki pulled a pistol from under the back of her jacket and pointed it at Tony. "Carefully Tony, I don't want to hurt you," she said. The peaceful force of her magic had become a raging torrent. Tony looked heart broken. He dropped the gun he had just pulled from the top drawer of the cabinet. He slowly opened the lower drawer and pulled out a lock box.

"They're already on their way," Dillon said as Tony began counting out hundred dollar bills.

"We're in a hurry now Tony, just give us a stack of fifties and a stack of twenties," Nikki ordered. Her growing anxiety gave a sharp edge to her magic, still powerful but more like what I'd felt from others.

He grabed the bundles as ordered and hurried to the counter.

"Now give me the twenty coins and be on your way to someplace that is not Poughkeepsie," he said looking at the items on the counter. Babat and Dillon dropped their coins on the counter as Nikki backed around the counter still pointing the pistol at Tony.

Kari hopped over the counter. "You better hope Chan is in a good mood when he finds out." She dropped her coins on the counter and handed the sword to Babat.

Tony winced at the threat, "I had no choice, they forced me to take an oath to delay you," he whimpered.

"Are we ready Dillon?" Kari asked picking up the bundles of cash.

"Do you know how to steal a car?" asked Dillon as his fingers stopped wiggling and started punctuating the air.

"Absolutely," she replied with a wide smile.

"Then lets go," said Dillon bolting for the stairs.

Everyone but Nikki made it to the stairs before me I turned in time to see Tony reach for his gun in the open top drawer. I winced at the sound of Nikki's pistol. The glass counter shattered and Tony dove to the floor.

"Stay down Tony!" Nikki called over the tinkling sound of the glass hitting the floor. There was no mistake that her magic had changed to a focused point. I had no doubt Tony would stay down.

"I'm sorry, it's part of the oath!" he called as Nikki ran to the stairs with tears in her eyes.

By the time Nikki and I got to the sidewalk a green Ford Explorer was idling at the curb with Kari in the driver's seat and the back door open. We hadn't even closed the door before the tires squeeled as the car catapulted forward.

"Isn't stealing the car of some innocent bystander a little over the line?" I asked, thinking of the unfortuante owner.

"Normally, I would agree with you" Kari said.

"But they need something to follow," Dillon said his fingers zealously working the air in front of him.

"Run this red light," he said to Kari and she blew through the intersection against the signal without incident. The black SUV behind us was not as lucky. I snapped my head around at the thunderous colision. The SUV looked like it had been tranformed into a large bumper on the delivery truck that had broadsided it.

"Well they're certainly following us," I said.

"Second left," said Dillon. He looked over his shoulder at me and said, "That's the point," as we screeched around the corner.

"So why do we want them following us?" I asked.

"Through the light and into the park," he said and then turned to me again. "We don't, but since our friend Tony has made sure they're following us we need to give them a false lead," he said. We swerved through another red light and into an enormous park with trees and open lawns.

"No cameras in Prospect Park, and the cameras in the Prospect Park subway station are about to have a major malfunction." explained Dillon, smiling. "Stop here please."

Dillon jumped out of the car as it lurched to a stop and began walking briskly across the lawn. Kari locked the car as we left to follow him. The owner would quickly get it back, unharmed.

We followed Dillon into the subway station as he relentlessly stabbed the air with his fingers. "Follow me," he said.

A train pulled into the station just as we reached the platform. I headed for the first open door.

"JJ," Dillon called. He wasn't getting on the train.

We joined the throng of people going out the exit at the other end of the subway station and boarded a Brooklyn bus number 43 just outside the station.

We sat together in the back of the bus as it pulled away from the curb.

"What was all that about?" whispered Babat.

"If someone were running from you and stole a car, you'd probably assume they wanted it for more than a twelve block joy ride. So the first thing they'll do is try to watch all seven roads out of the Park." he said. Almost on queue we heard a siren and held our breath. A police car, lights flashing, went through the intersection in front of the bus and kept going.

Dillon smiled and said, "If you then found the stolen car parked less than a thousand feet from a subway station you would probably check their security cameras. When they do, they will find video of us entering the station. Unfortunately for them, the cameras failed at the same time the train showed up. They'll probably assume we got on it and search the subway system. With all those options for a quicker escape do you think they'd even consider the possibility of us spending ninety minutes to use three different buses just to get to the Jamaica LIRR station?"

I was tired just listening to his explanaition of what we were doing.

"LIRR?" asked Babat.

"The Long Island Rail Road," said Dillon. "It's a commuter rail system that services the suburbs on Long Island."

"That's excellent," said Nikki punching Dillon in the arm again.

"You were awesome," said Dillon to her in reply.

"Yeah, that was some sick powerful magic," I said.

"I can't do magic," she said looking confused.

"But I felt it," I argued.

Kari gave me a curious look before turning to Nikki. "Not only were you exceptionally quick witted with the deception about Chan's location, but you also used some of the most powerful magic available. You were, in all ways, outstanding."

"Is that what you call waving a gun around?" said Nikki. She looked disgusted with herself and covered her face with her hands. I tried to comfort her by gently pulling one of her hands from her face and holding it tight. She stared at me in wonder and my heart skipped a beat.

"No, your weapons proficiency was also excellent but nothing compared to the formidable power of magic rooted in compassion," replied Kari.

That statement confused me. "I thought magic was just a force of will?" I said turning to look at Kari but keeping Nikki's hand in mine.

"It is. Which is why how powerfully you believe in your motivation determines how powerful the magic is," said Kari. "It is unusual that you are able to sense magic. Did you notice how different it felt?"

"Oh yeah, almost an irresistable force," I said and squeezed Nikki's hand.

"Indeed, Nikki is the most uniquely human person I have ever met. Her motives always seem to be rooted in love and compassion. When someone reaches out with true love and concern for your well being it is overwhelming. It is much easier to resist the will of someone who is only pursuing their own selfish agenda," she said.

I considered this statement and realized that the times my mother asked me to do things and showed her concern for me were the times I did what I was asked. They were also the times that defined how I preceived her.

"But I don't know magic," complained Nikki again.

"And how can you say shooting at him was motivated by compassion?" asked Dillon.

"It is so natural to you, you do not even know you are weilding such power." Kari said to Nikki. "And do you really think she missed by accident?" she chastized Dillon.

"OK, OK, enough with the praise for Nikki," Dillon fumed. "I'd like my money please," he growled.

As Kari covertly handed him a stack of bills I queried Babat, "What's with the sword?"

"I never would have been looking for it if I hadn't lost mine. It is worth many times what I paid for it," Babat said patting his side. "I would consider only the sword of Havorath more valuable," he said slyly, judging my response.

"Wow, that's a great find," I replied focusing on expressing the right appreciation without revealing the notion that the sword in my kamisan might be the sword of Havorath.

"Yeah," he said clearly disappointed at my response. "Don't tell Chan or he'll confiscate it for himself," he said ruefully.

"Bad news!" said Dillon and we all froze. "According to a breaking news report JJ and I have kidnapped his highschool heartache whose affection he was never able to win." He smiled as he glanced at Nikki and my intertwined hands and said, "one Nicolette Kovatu."

We all laughed.

12

Dillon said we should spread out because Nikki's picture was all over the news, so we each claimed a different part of the bus. The trip took longer than expected as the Friday evening rush hour kicked in. It seemed even longer sitting by myself in the back of the bus. Nikki glowed as she smiled at each passenger and chatted with the driver. She looked like anything but a kidnap victim. I wanted to talk with her and hold her hand again. The odor of the guy next to me made me realize how nice her perfume had smelled.

After a woman who smelled like she was coming home from the gym, a man who smelled like urine, and a fat lady who smelled worse than both combined, we arrived at the Jamaica Queens train station. I'd spent the entire trip sitting in the stench of others while unsuccessfully trying to come up with a way to save my mom without helping Kari and Chan cause an economic crisis.

Dillon followed Kari like a puppy as she went to buy tickets to Hicksville. I'm sure Kari recognized how unhappy I was when I snatched the ticket from her and headed for the train. I waited for everyone to board and briefly considered going it alone until Nikki boarded the train.

One half of the car had forward facing seats the other half backward facing seats. Kari and the others selected seats in the forward facing half of the car. I found a backward facing seat next to the window. If I couldn't sit next to Nikki I didn't want to see any of them.

The train had barely left the station when Kari sat next to me.

"I thought we were supposed to stay separated," I said defiantly.

"What is wrong JJ?" she asked.

"I don't know if I can trust you enough to answer that question," I responded.

She looked hurt. " I have done nothing but look out for you."

"All the while plotting to help Chan destroy the economy," I added.

"Oh, I see," she replied. "Will you try something for me?"

I didn't trust her. "Depends on what it is."

"Pretend you are the dragon in southern England five or six hundred years ago."

"And why would I do that."

"Just play along and see if you can understand where the Cyngor am Ryddid is coming from."

"OK," I sighed, "I'm a dragon."

"Of course you need to eat. So when you get hungry you fly out and feed on the cattle or sheep of the peasants and take anything that looks valuable for your hoard. The problem is your hoard is not growing very fast because peasants do not have much. Every once in a while you attack the castle of a local lord and get a little better haul but doing that is dangerous. You never know when someone will have the right weapons to hurt you or when some peasant will get a lucky shot in your eye."

"Ok, doesn't sound like such a great existence to me," I said.

"Yes, and you are bored because you have been doing it for a very long time," Kari added. "So one day you find out that the dragon in China has amassed an enormous hoard and has not left his lair to feed in over five hundred years."

"How'd he manage that?" I asked.

"He cornered a very rich dwarvish merchant. This merchant was well known and highly regarded in the market. Unfortunately for the dragon, the merchant was not carrying any coins. Fortunately for the dragon he was carrying paper notes that were promises to pay actual coins to anyone who brought the paper notes to his palace. The merchant had created paper money because he was tired of carrying the heavy iron coins China used at that time. The dragon and the merchant struck a deal. The dragon spared his life and the merchant established a business of safe-guarding the coins of others. After a few raids by the dragon everyone in the nearby towns were desperate for a safe place to keep their coins. The merchant offered to keep their coins safe. Everyone trusted him, so they gave him their coins and he gave them paper notes that promised to pay them the coins he held for them. Of course almost no one collected their coins because the paper was easier to carry and everyone knew what it was worth."

"What you're saying is they used paper money."

"Correct and the dragon added the coins to his hoard. He took their money without a fight," Kari said.

"What does that have to do with the dragon in England or with the Federal Reserve? That's ancient history," I said.

"Well, let us go back to that dragon in England," she said. "He cornered the goldsmiths in his domain and got them to agree to do the same thing with gold in England, except they also made loans. A lord who wanted to purchase something would get a loan from a goldsmith. But the goldsmith wouldn't give gold to the lord. He would give one of these paper promises to pay. Then the lord would have to pay back the note plus some additional real gold as interest. That way the dragon's hoard would grow."

"Sounds like the normal lending process to me," I said.

"Yes, until one day the dragon caught his most successful goldsmith trying to steal real gold from his hoard."

"And killed him of course," I said.

"No actually, what happened was the goldsmith had issued more paper notes than gold he had to lend. He was trying to steal from the dragon so he could cover the notes. What the dragon realized was that almost no one collected on the notes so they could put more people in debt to the dragon simply by issuing more paper," she said.

"Wouldn't people catch on to that though," I asked.

"Certainly, dragons had to work through many different iterations of this scheme and they have gotten very good at it. All of them enslave a population in a hopeless circle of debt that does nothing but feed the dragon's hoard," Kari replied.

"So you're saying that's the dragon you're fighting and the Fed is the most recent iteration of that scheme?" I asked.

"Yes and no. It is definitely not the same dragon but the Fed is definitely one of the more successful iterations of that scheme," she replied.

"But the Fed is –" I started but was interrupted by a hard cough from someone standing in the aisle. It was Babat. He pointed at his phone in annoyance.

Kari grabbed her phone. I looked out the window. The seemingly endless parade of six story buildings in Queens had given way to the tree lined streets of Long Island. Through the periodic breaks in the trees, I glimpsed the sun set with its gold and red arms stretching under the ominously black clouds that had developed. A storm was imminent.

The phone Dillon had given me vibrated. The text message read, "r u ok? –n."

My heart jumped into my throat. I typed three different replies to Nikki but ended up settling for "we need 2 talk."

The clouds opened up and unleashed an absolute deluge as the train eased into Hicksville. The elevated station spanned one of the suburban roads filled with sedans and minivans. Although there was only a narrow gap between the top of the train and the covered platform I still got drenched leaving the train.

Several of the commuters looked at me longer than they should have as I left the station. Kari grabbed my arm, pulled me into the backseat of a waiting cab, and gave an address to the cabbie.

"Are you kiddin' me?" he said, indignantly as he turned to look at her. His eyes almost popped out of his head when he saw her. "That's just around the corner," he said dumbfounded.

"It is raining and you will be well compensated," Kari said in her sweetest voice and handed the cabbie a fifty dollar bill. The poor guy didn't stand a chance.

The cabbie was right. It was only a few blocks to the address. He stopped at the end of a driveway shared by two houses, their respective garages barely visible through the narrow gap between them. Hedges lined both sides of the driveway from the sidewalk to the corner of each house. They looked like small pine trees that had been trimmed into square blocks.

Other than the driveway and hedges the two homes were nothing alike. One was a two story gray plaster monolith. If it hadn't been for the covered porch that ran the width of the building it would look like someone dropped a slate pyramid on a dingy old box. The other had warm cream colored siding. The monotony of the red shingled roof was interrupted by various shaped windows protruding from the regular slope. The warm glow of lights in its windows made the black windows of the gray house look like bottomless pits that were waiting to swallow us.

We got out of the cab and dashed to the covered porch of the gray house, hunching our shoulders against the downpour.

"Where are the others?" I asked.

"They are taking separate cabs to the Stumble Inn," she replied. "We will join them when we have finished here. She pulled a cloth from inside her coat and handed it to me. "Clean yourself up. You look like your face is melting."

I looked at my reflection in one of the windows. Between sweating in the heat and the drenching downpour, the stage makeup was smeared across my face. I quickly wiped my face while Kari sat in one of the gray wicker chairs on the porch.

"Shall I ring the bell?" I asked, failing miserably in my attempt to imitate her British lilt.

"You can if you want. It looks to me like we may have to wait a while," she said, motioning to the other gray wicker chair.

I rang the bell without much hope. If anyone moved inside I couldn't hear it over the roar of the rain pounding the porch roof. There was nothing to do but wait.

After a few minutes, I dropped into the chair and watched the rain. The small concrete figurines in the flower beds stood defiantly unmoved by the storm. The swaying of the neatly trimmed shrubs and trees was as out of place in the lifeless yard as Dillon had been in the lobby of the Plaza. Across the driveway the children's toys, unintentionally left to bathe in the shower, seemed sad in their stillness.

In that stillness I became aware of a faint magical flow coming from inside the house. It was like floating in the ocean. The waves gently urged me to leave.

"Do you feel that?" I asked Kari.

She looked at me like I had just asked how purple smelled. "Feel what?"

"That magical pulse."

She looked confused. "You feel magic right now?"

"Yes, the house, or something in the house, is trying to gently nudge us away."

She smiled, "It is a rare gift to have that level of connection to magic. Maybe I should teach you some basics so you can better use your gift."

"OK," I said. I was so eager to learn magic that I forgot all about Kari's part in causing economic distress to the country.

She shook her head, "Not here; we can go in back for a little more privacy."

We ran down the narrow driveway, leaning against the wind that funneled through the narrow gap. Lightning flashed and for a brief moment I saw into the gray house. It was filled with books. The walls were lined with bookshelves. Stacks of books covered the tables and crowded the steps to upstairs. Despite the various sizes and shapes of the books, every pile appeared neat and organized.

We reached the small porch on the back of the house and shook the rain from our clothes.

"Now, I am not nearly as proficient as Chan, but you already know that," she said with a smile. "The key is to be creative and find something that would naturally fit. For example," she gestured to the rain, "the rain is being drawn to the ground by gravity. It would be very difficult to identify the will of each individual rain drop and convince it to ignore gravity and it is virtually impossible to overpower the will of the earth to convince it to stop having gravity."

I nodded. I thought of the force of Chan's will and tried to imagine how much more powerful the will of the earth would be. The thought frightened me.

Kari continued, "So if I wanted to affect some of this rain, I wouldn't do it directly. I would use the wind, which is already blowing, and squeeze it into blowing the rain away." She closed her eyes and lifted her hands to the wind. I felt the familiar surge of magic and the wind shifted. A section of rain now blew sideways. It blew faster, until the drops burst into a fine mist as they hit the graceful arc of fast moving air Kari controlled. She stopped and opened her eyes, panting.

"Your turn," she said after she caught her breath. "Just reach out to the wind and will it into a more narrowly focused space."

I closed my eyes and raised my hands the way she had and imagined the air forming an arc like Kari's. I concentrated on that image. I opened my eyes. Nothing had happened.

"Are you willing the air to do it or are you imagining the air is doing it?" Kari asked.

I closed my eyes again and pressed harder. My will reached out to the winds faint push. I tried to squeeze it but could no more get my will around the wind then I could get my arms around an elephant. Undaunted, I decided to try pinching the side of it rather than squeezing all of it. As soon as I felt the smaller portion of the wind's will I used my will to pinch it as hard as I could. The moment I did, a shrill whistle rang out and disappeared with a loud crack like thunder. Water pelted my face and I completely lost my concentration.

Kari stared at me in shock.

"What happened?" I asked.

"I've only seen something like that once before," Kari said. "You didn't channel the wind -- you broke it."

"But I didn't. It's still here. All I did was pinch it," I replied.

"What you did was separate a portion of the wind

from the rest of it. That created a vacuum that the rest of the wind rushed to fill," she said. "That was amazing."

I beamed at her praise.

The back door clicked open and a small cranky voice said, "Go away, you've caused enough trouble already." Kari swiveled and pushed on the door. The security chain kept it from opening more than a couple inches.

"Let us in old man," Kari said. There was a magical edge to the statement despite the fact that she hadn't used his name. I had expected the librarian to be some sort of incredibly powerful monster, like a sphinx. This old man was the least threatening creature I had met in the last three days.

"You're not wanted here," he croaked. "You'll bring the wrath of the dragon upon us all."

"We aren't leaving without a translation," I said over Kari's shoulder.

The old man made a choking sound in his throat, "And you brought him here? Are you mad?" he said and began pushing the door in vain as Kari held it open.

"Just tell us what it says and we will leave," promised Kari.

"No, go away," the old man persisted, continuing to push on the door. "There is no benefit to me, only trouble."

"Ok Tom, I will give you a dragon stone for the translation," said Kari and the old man stopped pushing on the door.

"Show me the stone," he said greedily.

"It is in a kamisan," Kari said. The old man paused

for a moment before nodding his head and letting us into his kitchen. As with the yard everything was clean, organized and lifeless. Unlike any kitchen I had seen before, this one was filled with books. Only the stove, the sink, and a small space on the kitchen table were unencumbered by the neatly stacked towers of bound paper.

"Use the bathroom for your kamisan," he said, beckoning Kari to follow him. With a nod Kari gestured to me to go first. I understood. She wanted me to retrieve the codex from my kamisan.

Tom led us to a door in the hallway between the front room and the kitchen. The bathroom behind it was so small I could sit on the toilet, wash my hands and touch my elbows to the door and opposing wall all at the same time.

I closed the door, pulled the kamisan from its protective plastic and touched my watch to the paper. The features of the tiny bathroom began to dissolve but something was wrong. Instead of the edges of the room turning black they became line art. I had anticipated the image of the chest appearing in place of the small sink but a clear image did not appear. Instead the chest shook so violently it was a blur. The magic was trying to display the box but couldn't make it fit in the tiny space. I had no way to stop it. I couldn't grab the edge of the chest lid to open it. Thin cracks appeared in the walls. I had no choice but to open the line art door to the room. I grabbed the knob twisted it and pushed the door open.

The image of the foot locker flew out the door before me and landed in the hallway. The blackness pushed me off the toilet and onto the hallway floor. I knelt in front of the foot locker and wondered what Kari and Tom had experienced when the door opened. The black edge of the kamisan gave no hint of the kitchen where they had been.

I opened the foot locker and was astonished. The contents looked like a child's scribble rather than the perfectly ordered images I had come to expect. The image of my father appeared and started his little spiel. I reached into the kamisan and watched my fingers grasp the closest item. It was half way out of the foot locker before I realized it was a book. I set it on the floor and tried to lift the entire massive scribble out in one lump but the pile wouldn't move. Only one item could be removed at a time.

Finding the codex proved a miserably tedious task. By the time I located it, the pile of stuff I had pulled from the chest filled the hallway. I promised myself that I would take the time to examine each item later.

To find the key to the case would require organizing the entire foot locker if for no other reason than I had run out of space for items in the hallway. I put the individual items back and took others out. Murphy's law was in play and the very last part of the scribble turned out to be the mess of keys that had fallen from their hooks. None of them was the right one. Then I realized that I had left the key in my jacket pocket that morning. I had just wasted over thirty minutes searching for something I already had. I placed the remaining items into the foot locker as quickly as I could and shut the lid.

The white paper disappeared into darkness and the blackness surrounding me brightened only slightly. For a brief moment I thought I was cursed to be stuck in the kamisan forever. But as my eyes adjusted, the outline of the hallway and the piles of books in the rest of the house came into view. No one had bothered to turn on the lights when the last vestiges of daylight had vanished and only a portion of the light from the streetlamps filtered through the front curtains. The rain had stopped so there was no sound in the dark house. Kari and Tom stood perfectly still at the end of the hall near the kitchen.

"Hello?" I called sheepishly.

Tom snapped on a light. "What were you thinking boy!"

If he was half as dangerous as Babat said, his anger should have terrified me. But it was Kari who frightened me. The only time I had seen her that angry was when Sati died.

"I'm sorry! It didn't fit in there," I complained.

Their anger immediately turned to shock. "It didn't fit?" pondered Tom.

"How big is the box?" asked Kari

"A little bigger than a foot locker," I answered with the obvious answer.

"The size of a foot locker?" said Tom his eyes wide with wonder.

"What happened when I opened the door?" I whispered to Kari, not wanting to disturb Tom's train of thought.

"When you activate a powerful kamisan anyone in the room becomes an inanimate part of the kamisan text. It is very uncomfortable because you cannot see or hear anything and you are not breathing. You cannot move or feel your body."

"But you can still think," added Tom. I tried to

imagine the horrible condition I had forced upon them for the last forty minutes and shuddered at the thought.

"Horrible, nasty devices, created by the dragon to imprison and preserve humans he found valuable," said Tom. He glared at the codex then wheeled on Kari. "And that case doesn't look like a dragon stone."

"That would be in my horrible, nasty device," she said to him and headed for the bathroom.

"I assume yours will fit in that space?" said Tom. "I don't want to go through that again "

Kari stepped in and closed the door.

"The dragon actually stored people in kamisans?" I asked.

Tom laughed. "No, until today I'd never heard of a kamisan big enough to hold a person. The dragon used to pay guards to open a kamisan within the prison. While the guard slept and enjoyed a day's rations, the prisoners remained in oblivion, never aging, waiting for those few precious minutes of life at the changing of the guard. It was a clever guard who discovered that kamisans had the more humane use of sending messages and storing items."

Kari stepped from the bathroom and held up a beautiful fuchsia stone the size of a baseball. It glowed gently in the light of the kitchen. Tom swallowed hard then licked his lips.

"The stone for a full and accurate translation of the text," she said.

"Yes of course," said Tom, reaching for the stone but Kari held it to the side.

"Not until I know I am going to get what I am paying for." She nodded to me.

I quickly pulled the key from my pocket and

opened the case where it sat on the floor. Disappointment flashed across Tom's face. He turned back to Kari and said, "This is a rare volume in dragon script. It will take some time to translate." As if punctuating his statement, the wind outside picked up, making the windows whistle.

"You old fool, even I could see that. You are unable to read it." Kari said indignantly.

I looked at the codex. The characters on the front cover twitched as if anxious to reveal their secrets.

"I... I... of course I can. That's a... a transcript of early dragon history," he said, stumbling. Kari laughed and put the stone in her pocket.

A minivan passed the kitchen window. Kari and Tom froze. The wind was eerily silent. Three children piled out of the van.

"What was your favorite part of the movie Mom?" a young boy said.

"My favorite part was sharing popcorn with you," replied the woman who was stepping out of the front seat.

"Mom!" all three of them complained together.

"OK guys brush your teeth and go to bed. You need your sleep for soccer tomorrow," called the Mom. The air wavered with the energy of her magic.

"I'll get her to translate it," whispered Tom.

"I can do that myself," said Kari, pushing past him. "Come on JJ. We should have waited for the librarian." She nodded to me. I grabbed the codex and followed her to the back door.

"The librarian's a soccer mom?" I asked startled at the realization.

"Soccer moms are the most powerful single group

in this country. If I had the choice between the US military and the US soccer moms, I'd take the soccer moms." Kari said. She smiled as we walked outside to meet the librarian.

13

The librarian had entered the back door of the cream house by the time we made it off Tom's back porch. The wind blew so hard it had knocked over the garbage cans by Tom's back steps. Garbage spilled into the driveway. It almost knocked me off my feet.

"So Tom is just the Adjunct?" I yelled over the howling wind.

She nodded and put her finger to her lips to silence me. As we crept toward the house my whole body tingled at the magic. A loud clang reverberated around the houses. Kari and I froze in the middle of the driveway. The glow from the streetlights silhouetted a piece of siding that had come loose from the librarian's home. The wind pummeled it against the house.

A dark shadow seeped from the hedges at the front of the driveway and blocked our view of the sidewalk and street.

"Look out!" yelled Kari as the cloud shot toward us. I turned away from the cloud, ducked my head below my shoulders, and covered it with my hands. My watch expanded into the round shield. Something small pinged off its surface and drummed on my back and legs. I didn't feel any pain, but felt very tired. The armor had drawn on my will to live.

Kari gasped and fell to the pavement. Thousands of pine needles protruded from her back and her white jacket began to turn red with blood.

A pile of needles littered the ground behind me.

The librarian walked down her back steps and stood at the edge of the driveway. Her sun bleached hair fluttered in the fading wind. She looked down and said, "Nice to see you again Kari."

"Nice to see you too Liz," gasped Kari, writhing in pain. "How's George?"

"We've been divorced for three years now. He couldn't handle the mystery of our world bringing in more money than he did," she said sadly. "Oh do hush up!" she barked at the piece of siding clanging against her house. It quickly fit itself back into place.

"And what have we here?" she said, looking at me. "Ah, you must be the teenage weapons and explosives expert turned terrorist and kidnapper." She smiled at me but it quickly faded to a look of dangerous concern. "And how is it that you are not in the same condition as our dear friend Kari?"

"Speaking of which would you mind healing me?" groaned Kari, slumping to the ground.

"I'm trying to decide that now," Liz said to her calmly before turning back to me.

"Dragon armor," I said through gritted teeth. I didn't like that she knew Kari but seemed perfectly willing to let her die.

"Well, you certainly didn't get it from Chan." She tapped her lips as she gazed at the sky in thought. "Unless you are an exceptional thief?" She sized me up as if determining if that was a possibility. I felt my face flush with anger. "Oh, I give up. Where did you get it?"

"A gift from my father as well as this codex that we want you to translate. Now either heal her or deal with me," I said, drawing my dagger as I stood.

"Oh, I like him," she said to Kari as she bounced on the balls of her feet. "He's feisty." She smiled.

Kari's eyes glazed over.

"And why do you want me to translate that codex for you?" she was suddenly serious. It was as if she was trying to put on a show. I felt like I was talking with Dillon.

"I don't care if it is translated or not. I am trading it for the life of my mother. It's Kari and Chan that want to know what it says," I spat.

This took her by surprise. She looked at me with curiosity. Kari completely collapsed on the pavement.

"I need Kari to save my mom. Now heal her, Liz," I said putting all the will I could muster behind the statement and brandishing the dagger. The magical force pushed out from me and slammed into an unyielding invisible wall between us. She smiled at me. I pushed harder and her smile faded into a quizzical look. I felt the wall begin to slide ever so slightly.

"You have a great deal to learn about magic," she said.

My will faltered. The unstoppable force of her will rushed toward me. I gasped. Her will was so powerful I knew it would not only overwhelm me, it would extinguish my entire existence. It was more terrifying than Chan, more terrifying than the bull, more terrifying than anything I could imagine. At the last possible moment the force stopped. It hung over me while Liz pondered. I couldn't move. I couldn't breathe. Yet, the only thing I worried about was what would happen to Kari, Dillon, Nikki, and my mom.

"I will heal Kari for the sake of your mother, not under the duress of magic," Liz said. The force dissipated.

"Thank you," I said with the depth of gratitude that can only be expressed to someone who spared your life for no reason other than mercy.

Kari's white jacket was entirely crimson with the blood she had lost. Liz knelt next to Kari and ran her hands over the pine needles stuck in her back. As her hand passed, the needles began to melt as if they were lit candles. The magic felt like a churning hot tube that was boiling over. The blood in Kari's jacket gathered together at each needle. It looked like pink polka-dots just before the needles completely melted and Kari was left lying on the driveway as if she had never been injured.

"Shall we go inside and get out of this dreadful weather?" Liz stood, turned, and headed toward the back door.

I helped Kari up, who was still a little wobbly and we walked into Liz's house.

There were no books in this kitchen. It was warm and cheery, full of life. I felt like I had just walked into my mother's kitchen before it had been turned into a pile of ash. The memory caused my throat to close and the details of Liz's kitchen became blurry as my eyes watered.

"Wait here 'til I get the kids in bed," Liz said, rushing from the room.

Kari and I sat at the kitchen table. The codex case looked out of place on the chipped and worn laminate kitchen table. We both chuckled at the machinations her kids went through to avoid going to bed. After several minutes of cajoling her children, including an artful parry of two "I'm thirsty" requests, Liz joined us at the table.

"So, what's so important that you need translated?" she asked Kari who motioned to me.

I snapped open the case. The letters on the cover danced frantically. I was certain they wanted her to read them.

"Where did you get this?" Liz opened to a page in the middle of the book that looked like some sort of table. The letters leapt all over the page. The characters in the last two columns began forming numbers. At times it looked like a checkbook where the first column showed either a positive or negative number and the last column changed based on that value.

"It's an accounting ledger," I said.

Kari and Liz looked at me like some jack-in-the-box that had surprised them. I was getting really tired of people looking at me like that.

"Why didn't you tell me you could read part of it?" asked Kari.

"Can't you see it now?" I asked.

"No, it looks the same to me," Kari replied.

"But the characters are dancing all over the place. Isn't that Liz translating it?"

Liz smiled. "I have done nothing, but you are right. This part of it is an accounting ledger. This particular page appears to outline some early dealings of the Federal Reserve," said Liz.

"Babat would love to hear that," I mumbled under my breath.

"How is Babat?" Liz asked eagerly.

"Um, he's fine," I replied, surprised at how mentioning Babat had completely distracted her from the codex.

Liz seemed lost in thought before Kari brought her back, "Liz? The codex?"

"Oh right," she said, turning more pages of the codex. "I'm sure Babat would love this," she said. It still didn't sound like she was concentrating on the codex.

"Oh, that's what I was going to ask you on the train," I said to Kari, remembering our interrupted conversation. "How can the Federal Reserve be the dragon's tool when it's a government agency?"

Kari looked at Liz who was shaking her head.

"It was the last question on my final government exam. The Constitution says Congress controls the money," I said, pleading my case.

"That is what it says in in the Constitution but the Federal Reserve is not a government agency," Kari said.

"That's not entirely true. It is privately owned but congress confirms whomever the president nominates to the Board of Governors," Liz replied.

"Not hard to figure out who is pulling the strings for the nominations to those seven spots," Kari said sarcastically.

"So it *is* a government agency," I said.

"No it is a legalized banking cartel," Kari said. "The Fed themselves even say they're 'independent from the government'," she added, making little quote signs in the air with her fingers.

"You would think that a high school graduate would have some idea of how the monetary system of his own country works," said Liz, her voice dripping with disappointment. "And that is why good people like Babat end up blindly following Chan on his crusade to end the Fed?"

"You cannot deny that allowing a private organization to define US monetary policy in secret meetings has allowed the dragon to amass its hoard," Kari replied.

"Sure, but that doesn't mean you have to scrap the Fed." Liz said in that tone all mothers use when they have reached the limit of their patience. "But we could argue about that all night," she pre-empted Kari's reply before turning to me. "You should read up on it and make up your own mind. Be careful to stick to the facts. There are a lot of crazy conspiracy theorists out there floating enough fiction to make anyone's head spin."

"Ok," I said sheepishly. I half wished they would continue their discussion so I could better understand what was going on. But there was no way I was going to push Liz and the last thing I was going to do was study. I'd hated history in school and had no intention of developing a new appreciation for the subject. Then I remembered that my plan for avoiding college by working for Nikki's dad wasn't going to work out and my heart sank.

Liz noticed my frown. "Of course you can read about what really happened behind the scenes in here," she said slapping the pages of the codex.

"I can't read that," I protested.

"But you will, that's why the text dances for you," she said with a grin. "And this is a pretty good read. It details most of the early tricks the dragon used to leverage the Fed for his major power grabs." She began flipping through the pages again.

"That makes no sense," said Kari. "Why would the dragon care about a book, written in dragon script that details past successful ploys?" I got the feeling she was trying to direct the conversation away from my developing ability to read the codex.

"But you said so yourself," Liz answered. "The details of the Fed are secret. The truth of any secret plan is dangerous to those who wish it to remain secret. Otherwise they wouldn't be keeping it a secret."

"No one would believe it," Kari replied.

"People seem to have a natural sense of when something rings true; or false for that matter," Liz said dismissively as she continued to thumb through the codex.

Kari launched into one of her breathless rants. "But the dragon controls the media outlets. If we publish it online he would have it declared a terrorist site and have it removed. Why would he go to the extreme of calling out harpies over something so easily squashed? We figured it had a layout of the lair or..." Kari paused.

Liz was frozen, staring at one of the first pages in the codex. "This is why," she said so softly it was almost inaudible.

I craned my neck to look at the page. The characters on it danced like popcorn in a popper. Every once in a while words would form and then quickly disappear.

"This lists the true magical names and locations of every dragon on earth," Liz whispered in disbelief.

Kari gasped and then froze. Liz looked at Kari with the grin of someone about to lay down the winning hand in poker and said, "Including his."

"The most powerful magical tool anyone could

have against the dragons," said Kari, her whole body rigid with excitement. She looked at the codex in complete awe. Now I understood why the dragon wanted it back. Not only would he want to protect his name but I imagine the other dragons wouldn't be too happy if they discovered he had revealed their names.

The warning clang from the siding split the silence. We all jumped. Kari sprang to her feet, blades drawn. Liz froze, waiting to hear if it would clang again. I wondered what unwelcome visitor had just arrived and hoped it wasn't Inicma.

It clanged again. "We need to get you out of here," Liz rushed. "Officially the archive keeper is neutral. If a goon finds you here with that codex I will lose all protections." She quickly crossed to a door on the far side of the kitchen. "Wait down here and if anything happens you have my permission to go through the library. It's behind the saw."

I snapped the case with the codex shut and followed Kari toward the door.

Kari stopped at the top of the stairs. "What is the dragon's name?"

"I am not going to endanger my children," said Liz, pushing her through the door to the basement steps. "Ask him." She pushed in me after Kari.

"But I can't read it," I responded.

"You will," she said as she shut the door behind us. I knew getting the dragon's name would count as the critical information I had agreed to get for Chan and wished desperately that she would have just told us what it was.

We were standing on some painted wooden steps with old blue indoor/outdoor carpet on them. Bare light bulbs showed a jumbled basement that included old toys and boxes labeled Xmas. A shelf with different colored glass bottles and a workbench with tools hanging in outlined spaces on a peg board lined the walls. Next to the workbench stood a large table saw.

"I have an idea," Kari said. She darted to the to the shelves and selected a green bottle with a round bottom and tall narrow neck. "Put the codex in your kamisan and give me the case."

"I don't have a room to go into," I said, looking for a way to get out of the room she was in.

"I will be fine. Just do it quickly," she replied. Her whole body seemed to vibrate as she anxiously watched me pull out the kamisan.

I touched my watch to the kamisan. The basement disappeared and I opened the chest. While my father's image gave its instructions I opened the codex case, and placed the unprotected codex in the kamisan. The image of the ax on the back wall definitely vibrated this time. I didn't have time to play with it. My father had just finished expressing his love for my mom and I quickly closed the footlocker.

No sooner had Kari regained her color than she grabbed the open case from me, put the green vile in it, and closed the lid. I looked at Kari apologetically as I stuffed the plastic bag with the kamisan back into the pocket in my armor. She just smiled, holding the case in both hands like it was a prize at the fair.

Upstairs fell silent. An ominous stillness filled the emptiness left by the silenced alarm.

"Let's find the door," Kari whispered. We searched everywhere around the large table saw. She turned the wheels and slid the levers. I tried pushing it and pulling it. Kari stopped me before I could kick it.

The back door to the kitchen opened. We held perfectly still and listened.

"I want to know where they are," came a slow hissing voice.

"Harpy," whispered Kari.

"I told you, I don't know," said Liz.

Kari held up the case that now held the green bottle and whispered, "If things go wrong and this case isn't what I think it is we are going to die very quickly."

At that moment, the hand-saw hanging on the workbench swung to one side. The workbench slid forward like a giant vault door until it revealed the spiral staircase behind it.

A black shadow stood on the top step, blocking our exit. "I can get you out of here," Tom said. He stepped forward and the light revealed his wicked smirk.

"They were here. I can feel it," said the slow hissing voice from just beyond the basement door.

"Yes, they were here but as you can see I asked them to leave," said Liz calmly. I was impressed that she was able to say words that were absolutely true in a way that made it sound like we had long since left.

Tom looked at Kari and his smirk became a sneer. "It will cost you the dragon stone."

Kari scowled at him.

"Mommy, what was that noise?" a faint little girl's voice called from somewhere above.

"It's nothing honey, I'll be right up," Liz called sweetly back to her daughter.

"Get out of my way," Kari growled softly as she reached for one of her blades.

"Ught, ught," scolded Tom, moving his hand

forward to reveal a pistol like I had seen the Germans use in old World War II movies.

"Perhaps I will just take a look around the archives myself," hissed the voice from upstairs. My heart raced. I looked over my shoulder to see if the door would open.

"Here she comes, now give me the stone," Tom hissed angrily.

"If all you want is a library visit you will have to see Tom while I tend to my children," said Liz. It sounded like her voice was right at the top of the stairs.

"Perhaps, you should get back to your place before your client arrives," said Kari as she smiled smugly at Tom.

"Oh, she won't hurt me. See, I'm the one who told them you were here," said Tom.

I sighed. We had no escape.

"I have already talked to Tom and know they are here," hissed the voice irritably.

"Then he should be able to locate them for you because I don't know where they are," replied Liz, raising her voice. It was impossible to tell if she was upset with the harpy or with Tom.

"Now give me the gem and I will let you pass," said Tom.

"Mommy, who are you talking too," the little girl said.

"Go to bed sweetie, I'll be up in a minute to tuck you in." There was no edge to Liz's reply.

"If you don't let me through that door then *I* will tuck your children in," the voice hissed back.

Kari reached into her pocket and slowly pulled out the gem.

"Am I mistaken or did you just threaten my children?" I heard Liz say in an ominous tone.

"You are not mistaken. Let me pass or they will pay for your insolence," hissed the voice.

There was a moment of silence. It felt like every hair on my body stood on end before the magical energy upstairs was released. A tremendous explosion shook the house. Kari took that moment, when Tom was surprised, to lunge forward and slam the metal case into his chest. The sound of breaking glass from inside the case was quickly swallowed by the earsplitting crack of Tom's gun. Kari drove him back to the stairs and brought the case down on his arm. The gun fell from his grasp, clanking on the metal stairs as it bounced out of sight.

"Follow me," Kari called as she launched herself down the stairs.

Tom threw a wild punch at me as I approached the stairs. I used Babat's training. I stepped inside the punch and lowered my shoulder. Tom's arm bounced off my shoulder as I drove him back. He cried out in pain as he bent backwards over the railing. I sprang away from him and rushed down the stairs.

I caught a brief glimpse of Kari, grasping the center post. She spun down the steps five at a time and disappeared like she had swirled down a drain. I tore down the steps as fast as I could; taking three steps at a time on the curving stairway. There was no way I could keep up.

Tom screamed in fury. His slow hobbled steps echoed on the staircase above.

The steps of the staircase became irregularly spaced as they plunged through the earth. I almost fell more than once. The stairs periodically gave way to a narrow tunnel cut through stone, which would lead to yet another set of stairs. I was on my sixth set of stairs when another thunderous explosion shook the staircase so violently that I lost my balance and fell over the railing.

14

I knew I was plummeting to my death. I grasped at the stone as it rushed by but it was just out of reach. I tumbled through the air until I landed, gently, on top of a large wooden bookcase.

Bookcases, identical to the one I was on, filled the room as far as the eye could see. There were no walls. The only distinguishing characteristics were the two spiral staircases that went up through two holes in the stone ceiling. Both staircases were more than a football field away from me. I wondered how I could possibly have fallen so far from the steps. Above me was only hewn stone.

"Kari?" I called peering over the edge of the book case. I was more than thirty feet from the ground.

"I'm over here," her voice wafted up from between some shelves not far from me. The shelves were not in neatly ordered rows. As I tried to find a way to get to Kari on the tops of the book cases it became clear that this was a labyrinth beyond my abilities.

"This place is a maze," I yelled to her.

"It contains all the known magical history in the world and is organized that way. Let me guess, you are in American Banking," she said, but it seemed to come from a different direction.

I pulled a book from the top shelf. *A History of US Fiat Currency*

"Yeah, how did you know?" I called.

"We enter the library based on our needs," she said from a different direction. "The library takes on the attitude of the librarian. So based on the conversation we just had with Liz, I guessed that was where you would land."

"Great, so how do we find each other?" I asked.

"I would guess we have to get our needs to align." Her reply was such a faint echo I couldn't tell where it was coming from.

"You would guess?" I asked indignantly. Kari had been my source of endless expertise but now she didn't sound at all confident.

"Well, I have only been here once and was accompanied by the librarian, so there is a lot I don't understand," she said from just a few rows to my left.

"OK, so what section are you in?" I asked.

"Um...I would rather not say," she replied. I was astounded. Kari was never at a loss for words.

"Well since you already know a ton about US banking history, it doesn't seem very likely that you will convince the library you need to be here. So I need to change my need to match yours," I said.

There was no reply.

"Kari?" I called.

"I heard you. I am just trying to find a better alternative," she replied and it sounded like she was right at the end of the book case. Now I really wanted to know what section she was in, regardless of need. I crawled to the end of the book case and peered over the edge. I expected to see her but only found a ladder instead.

"Oh alright, I am in a section about how to forgive others," she said from far to my right.

I probably would have asked her a million questions about why she was in that section if it hadn't been for the screech of a harpy. It echoed through the cavern and filled my heart with dread. "Thank you for telling me your location," hissed the harpy. The flutter of wings sounded like it was right next to me. The harpy's voice was higher, more menacing than it had been when talking to Liz.

I wondered if Liz was ok as I quickly swung myself over the edge of the book case and scrambled down the ladder. I figured if Kari was magically moving around so I couldn't find her, then I should be moving around so the harpy couldn't find me.

The harpy's next screech sounded miles away.

Even though I couldn't read most of the titles I knew that every book I passed dealt with banking. *The History and Impact of the Bank of England, Fractional Lending for Dolts,* and *Gold, Silver or Fiat?* were some of the English titles I passed. I wondered why the library didn't think my most pressing need was how to rescue a dragon abductee or how to escape harpy attacks. Then it occurred to me there probably wasn't much written on either subject because there probably weren't many who had successfully done either.

I reached the bottom of the ladder and turned away from a thick tome labeled *Greenbacks: Fiat Boon or Fiat Bust* and started running.

The energy from the books made my head spin. I didn't care where I was running I just wanted to get away from the banking books. Just standing in the aisle with them made me sick to my stomach. I took my first left and felt relief at not having to worry about that section. I turned right at the next intersection and slammed into another old ladder. I took a quick look to see what section I was in and came face to face with *Greenbacks: Fiat Boon or Fiat Bust.* I was right back where I started.

My head was splitting. Everywhere I looked the magical letters on books were spinning, and vibrating. I dropped to my knees, dizzy from the letters' motions. It felt like my head was a water balloon that someone was trying to overfill with magical knowledge. I closed my eyes and wrapped my arms around my head in an effort to keep it from exploding.

The world spun around me with my eyes closed so I couldn't tell which way was up or down or if there was any way at all. I thought I was still on the ground but pried my eyes open just to be sure. I was still in the library and was face to face with a particularly colorful book binding. The characters danced on the cover. I blinked, then blinked again. The title read, "Fiat Currency Review."

As soon as the letters settled into place the pain disappeared and the room stopped spinning. The chaos was replaced by perfect order. I could read the title of every book. I knew which titles were magical, which were French, which were German yet they all appeared as perfect English to me.

I could also feel the magic that redirected every path back to this spot. It was like an invisible river of energy that flowed around the book cases, twisting space and carrying any path back to where I stood. The library would keep me here until I had learned what I needed.

"What does it mean that I can read everything now?" I called to Kari. There was a long pause.

"I'm not sure," Kari called from far away. She must have been really stressed because her attempt to lie failed miserably.

The thud of the harpy landing on a bookcase echoed above me. The magic of the library swept the harpy away in a swiftly moving magical current before I could look up to see how close she was. "I will find you," she hissed from farther away.

The harpy's current had been different from mine. Almost like, the currents that affected me were one color and the currents that affected the harpy were another.

I looked back at the books in front of me. "Kari, the library seems fixated on teaching me about fiat currency. What is that?" I asked.

"Fiat is Latin for 'let it be done.' So Fiat currency is money that only has value because the ruling class says it has value," Kari said. She was only a couple aisles away.

The magical flow that kept me in this section began to subside.

"So instead of the money being based on Gold or Silver the money only counts because the government says so?" I asked, trying to clarify.

"Now I have you," hissed the harpy. It sounded like she was between me and Kari, but I had no fear of being found. The harpies current flowed away from me while Kari's current was parallel to mine.

"Yes, and in the case of the US currency that value

is mostly controlled by the Fed," Kari said. The magic of the library swirled around me and whisked me away to a different section. There was no physical movement but the magical current was unmistakable. The books on fiat currency disappeared and were replaced by books on the Federal Reserve and books on the Cyngor am Ryddid.

"Where are you boy?" squawked the harpy from far away.

I smiled at the harpy's struggle with the magic and resisted the urge to taunt it. "Ok Kari, I think the library is trying to get me to make a decision between the Fed and the Cyngor am Ryddid," I called.

"But that is not an either or decision," she called, farther away than ever.

"Well apparently, Liz thinks it is and I have to say that I agree with her," I called.

"The decision is between the dragon and the Cyngor am Ryddid," she said, her position hadn't changed.

"And trust me boy, you want to side with dragon," hissed the harpy.

"Kari, you've made it clear that no matter who wins the economy is going to tank because whoever wins determines what happens with the Fed. So the Fed is a part of this," I replied pretending not to hear the harpy.

"Look, you may not believe it but I know that the Fed was created to fill the dragon's hoard and subject people to mounds of debt and taxes that would enslave them to the dragon. And I know it has been very successful," Kari said.

"And my master will always be successful at

defeating riff-raff like you," hissed the harpy.

"Let us take Liz's advice and stick to facts anyone can find in a regular library," Kari said still in the same location. "Officially the Fed was created to provide monetary and economic stability. Just look at US economic history since it was created and you'll see it has failed in that mandate."

The magic washed over one side of the aisle and the shelves were instantly filled with books on US economic history.

"Ya know Kari, I've always hated history. Even if I wanted to, there's no way I could dig through all the economic history books that just appeared in front of me," I replied.

"Oh, I love history, particularly when it leads me to my prey," hissed the harpy. I felt a subtle shift in the harpy's magic but was confident it would not find me.

"Well, the great depression happened after the Fed was created and we certainly are not in a good place now," Kari said.

I could feel the truth in her words but I still didn't like siding with the Cyngor am Ryddid when it meant economic catastrophe. I wondered how my mom would feel about Chan's plans and knew she would not agree with anything that would add to people's suffering. "How could my father be showing my mom that he loved her if he was trying to plunge the country into chaos by destroying the Fed?" I asked myself aloud.

"Your father did not want to destroy the Fed. He wanted to keep it but without the dragon and with enough controls that greedy power mongers couldn't abuse it," Kari replied.

That was the most rational thing I'd heard about this whole mess. "Could that be done?" I asked.

The harpy laughed menacingly. "You are all fools," it screeched.

"That is what Pete is hoping for, but nothing happens while the dragon lives," Kari replied.

The magic changed the books on the shelves before I realized I had made a decision. I could give Chan the information to slay the dragon as long as there was some hope that someone more reasonable, like Pete, would keep the economy from crashing. I was now surrounded by books about the organization of the Cyngor am Ryddid. Kari's magical flow was now very close to mine.

"Who do you need to forgive?" I asked Kari. There was a long silence but I could feel that she was close and knew that she had heard me.

"My parents died slaying the dragon that was behind Apartheid in South Africa. There are a great many people I need to forgive." The shame in her voice hurt my ears. The sorrow of her loss was amplified by her guilt at failing to forgive.

My sorrow for her loss constricted my chest. She knew the pain of losing a parent. I wondered if I would be as bitter if Chan failed to save my mom. "I'd guess some of them are in the Cyngor am Ryddid?" I asked. A small portion of our currents now intersected.

"Yes," she replied, equally ashamed.

"And you've done a lot of research to know who they are huh?" I asked. The currents were close I just needed to find a way to make the library connect them.

"Yes, what are you getting at?" She was getting upset at my probing into parts of her past she wanted kept private.

"He's trying to get your last confession before I kill you," the harpy cried.

Then it occurred to me. The library needed to be told how the currents would connect. I didn't have a pen or paper but knew where I could find some. I pulled the kamisan from its plastic pouch and touched my watch to it. The blackness filled the library and the foot locker top appeared. I wondered what the harpy would think of being stuck in its master's device.

I dug through the disorganized pile I had dumped in the corner of the chest. My father had long since finished his little speech before I found an old fashioned quill, a bottle of ink, and some ancient parchment. It was strange to feel the magic in my hands as I held the quill over the paper. It took a few tries to figure out how the quill and ink worked. I knew what I was writing was magical so the library would understand it, but I had to concentrate to have letters be English as well. I needed Kari to be able to read it too. Eventually I wrote:

While working to forgive those in the Cyngor am Ryddid, Kari Tiesos told Michael Jefferson Jones the role of a squire was to defend the dragon slayer.

With new found appreciation for the magical ink and quill I placed them neatly on a stack of books in the back of the chest. The ax on the back panel shook as if it were going to leap out of the box. I watched it for a moment wondering if I would even be able to lift such an imposing looking weapon. The harpy would undoubtedly try to follow us when we found a way out and my little dagger hadn't been much help last time so I decided to give the ax a try.

I reached for the ax and it flew into my hand. As I lifted it from the foot locker, the double bladed head grew to be wider than my shoulders and turned a brilliant sky blue. The wooden handle was a highly polished deep brown wood with two silver bands evenly spaced. From the silver cap on the end of the handle to the tips of the blades, the ax was as long as one of my legs. Magic pulsed through it. Despite its enormous size, it was as light and easy to wield as my dagger. It was definitely coming with me.

I leaned it against my side while I closed the lid to exit the kamisan but as soon as I leaned forward the ax snapped to my back as if drawn by a magnet. I froze at the surprising motion. The blade rested flat against the small of my back while the handle protruded above my right shoulder. The ax felt as comfortable as a warm blanket and much more reassuring. I snapped the chest shut and stood as the blackness disappeared.

When the library came into focus Kari asked, "What are you doing JJ?"

I placed the parchment on the shelf in front of me. The tan parchment melted into a puddle that looked like vanilla pudding. The puddle rippled slightly before a narrow, leather bound portfolio began to silently grow from its center. The puddle shrank as the portfolio grew until finally the puddle was gone. The title on the edge of the portfolio read, "The Writings of Michael Jefferson Jones." I could feel the magical connection between our sections.

"I think I just forged a link between our sections," I said reaching for the book.

"I guess you did," she said.

When my fingers touched the book most of the other books on the shelves faded away like a bad dream, until the shelves were nearly empty. As the books disappeared from the shelves, Kari appeared at my side, her hand on the same book I had just written. The magical current that had seemed like a river flowing between and through the bookcases now felt like a shallow stream at my feet.

She smiled at me. "That was brilliant."

I felt my face flush. "Now, how do we get out of here?" I scanned the aisle of nearly empty shelves. There were only two books close enough to see the titles. One was an enormous volume entitled, "Dragon Conspiracies" and the other was a miniscule pamphlet entitled "Farewell." Kari and I looked at each other in disbelief and then simultaneously reached for the pamphlet. The moment we touched it, the library disappeared and we were standing on a spiral staircase.

"This place makes no sense!" screeched the harpy in the distance.

Kari and I chuckled as we started up the stairs.

"That was creepy," Kari said

"Once you get used to the magic it isn't that bad," I replied.

"What magic?" Kari asked with that surprised look I hated.

"You know the headache and dizziness when you're first surrounded by all the magic," I replied.

"As I said, it is very rare to be able to feel the magic so acutely. In any case I have never heard of it overwhelming someone to the point that it would be painful unless they were specifically targeted for pain," she said.

"Ya know Kari, I used to like you, but now you've gotten all cryptic on me," I teased.

"Quiet please, we are almost there," she replied with a teasing smile.

We had only climbed two flights of stairs before they stopped at a dimly lit narrow hall. At the end of the hall was a stone wall with a small brass door handle in the middle. Kari drew one of her blades, still holding the steel case in the other. I turned the handle to the door and it silently slid to the side. Light poured through the doorway accompanied by the wailing of the wind from outside. A wave of magical energy washed over me that told me it was no ordinary wind.

We emerged into the glare of uncovered light bulbs in a basement filled with stacks of books and boxes. The steps on the far side of the basement were blocked. Tom sat on them, his gun in hand and pointed our direction.

"Take one more step and you're dead," he said.

We froze where we were.

"That really hurt," he said, rubbing his back with his free hand. "So I think I will return the favor. You wanted to know why you can suddenly read the dragon scripts?" his sneer sent chills down my spine. "The only way a person comes by that skill is to be given it by the dragon," he said, "or to inherit it." He enunciated each syllable of "inherit" individually. Each felt like a dagger to my chest.

The uncovered light bulbs seemed to burn the realization into my tearing eyes. I had inherited my mother's magical gifts.

My chest seared with pain. I had her gifts because

either Inicma or the dragon had killed her.

Hatred erupted within me.

"I think I'll be taking that dragon stone now." Tom leveled his gun at Kari. His eyes narrowed and his arm flexed. He was going to kill her.

Anger burned in the pit of my stomach. It roared through my chest and into my head. Without realizing what I was doing, I rushed forward pulling the ax from my back with my right hand. I raised my arm in front of me. The watch burst into the round shield. I lifted it to cover my face. The portion of the shield that would have blocked my view became transparent. Tom's face shone with horror. He pointed his gun at me and squeezed off a shot. The bullet rang as it bounced off the shield.

As I neared Tom everything seemed to slow down. My rage faded. I was about to split him in two at the waist. I didn't want to kill anyone. The ax was already in motion. I remembered Babat's instructions about keeping the edge of a dagger toward an opponent and did the opposite. At the last moment I twisted my arm so the ax hit Tom with the flat of the blade. There was a sickening crunch as the force of the ax propelled him from the steps to the basement floor. His gun flew from his hand, slid across the floor and lodged under a book case.

"Wow, I do not know where that came from, but we must go," Kari said, urgently pushing me up the stairs. I didn't care about getting out of the basement. My mom was dead. I had no reason to continue this nonsense.

Kari pushed me through the door at the top of the stairs and into Tom's kitchen. The only light was a faint glow through the back porch door. The incredible wind from outside shook the windows. I could taste the magic in the air as Kari opened the back door.

Liz stood in the middle of the driveway highlighted by the headlights of her mini-van. She was staring intently down the driveway toward the road and was swinging her hands in the air in alternating circles. Babat was right; the magical power that enveloped her made it obvious, she was scary.

The wind sounded like a freight train and threatened to carry me away. I put the ax back in its place on my back and held fast to the porch railing. Kari pulled me down the back porch steps to stand next to Liz, where the wind was almost nonexistent.

The driveway between the houses was covered with the slashing bands of a whirling tornado that was full of pine needles, metal siding, and shredded garbage cans. The back half of the first floor of Liz's house was missing.

Liz looked at us briefly before she stopped moving her arms. She held her hands out to the side, her fingers curled toward the sky as if each hand held a large weight. The noise of the tornado stopped and the gray swirling mist dissolved to reveal several SUVs, numerous goons, and two harpies suspended in midair. "The library," Liz said in a loud voice as she turned her hands over in front of her chest, as if she were throwing the weights to the ground in front of her, "is closed." Both houses folded in upon themselves like they were being sucked into the ground. The goons and SUV's fell into the roiling flow of splintered wood, broken stone, and twisting metal. The harpies shrieked in horror as pipes from the houses shot into the sky, wrapped around their legs, and pulled them into the tumult. The roar continued until the houses, trees and shrubs had all been consumed by the frothing pits where the houses had been. Silence fell and all that remained was the grass, the driveway, and two perfectly smooth concrete slabs on the ground, like flat grave markers commemorating where the houses once stood.

Liz turned to get into her van. The wide eyes of her three children stared at her in wonder.

"Wait!" said Kari stepping toward her. She paused when Liz glared at her. "Take this," she said offering her cell phone to Liz.

Liz paused at the door of her mini-van and looked at the phone skeptically.

"So you can reach us if you want. It has Babat's number in it and is a clean line," she said.

"Thank you," said Liz, her expression softening as she took the phone.

"Please tell me the name?" asked Kari desperately.

"Avarice, Diluter of Liberty and Ouster of Charity" Liz said softly as she shut her door. The mini-van shot forward cutting across the lawn, veering onto the street with its tires squealing and sped away into the darkness

15

Kari and I stood for several minutes looking at the desolate space around us. The sheer power I had just witnessed temporarily drove Tom's revelation about my mom from my mind.

"Sorry about your case," Kari said handing it to me.

"Why, what's wrong with it?" I asked.

"That was a vile of poison. I heard it break when I pushed past Tom so the only thing you could use that case for now is a trap."

"That's OK, if we had to give something to a harpy I couldn't think of a better gift," I said and smiled at her to make sure she knew I meant it.

"Do you think we can get a cab this time of night?" Kari asked looking at the desolate street.

I shook my head. "In Hicksville? Probably not."

"Well, we better get moving then because it is a long walk to the Stumble Inn." she said. As we walked down the driveway she asked, "So are you going to tell me about that ax that appeared from nowhere?"

"Oh, good point, I should probably put it back in the kamisan before someone sees it," I replied looking around and wondering what would happen if I opened the kamisan outdoors.

"First of all, unless you want to wreak havoc on Hicksville I would leave your kamisan where it is. Secondly, if I cannot see that ax, then no one else can either," she said casually.

"What do you mean? It's magically stuck to my back. Of course you can see it." I replied.

"If it is on your back right now then it is invisible and I would not so easily part company with such a magnificent weapon."

We walked under the midnight shadows of the trees in silence as I considered the magical weapon on my back and the incredible power of the librarian. Then I remembered what Tom said and the pain brought me to a halt. The grief felt like an enormous weight on my chest that would crush me. I almost wished it would crush me. I'd rather that than continue to suffer the pain in my chest.

"Is something wrong?" asked Kari.

"Why didn't you tell me my mom was dead?" I forced the words from tightening throat.

"We do not know that she is dead," she replied softly and patted my hunched shoulder in comfort.

I shrugged away from her touch. "Tom said reading dragon script only comes through inheritance." I looked at the ground to avoid making eye contact with her. Bursting into tears in front of Kari was a shame I did not want to endure.

"That was quite cruel of him," she said and I heard a small glimmer of hope in her voice. "While it is true that such skill is only obtained through inheritance, magical inheritance can be achieved in many ways that do not require death," she explained.

I looked up and saw the hope in her eyes and my heart rebelled against the agony it felt. The hope that she still lived lifted the weight from my chest. I clung to that hope.

I would get her back unharmed or would spend the rest of my life making sure every sordid detail of the codex was revealed until the dragon ran in fear of its peers.

📖 📖 📖

It was nearly one in the morning when we reached the dilapidated old motel. The Stumble Inn sign hung from a rusty metal pole in front of a tiny wood panel building with windows full of neon beer signs. Behind that sat two long squat one story buildings on either side of a parking lot that had decayed from asphalt to gravel. The fresh coats of white and turquoise paint on these buildings did little to hide the scars from years of abuse.

"Why did you want us to stay here?" I asked Kari as we walked toward the office.

"They will rent rooms for cash," she said. I nodded, understanding that she didn't want to use a credit card because it could be tracked. "And they have excellent food," she finished, smiling at me.

I waited outside while she went into the office and returned with a room key. We rounded the corner and Kari smiled at the Mylar balloon bumping against one of the doors. "I guess we know which room they're in," she said. I smiled at the thought of seeing Dillon and Nikki again.

When we arrived at the door Kari reached for the balloon but it shot away. She chuckled. "I guess Chan remembered that I am not his squire anymore."

Babat opened the door before Kari could knock. Much like its exterior, the room showed the age of the motel. It had two sagging beds and a beat up desk that Dillon sat at, drumming away on his laptop. The burning scent of bleach did little to obscure the dank smell of mold.

"How did you know it was us?" Kari asked as we stepped inside.

"Brain child over there has been tracking you by your phones," he said motioning toward Dillon.

"Dude, what happened? Did you decide to go for an evening stroll through the picturesque monotony of Hicksville?" asked Dillon, never looking up from his desk. Nikki rolled her eyes.

For a brief moment I felt like we were back in school, without any worries. "Yeah, we didn't think a cab was a good idea since my disguise washed away."

Nikki got up off the bed where she'd been sitting and not so gently punched my arm. "Why didn't you tell us you were ok," she said wiggling her phone in the air.

I smiled at her. It was so nice to see her and know that she was thinking about me that I didn't rebuff her with the fact that we had been busy trying to stay alive.

"Why didn't you just steal a car?" Dillon asked.

"Because we were not fleeing an immediate threat so it was not necessary to inconvenience some innocent bystander," scolded Kari, who was holding the door open for the balloon.

Dillon looked up at her and his eyes went wide, as if he had forgotten what she looked like. He smiled and turned back to his computer. "Gotta get over that wow factor," he said under his breath but everyone in the room heard it. Kari smiled.

Babat looked like a lost puppy as the balloon floated toward him. He glanced back and forth between Kari and the balloon. As he touched it, the balloon dissolved and a small piece of paper appeared in his hand. "It's just a bunch of numbers." he said, sounding very confused.

"Let me see that." Dillon snatched it from him. After a quick glance he turned to his computer and quickly stroked the keys.

I sat on the bed next to Nikki, our hands interlocked so naturally it was as if they had years of practice finding their way to each other. My heart jumped up in my throat but I couldn't tell if it was from joy or horror.

"Looks like we're headed to the Bronx tomorrow" said Dillon.

"Where precisely?" asked Kari.

"Kingsbridge armory at 10am" he replied.

"Well it has been a long day for all of us. I suggest we get some sleep and head out in the morning," said Kari. I felt like I was being mothered.

Dillon flopped on one of the beds and said, "Plenty of room here," to Kari, patting the bed beside him. Nikki put her free hand to her mouth but failed to suppress her laughter.

"Nikki and I have our own room," Kari replied with disdain. Dillon's smile never faded.

"And shall the warrior princess of death force us onto mass transit tomorrow with her new found moral objection to grand theft auto, or shall we ride in style?" he asked in a mock pleading tone. Nikki rolled her eyes again. "I saw that Nikki," he remarked without taking his eyes off Kari's face.

"I believe I made it clear that I will only do that when absolutely necessary," she replied.

"Everyone sleep-in tomorrow," said Dillon conspiratorially.

"Enough with this silliness, I want to know what happened," said Babat.

"Yeah, and why is your phone in New Jersey?" said Dillon glancing at his laptop.

Kari explained the events with the librarian. Babat seemed to perk up at her description of Liz's reaction to his name. When she got to the point where Tom told me about my mother Nikki leaned her head against my shoulder and I felt my heart rate increase. After that I wasn't paying much attention to the story.

"Now, I really think we should all get some rest," said Kari beckoning to Nikki.

"Um," Nikki began, looking at me. "I ..." she was looking for the right words. My heart pounded in my chest. I wasn't sure what to say. I knew I needed to talk to her but the thought of trying to explain our new relationship was terrifying. Even more terrifying was the thought that I would say something wrong that would ruin what we had. I considered letting Kari take her to the other room but decided that was the coward's way out. After what I had been through I was sure I wasn't a coward.

"I'd like a minute to talk to her first," I said. Kari nodded and gave Nikki a key to their room.

Nikki and I followed Kari outside and watched as she entered the room just a couple doors down. My mind was a complete blank as I stood outside this crappy little motel in the middle of the night holding Nikki's hand. I had never been good at talking to girls … except for Nikki … and that had only been because I'd never realized how amazing she was. Now that I saw her clearly, I wasn't sure what to say.

"Nikki," I began, but she looked up at me with those enormous eyes and I completely forgot what I was going to say next.

"Yes?" she prodded.

"Look, I don't know what this is," I said shaking the hand that held hers. "But I am so grateful for all you've done." That sounded really stupid and I regretted saying it the moment it came out of my mouth. "I mean...thank you...for being here with me... I mean for me...I mean..." She put the hand I wasn't holding against my lips to stop me from talking. Her fingers were smooth, soft and tender.

"I will always be here for you," she said, then quickly kissed my cheek and walked away toward her room. I stood there stunned, both at what she had said and at the display of affection. I wanted more. I missed her touch. I wanted to hear her voice and look into her eyes. I wanted to be with her but the door had closed and I was left standing in the dim light of the parking lot, alone.

Dillon and Babat had claimed both of the beds by the time I got back to the room, so I set my ax next to the couch and lay down. The poisoned case sat by the bed and I decided I should put it away before going to sleep.

I went to the little bathroom, shut the door, and entered the kamisan. After putting the case away I pulled out the codex. The text on the cover no longer danced but read "Alpha Volume." The first page was labeled "The Dragon Pride." It contained a simple list of cities and dragon names in no particular order, starting at Apiarity and ending with Hubris. I found it interesting that almost all the dragons were named for vices but didn't pay much attention to them.

I knew which one had my mom.

I flipped quickly through the pages until Inicma's name jumped off the page at me. It was in the section that had looked like a recipe book to me before I could read it. Each entry listed what I assumed was a goon. It described them, what they were paid and most importantly, it gave their actual names as well as their operating names. I now knew that Inicma's full name was actually Zurdo Veijo. This information would certainly turn the tide of any battle.

I turned several more pages and found a set of construction plans for adding an entrance to the dragon's lair. I didn't understand all the blue prints but I understood the one with the overall layout of the lair. The dragon's lair was under Central Park. Its vast network of tunnels permeated nearly every corner of the park. That made perfect sense. It was the only part of Manhattan that didn't have subways running beneath it.

I stared at the corridor labeled 'to dungeon.' That was where I needed to go. I tried to picture the tunnel in my mind.

Mom and I were running from the dragon's lair. As I looked back to see how far back the dragon was, it snapped Nikki up in its claws, her kind wide eyes still staring at me. The dragon laughed like rolling thunder and said "You think knowing some names will save you and your little friends?" His voice was so low it shook the walls of the tunnel.

My eyes snapped open as I woke from the dream. I lifted my head from the codex. I was still in the kamisan. I looked at my watch. It was eight o'clock. Some part of me noticed that the second hand was now stuck on the five. I quickly returned the codex to the chest and closed it. When the bathroom reappeared Babat was standing in the doorway blinking his eyes in the light.

"Sorry," I said, pushing past him into the motel room. Sunlight shone through the front window.

"What was that?" Dillon asked in a daze.

"That's the kamisan and we're late" I rushed for the door to the room.

"Excellent! You really did sleep-in." he said. "No way to get to the Bronx in two hours if we use mass transit," he added.

I opened the door to find Kari and Nikki standing there. They looked like Athena and Aphrodite. "What happened?" asked Kari in a rage.

"I fell asleep reading in the kamisan," I replied. Kari paused for a moment to process what I had just said. She looked at Babat. He was still standing outside the bathroom in his boxers with a stunned look on his face. Kari burst out laughing and said, "I will go find a car to steal. It is the only way we will get there on time. You guys get ready."

"Yes dear, whatever you say, dear," Dillon replied sarcastically. Kari glared at him and for a moment I thought she was really going to yell at him, but Dillon just smiled at her until she left.

Dillon, Babat, and I quickly got ready and by the

time we left the room Kari was waiting in a minivan just outside the door. I climbed into the back seat with Nikki. They had been kind enough to pick up doughnuts while they were out stealing the car and we devoured them as we headed toward the Bronx.

When I told Kari that the codex did contain a map of the dragon's lair she practically floated out of the car in elation. Kari, Babat, and Dillon began peppering me with questions about it, but I couldn't remember much besides the fact that it was under Central Park and that the dungeon was on the west side. Dillon started air-typing and sharing what he found. He talked about how it made sense that each entrance to the park was called a gate with a different name and function. Kari and Babat lamented Chan's choice of hotel. It had placed them essentially on the dragon's front door step. They began speculating on challenges in assaulting the lair. None of them talked about the challenges we might face in rescuing my mom. I tuned out of the discussion rather than start an argument over their baseless speculating.

The Whitestone Bridge spans the Long Island Sound to connect Northern Queens to the Southern Bronx. As we crossed it I looked out over the Manhattan skyline. It was my home. With the soaring sky scrapers and modern technology it was hard to imagine a dragon living in the middle of the city I loved.

Dillon gave his normally flawless directions and we arrived at the Kingsbridge Armory in the Bronx just before ten o'clock. The former National Guard Armory looked like a large brick castle with towers and parapets surrounding a large arched roof in the middle.

The chain link fence that stood in front of the existing wrought iron fence was out of place for such a majestic building.

Babat touched the rusted lock on the gate and it popped opened. We followed him up the steps and through the elaborate iron doors.

The hallway was beautiful. Despite some minor chips in the plaster the vaulted brick and plaster arches were breathtaking. It seemed such a waste to have this magnificent building go unused. I wondered what type of politics had gotten in the way of it becoming the center of the community after the National Guard left.

Deacon Pete sat on a chair on the far side of the hall as we entered. "I've been waiting for you. Are you ok?" he asked with a smile of genuine concern.

"Hi Pete," I said. "Yeah, we're all fine."

"Oh, I'm so glad you're OK," said Nikki running to him and giving him a hug. I felt a small pang of jealousy at their touch.

"Your friend Joe made sure of that," he said to me motioning toward the door. I turned around to see Joe standing guard. He looked as healthy as he had when we first met.

"Hey JJ, those driving tips were real helpful," he said closing the doors.

"You gave someone driving tips? And they actually worked?" Dillon asked in shock.

"Actually, I just quoted you," I replied.

"Well, that makes more sense," he said, smiling to himself.

"You look well, but how do you feel?" said Kari with a wry smile as she gave Joe a hug.

"I feel good. You feel good too," he said holding

her closer.

Dillon's ears turned red. He definitely did not like what passed between Kari and Joe.

I decided to change the subject. "Hey Joe, I never got to say thanks for taking on Inicma for me. I didn't know what I was getting into." I looked at the floor, trying to hide my embarrassment.

"Happy to do it. I can't wait to get another crack at him," said Joe smiling.

"Where's Chan?" said Babat, sounding very official and annoyed with the friendly greetings.

"I think he's in the parade hall," Joe glared at Babat as he pointed down the hall. I got the impression he didn't approve of Babat replacing Kari as squire.

"I'll show you the way," said Pete. Kari reluctantly left Joe and came with us as we followed Pete around the corner and into one of the largest rooms I had ever seen. We stood on a wide walkway more than ten feet above a floor the size of four football fields that was covered in a mass of wings and golden fur. I paused to make sense of it as Babat moved on. It took a moment to realize that the wings and fur belonged to hundreds of creatures with the back legs of a lion and the head, wings and talons of an eagle. The head of each creature was more than twice the height of the men walking around them. The name "ryder" suddenly took on a new meaning for me.

"I wondered where he could possibly hide the griffins," Kari said. "This is a perfect location."

"Oh they're beautiful," Nikki said.

"They are the only remaining natural enemy of harpies and dragons," Kari said. "and an absolute riot to ride," she added with a smile.

"Well, Mr. Jones what do you think of my crazy conspiracy theories now?" said Mr. Morgan from behind me. I jumped at the sound of his voice.

He continued without waiting for a reply, "Did you know that the school district censured me for telling a class that the Federal Reserve was controlled by private interests and was not constitutional? I mean how constitutional can it be when the entire country's monetary policy is created by twelve people, five of whom are privately appointed and the other seven appointed by..."

"And putting the monetary policy in the hands of politicians will just let that bunch of crooks run the country into the ground," interrupted Pete.

"That's why we have to be on the gold standard," Mr. Morgan retorted.

"And who do you think has all the gold?" rebutted Pete.

"If the dragon didn't control the curriculum of every major college ..." Mr. Morgan began but I wasn't interested in listening to two old men argue about something I had already heard too much about.

"Nice to see you're doing so well, Mr. Morgan," I interrupted.

He looked at me with a start, as if he had forgotten I was there.

"Yes, well the combination of magic and medicine does wonders," he boasted, puffing out his chest. Nikki suppressed a laugh.

"I take it the cost of rescuing Mr. Gottschalk has paid dividends?" he asked Kari. Dillon turned to look at her, anxious for her reply.

She didn't get a chance to respond. "You lost four

men!" Chan screeched. Nikki took my hand as I turned. Chan's face was purple and was so close to Babat's they looked like they might touch. Babat's mouth moved but they were too far away for me to tell if he actually said anything. "You were supposed to get the tools I needed not lose my best men!" Chan's squeal echoed around the enormous room that had become suddenly quiet. "That book better be worth it!" he said through gritted teeth before turning his back on Babat.

"What is his problem?" I asked more to myself than to anyone in particular.

Mr. Morgan answered. "It's been more than two hundred years since a dragon slayer has survived slaying a dragon and we're launching the assault on the lair tonight."

16

Chan's anger quickly disappeared when Kari described the demise of the goons and harpies at Liz's hand. He became almost giddy when she explained that the codex contained the dragon's name and a map of his lair. But his elation disappeared when he learned it was in dragon script and that I was the only one who could read it.

"You are about to become very popular," Pete whispered to me. His prediction was quickly realized. After visiting a private room to use my kamisan, I was ushered to a large conference room. No less than twenty ryders sat around the long table in the middle of the room. Half had laptops. The other half looked too muscle bound to put their hands close enough together to use a keyboard. They all had weapons. Kari, Dillon and Nikki stood at the back of the room. I bristled that Chan treated them as too insignificant for a seat at the table.

"OK JJ, what does the codex say?" Chan asked.

He hadn't even given me time to be escorted to my seat. Just to annoy him I took my time. I sat in my chair and played with the height adjustment until I was comfortable. A stack of blank papers and a cup of pens had been placed in front of my seat. I pushed them aside, set the codex on the table and said, "The dragon's name is Avarice, Diluter of Liberty and Ouster of Charity."

"Yes, yes Kari already told us that," Chan said.

I was glad I could irritate him as much as he did me.

I started at what I thought would be most valuable in the upcoming battle. "Very well, there is a list of Avarice's goons, their descriptions, and true names. This includes …"

"That is irrelevant," Chan interrupted. "The codex is almost twenty years old. Most of those goons are probably dead, particularly after the librarian's success."

"Yes, but it –" I tried to tell him that it had Inicma's name, but he interrupted me.

"No 'buts', we want the layout of the lair," screeched Chan.

"Are you sure you wouldn't rather have me read you bedtime stories about the early dealings of the Fed," I replied with as much sarcasm as I could force through my clenched teeth.

Chan actually paused, a longing look in his eye. "We'll get to that later. For now just draw the lair if you have no other useful information for us," he spat back.

If that was the only thing Chan needed for me to meet my end of our deal, then that was all I would give him.

I spent the next several hours copying the pages of construction plans onto the blank pages. Although drawing had never been my strong suite I found it easy to create highly accurate reproductions of the plans. I suspected this was another skill I had inherited.

The ryders in the room couldn't agree on what the plans meant. Some believed that the new exit the codex talked about was one that they already knew about beneath the sewage treatment plant on Ward's Island. Others thought it was a previously unknown exit. Many of them began to question the accuracy of my drawings.

Dillon snapped a picture of my drawings and quickly showed how they perfectly aligned with his subterranean maps of Manhattan. He became the center of attention. While he argued with them about a third entrance and how suicidal an assault through the City Hall subway station would be, I thumbed through the codex.

When I got to the last page I found a plain white piece of paper that was not bound as part of the codex. The instant I touched it, words began to form on the page. For a moment I worried it was another kamisan but the room did not begin to fade and the words became clearer.

The page was titled "The Last Will and Testament of Bewirken Managito." My heart raced as I opened my father's will. It read:

"I Bewirken Managito do hereby incant that the following shall occur upon my death: All my material possessions, except any obligations owed to Peter Fidelis Coney for fulfillment of his oaths, shall become the property of Samantha Lee Meikleham." I wondered if this meant Pete and what oaths he was under. The will continued, "Stewardship of all my magical skills, items, and accoutrements shall remain with Samantha Lee Meikleham until a descendant of mine attains the age of eighteen..."

My heart imploded. I wouldn't be eighteen until Monday. That had to mean that my mom died last night. The tears crowded my eyes. "Excuse me," I said to the group as I took the will and got up to leave. Dillon continued shouting about something being the reason there was no 1st Avenue subway and I stepped away.

"What's wrong," Nikki asked, reaching for me as I passed her and Kari.

"I need a minute," I said, waving her away. I just wanted to be alone. I wanted to find a place to let the pain in my chest consume me. My eyes began to water and my chest felt tight as I walked the hallways. The sensation wasn't new. Twice in the last three days I had believed that my mom was gone for good. I leaned against the corner of the hallway, slid to the floor in the corner, and put my hands over my face, trying to regain my composure. I was tired of relying on other people, tired of looking to Kari for answers, tired of arguing with Babat and Chan. I had promised myself that if my mom died, I would expose the secrets of the codex and ruin the dragon and all who supported him. I had my father's gifts. Now was my time to act.

"What's wrong JJ," Pete asked in a sensitive tone. My glare did nothing to deter him. "I would have thought you'd be helping plan your mother's rescue."

"It doesn't matter," I said flatly, "She's ... dead." Even with experience from the last three days it was hard to say. Putting it in words made it more real somehow. The pain and emptiness was overwhelming. I blinked backed the tears, using the agony to fuel my hatred of the dragon.

Pete's reply was too dispassionate. "You don't know that. I don't think—"

"I DO know, Pete," I corrected.

Pete took a step back. His eyes filled with fear. Only then did I feel the magical force my anger had created. It flowed from me like a jack hammer and Pete's defenses were crumbling. The magnitude of the power startled me. I took a deep breath and let the force dissipate. If I now possessed that kind of power I would need to be more careful about my emotions. I didn't hate Pete, yet I had almost destroyed him. I took another deep breath before offering him the will as proof of my mother's death.

He hesitated before coming close enough to take it. "Well, I'm glad old Barry remembered our deal," he said as if he had received good news.

"What are you talking about old man?"

"Well, that is one thing you have right JJ. You're probably wrong about your mom but I *am* very old," he said.

"What do you mean?" I asked, wondering how I could possibly be wrong about my mom again.

"I was born in 1680 so am well over three hundred years old," Pete said.

That wasn't the answer I was expecting. My mind raced for a possible explanation. "Please don't tell me you're a vampire, 'cause I just don't think I could handle that."

"No, vampires and werewolves are pure fantasy. But being imprisoned in a kamisan is very real and very frightening," he replied.

"I thought dragons only did that to people with special skills." I realized too late that it came out as an insult.

Pete looked into the distance and said, "I am the son of John Coney. He was a great silversmith. Avarice took me from the hospital in my infancy. He had his goons provide another infant for my parents to bury and kept me as his prisoner. When my father died his talents passed to me. The dragon put me to work creating all sorts of devices." He looked at me, smiled and said, "None as amazing as I created with your father."

"So what happened? How did you escape?"

"Your father freed me almost twenty years ago. We made an oath. He promised me enough silver to start my own shop and I promised I would do my best to look after his young family."

"Why didn't you look after my mom then?" I spat, the pain of her loss still too raw to remain civil.

"As I told you before, I promised to look after his young family. Had I engaged Inicma I would have died and you would have been left on your own. The best I could do for the youngest in his family was to be there for you," he said.

I nodded, unable to speak, as the reminder of my mother's death consumed me. Kari had said the wording of agreements was very important. I understood his decision, but still wasn't happy with it.

He placed a hand on my shoulder. "I think it highly unlikely that Inicma has harmed your mother."

"How can you say that? It says my dad's magical powers transfer to me when I turn eighteen. I have his power but my birthday isn't until Monday," I explained, annoyed that he hadn't caught that when he read the will.

He looked like he was trying to hold in a burp. "Actually," he said, feeling around in his jacket pocket "you are eighteen." He held out the envelope he'd just pulled from his pocket.

I couldn't speak. How could my birthday not be my birthday? As I opened it he said, "It took quite a few rounds of some not so nice magic to get the doctor and nurse to modify your legal birth certificate but a record of magical naming must have the correct birth date."

Inside the envelope was a piece of parchment half the size of a regular page. It had my full name and listed my birth date as June seventh.

A wave of hope washed over me. "Why didn't you tell me?" I tried to sound angry but was too relieved. There was still a chance to save my mom.

"Your mother swore me to secrecy. We didn't want anyone knowing that you had a dragon slayers birthday." I didn't have time to process that before he continued. "It seemed like moving it a couple days would keep you off the radar of the Cyngor am Ryddid so you could live a normal life." He smiled at me. "And it worked until this week. We'd hoped that you would open the kamisan, pull out the codex, and go away to college," he made a motion with his hand like a plane taking off.

"Yeah, well it's gotten a little more complicated than that," I replied.

"Neither of us had ever seen Barry's will. I imagine you were wondering what was happening to you at midnight," he mused.

I realized that was precisely the time the magic overwhelmed me in the library. "Yeah, you could say that."

"I have to admit I am a little worried that, with your father's skill, you may end up the dragon slayer Chan aspires to be."

"I will not let that happen," I said and I felt my desire magically solidify into an immoveable resolve. I had just gone through the agony of losing my mom for the third time. I was determined not to go through that pain again. My thoughts jumped to my dream where I rescued my mother only to have the dragon kill Nikki. "I am not dying today. My life just became worth living."

"Look at that," Pete said as if finding a piece to a puzzle.

"What is it," I asked. I was surprised at how commanding my voice had become.

"This will was written prior to your parents' marriage. That means this is the first magical record of your mother's name," he said

"So?"

"That's the reason I safe guarded your birth certificate. If you have the first magical record of a person's name you can change their name." He and I stared at each other for a moment. "Undoubtedly, Inicma got your mother's name from the marriage certificate; he may even have the certificate with him."

"But with this I could change her name and break his spell on her." My heart raced. I snatched the will from him and marched down the hall. I had a way to save my mother. Nothing was going to stop me.

Nikki and Kari waited by the doorway of the conference room. I put my hands on either side of Nikki's shoulders so she had to look back into my eyes.

"I'm sorry. That was very rude of me. It won't happen again." She blinked twice in disbelief. "You need to get ready," I said to both of them, "We're leaving."

I strode into the conference room. Nikki and Kari followed.

"Good news, they finally saw the light and have a reasonable strategy for the attack." Dillon said cheerfully. His expression dropped when he saw my face. Any doubt about whether I had fulfilled my obligation to Chan was erased by Dillon's statement.

"Chan, I have kept my end of our deal. You have the critical information for your attack. Yet, not once have I heard you talk about how you are going to save my mother. So tell me, what are your plans for honoring your end of the deal?" The room fell silent and everyone stared at me. I didn't care.

"I have none," he replied flatly. I wasn't surprised.

"You mean you are not going to honor our agreement?" I pressed.

"How dare you question my honor? Your mother is already dead or you would not be able to read the codex," Chan seethed.

"She is not dead," I said holding up the will. "I have inherited those gifts from my father."

Chan paused, surprised at this new evidence. "It doesn't matter." He waved his hand in the air dismissively. "I agreed to do what I could to save your mother. With the losses we have suffered I cannot spare anyone else." The magic of our deal swirled around him, reprimanding him for his remark. His tone of voice became more plaintive. "I hope she survives our assault and is returned to you unharmed. If the opportunity presents itself I will do what I can to save her without jeopardizing the larger mission." I could tell from the change in the magic that he thought this met the terms of our agreement. I didn't.

I fought to control my anger. I hated him, but he still opposed the dragon. Now was not the time to make another enemy. "You need to delay your attack so you can get the resources and create a plan that will save her."

"I can't" he squealed. "Today is my birthday," he said more quietly. I felt a flutter of fear in my chest at the knowledge that Chan and I shared the date. "All successful dragon slaying has occurred on this date. We must strike before midnight or lose the opportunity." Some of the ryders in the room cheered.

My anger surged. An overwhelming urge to grab my ax and teach Chan a lesson washed over me. I could feel Nikki's concern in the magic of the room and drew on it to maintain control. "Then I will wish you the best of luck and be on my way," I said, stepping forward and grabbing the codex.

"I'm afraid I can't let you do that. I will need the information in that book to reverse the hundreds of years of damage done by Avarice," he said. My control wavered.

"Since 1913 actually," said Dillon quietly. Kari suppressed a chuckle and I regained control of my anger.

Chan scowled at Dillon. "This isn't just about the Federal Reserve. That book may have the evidence we need to do away with all the world's central banks," Chan barked at Dillon. He sounded like a lap dog with an inferiority complex.

"You're mad if you think the world will accept the

elimination of central banks," said Peter from the doorway. "International business requires their central clearing function."

"We cannot give away our only evidence of the dragon's treachery. There is too much to be learned from the truth in that book," Chan argued.

"And it is of no use to you because I am the only one who can translate it," I replied.

Chan stared at me intently. I could see the realization settle into his face. For a moment I thought he would agree to let me take the codex. Then his mouth turned up in a villainous smirk. "You're right," he said. "Seize him!" he screamed.

Two of the burly ryders grabbed me, twisted my arms, and pushed me against the table. One of them shoved my head down. Pain shot throw my cheek as it slammed into the hard wooden surface. I knew it would leave a bruise.

The codex fell to the floor.

Nikki gasped and reached under her jacket. Kari was too quick for her. She caught Nikki's hand before she could reach her gun.

"No!" Kari yelled. "Nikki listen to me," she bellowed. Nikki instantly stopped, obeying the magical command.

Anger seethed through me at Kari's use of magic to control her. "We need to let Chan have the codex for the greater good," Kari said and the fight in Nikki's face dissolved. I couldn't believe how easily Nikki listened to her. I wondered what kind of magical promise Kari had extracted from her. Whatever it was, it superseded her commitment to be there for me.

I reached for the magic of Nikki's concern to calm

my anger. It was only an empty shadow of what it had been.

My heartbeat pounded in my ears. I fought against the iron grip of the ryders, raising my head. They slammed me back to the table and this time I was looking at Dillon. He stared longingly at Kari before looking at me apologetically. The thought of him turning on me for Kari added fuel to my rage.

"How could you!" I bellowed at him. "How could you side with her after all we've been through!?" The strength of my outburst hurt my throat. I struggled in vain against my captors as they held me to the table. "So much for the fight for liberty, huh Chan?" I loaded the question with as much acid accusation as possible.

"The truth is more valuable than a single life. Surely you can see that?" he replied.

"No," The heat of my anger was searing my temples.

"I regret imprisoning you here. We will move you to more comfortable accommodation for the translation after I return," he said coolly.

"You mean IF you return," I spat.

"WHEN I return from slaying Avarice the codex's secrets must be published," he screamed. "Take him away," he ordered.

His men dragged me toward the door. "You are no better than the dragon," I accused. His reaction told me this was the right insult. "You use your secret club for your own comforts and to steal from and imprison an innocent kid like me; all in the name of liberty."

"You will never understand the burden of being a dragon slayer," he said turning from me and waving his hand in dismissal.

"You're not the only one who's got power because his birthday is today," I called as they dragged me to the door. Pete bowed his head in defeat. I had betrayed the secret he had kept for so long.

"Whatever skills you inherited from your dearly departed father, they are not powerful enough to save your mother, just as they were not powerful enough to save his filthy dwarfish hide," Chan chimed his insult dismissively.

The rage flooded through me and burst my control. My desire to kill Chan pushed all other thought from my mind. I saw nothing but him. My feet found the floor and I sprang at Chan. The ryders who held me crashed into the sides of the doorway as I sailed through it. I reached for my ax as I landed in the middle of the table. Chan reached for his sword but he wasn't quick enough. I was going to split him in two.

Kari moved so fast she was only a blur. "You do not want this fight," she said as she slammed into me and we crashed to the floor together.

"Traitor!" I yelled, swinging my elbow up and narrowly missing her face.

"Go and we will free you," she whispered as we wrestled. She said it so fast and so quietly there was no way anyone else could have heard it. My shock at her instruction brought an abrupt stop to my struggling and she pinned my arms behind my back.

"Oh man, is that all I had to do to get her to tackle me?" said Dillon and all the ryders laughed.

"Do any of you have handcuffs?" Kari asked. One of the ryders quickly handed her some.

"How come you never asked me that?" said Dillon, his fingers twitching frantically.

"Because you are a stupid child," she glared at him as she gently put the cuffs on me. They were so loose I thought they would slip off.

"Eewwwww." Dillon wiggled his fingers in the air, pretending to be scared. But his eyes were focused on something in his glasses. Then he nodded slightly.

"Come on. Off you go," said Kari as she and two ryders escorted me from the room.

17

Kari followed me all the way down to the dank sub-basement. It smelled of stagnant water and the walls were covered with flaking paint. She watched as they locked me in a cell, complete with iron bars and an armed guard.

I didn't have long to wonder when she was planning to spring me. A minute later Nikki came down the hall.

"What do you want?" the guard asked gruffly.

"Ah, I just wanted to say goodbye before I leave," she said in an innocent voice with a flirtatious pout. My jaw just about hit the floor.

The guard's defenses crumbled under her charm. "OK," but make it quick."

"Oh, but he can't even give me a hug." She made her pout even bigger. The guard looked confused. "Could you un-cuff him so we can say a proper goodbye?" She even blushed as she said it but I felt the magic. She didn't want to hurt him.

He didn't stand a chance. "Let me see your hands." He pulled out his keys, reached through the bars and took off my handcuffs.

"Thank you. Now would you be sweet enough to

turn the other way while I give him his goodbye kiss," she said sweetly. "I'm a little shy about public displays of affection," she whispered.

Since last night there had been several occasions when I had thought of kissing Nikki but not as part of some act. I was certain that I was blushing as well.

The guard obediently turned his back. Nikki pulled her gun from under the back of her jacket and pointed it at him. "Now I really don't want to shoot you but I will if I have to." The entire pretense was gone but the flow of her magic hadn't changed. The guard stared at her with a wounded look in his eyes. "All I need you to do is trade places with JJ so no one gets hurt," she said.

The guard obediently opened the cell and stepped inside. "I'll take the keys," I said and he quickly handed them to me. I closed the cell door, and tossed the keys down the hall before following Nikki.

"What no kiss?" I teased when we stopped at the bottom of the stairs.

"Later," she said.

I smiled.

The sound of sirens filtered in from outside. Whispered calls of "NYPD" echoed through the halls.

Moments later Dillon appeared at the top of the stairs carrying the codex. Kari was right behind him. I opened my mouth to ask what was happening, but Kari put a finger to her lips silencing me before I could ask.

We followed Dillon through the dingy basement until we reached a metal door big enough for a truck. Kari picked the lock and we all rolled under the partially open door and into the shade of a narrow alleyway. I followed Dillon's lead, calmly walking out of the ally and onto the sidewalk heading toward the elevated subway tracks. Behind us, a mass of fire trucks and police cars gathered around a nearby apartment building.

"What's the plan?" asked Nikki.

"Well Chan isn't going to send ryders pouring out of the armory with NYPD investigating a bomb scare in that building so we should be able to catch the four train that's about to arrive and we'll take it from there," said Dillon.

Kari mussed his hair. "You really are brilliant "

"Even though I'm a stupid child?" he scowled at her.

"You know that was just for show," she chided

"Like tackling me?" I said with mock contempt.

"After all we've been through in the past three days did you really think I had turned against you?" she replied.

I looked at the sidewalk. "You've known Chan longer and have many of his same beliefs. I thought you had sided with him and had Nikki under some sort of magical restraint."

"The only way to stop Nikki from helping you is to kill her," Kari replied. Nikki took my hand and I felt guilty for doubting her.

"And what about me?" Dillon asked.

"I figured you were too hung up on Kari to do anything," I said with much more confidence in my answer.

"Dude, there is no way I'd ever hang you out to dry for her. She's treated me like crap since we first met," he replied as we started up the steps to the empty car at the end of the train.

"No I haven't!" complained Kari.

"Oh, I must have hit a nerve because she used a contraction," Dillon said to me as if we were having a private conversation that she wasn't meant to hear. Nikki smirked.

"I'm with you, she's probably feeling guilty for calling you a filthy rapscallion before you saved her life," I replied in an equally private tone.

"I wasted my best laptop saving someone who called me a rapscallion," he lamented. "Wait, what's a rapscallion?" he said as he wiggled his fingers in the air. "Oh, I quite like that actually," he grinned as we boarded the train.

Kari's eyebrows knit together in disbelief. "Look JJ, I gave you my word I would help save your mom. So even though I don't think we should give the codex to Avarice, Chan had no right to break his deal with you."

"Oh sure give him an explanation," Dillon said and it sounded like he was genuinely hurt.

"OK, Dillon, I apologize if I have ever made you feel bad. You are, without a doubt, the most talented logistician I have ever met."

"I think I like rapscallion better," Dillon said twisting his face like he had just eaten something that tasted awful.

Kari chuckled. "Both of you saved my life. I will do whatever it takes to get your mom back."

"Hey, don't pay me back by saving his mom. Pay me back with a date," said Dillon. Both Nikki and Kari rolled their eyes.

"Yes! Simultaneous eye rolls," he gloated.

"So what's the plan?" asked Nikki impatiently. I wondered why she and Kari were looking at me.

"Wait, since when is JJ the idea guy in our merry

little band?" Dillon asked.

Kari smiled at him. "I am bound to protect him, you are his best friend - "

"And Nikki's his stalker. So what?" Dillon retorted.

"Do you really want to pick a fight with the gun toting daughter of a Ukrainian crime boss?" Nikki sneered.

I suppressed a laugh.

"Dillon," Kari commanded his attention. "We are all bound to JJ. It is his mother who is in the clutches of the dragon. And JJ has more power than he realizes."

Dillon looked skeptical.

"So," Kari continued, "JJ is the leader of our merry little band, Nikki and I are the muscle, and you are the brains." Dillon melted under her smile.

"I can live with that. So what's the plan?" he asked me. Nikki squeezed my hand.

I think I blushed at my unexpected new role, but was glad to have it. "We put Avarice under oath of death to return my mom unharmed in exchange for the codex."

"You mean like he did to Tony?" asked Nikki.

"Yep," I said, unable to read their reactions.

"Yeah, just a few problems with that," said Dillon. We all turned to listen. He paused to revel in the show of respect. "First, there's still the problem of us being wanted terrorists."

"and kidnappers," added Nikki. We all smiled.

"and kidnappers," agreed Dillon turning back to me.

"So we ask him to publicly exonerate us," I said.

"Uh huh." The skepticism oozed from him.

"Hey, they clearly own the media and the police so

they can create any story they want," I reasoned.

"Right," he responded, the word dripped with sarcasm. "Second, what's to keep him from killing us at the exchange?"

"We'll put that in the oath as well," I said. Dillon looked at me like I was crazy but didn't bother to argue the point.

"Third, how do we know his oath is solid and that he won't track us down later just for the fun of it?" he asked.

"Well, technically that's two more things," said Nikki. Dillon rolled his eyes while waving his hands in the air like she was hindering the progress of the conversation.

"You're right it is fun to make people roll their eyes," she said. Dillon stuck his tongue out at her and Kari actually laughed.

I marveled at how light the mood had become and realized we were enjoying a freedom we hadn't felt since making the deal with Chan. I worried that entering into an agreement with Avarice would feel even more oppressive but could think of no other way to get our lives back. "Look, they've gone to all this trouble to get the codex. I don't think it's unreasonable to ask for our lives to be put back the way they were in exchange," I said.

"Sure that sounds reasonable now, but Inicma doesn't seem like a reasonable guy," Nikki said. "How do we know the dragon won't just turn him loose on us?"

I hadn't thought of that.

"The oath could be magically written to cover all of Avarice's minions and validated by a third party," Kari said.

We all stared at her.

"Who would validate it?" I asked.

"I would recommend Liz. She might do it if she got amnesty from Avarice for killing his harpies. And she is a master at getting the language right in those types of contracts," Kari explained with more enthusiasm than I expected.

"Do you really think this will work?" Dillon asked her.

"Based on the dragon lore I know, this seems like the type of deal the dragon would make, but it will probably only work if we do it before Chan attacks," she replied.

"Exactly why we had to get away from Chan." I said. "Kari, will you call Liz?" I handed her my phone.

"Actually, I think Babat would have a better shot, but I can work on it." She began dialing.

"Dillon, can you find a way to contact Inicma?" I asked.

He looked at me like he was insulted. "If you want me to work my magic now, we better get off here or we'll lose signal," he said as the train stopped at Yankee Stadium. "The tracks go back underground from here," he explained as we exited the train.

The crowd in the stadium yelled "Charge" in response to the organ music as we exited the train. On the sidewalk below the station, the street vendors were ramping up. It must have been near the end of the game.

Nikki and I sat on a bench in the station while Kari talked on the phone and Dillon worked his unseen keyboard.

"Did I hear you say today was your birthday?" Nikki asked.

"Yeah, pretty wild to learn that you've celebrated your birthday two days late for seventeen years," I replied.

"No birthday party then?" she said with a glint in her eye. I wondered what she was driving at. Then it hit me. "Oh man, you were supposed to have your graduation party today. I'm sorry I ruined that for you."

She laughed. It sounded like music to me. "You were the only person I invited," she said squeezing my hand.

"Right, my stalker," I joked.

"Yeah, well, he's not far off. I've been chasing you for the last four years."

I stared at her in disbelief. "You've been chasing me for four years?"

"You didn't really think it was a coincidence that I always showed up when you were in trouble?"

I wondered if there was a reason the other girls had avoided me in high school. Then I wondered something else. "Does your dad know about this?"

"Oh yeah, I'm even registered for college in Utah 'cause I thought that's where you'd be. I figure he offered you that job to keep me in New York."

I stopped breathing. Her hand suddenly felt uncomfortable in mine. This was the type of behavior from psychopaths you read about in the papers, not from someone like Nikki. Then I realized how this explained so much of her behavior. In the same way every story about me getting in trouble included Dillon, every good story included Nikki.

She leaned against my shoulder. "Happy Birthday."

"OK, I think I have this set up," said Dillon. "You'll call Brad's old cell phone and leave a message for Inicma to call into a conference bridge in ... let's say a half hour. If I bounce the call through a few international nodes we should be able to keep him from tracing us too quickly."

"That's awesome," I replied.

"I was wondering how you felt about Lincoln Center," Dillon asked.

"Um, it's a nice place to go if you like ballet?" I guessed.

"I meant as a meeting place. Assuming Inicma gets Avarice to agree to this crazy idea, you need to tell him where we are meeting," he said.

"So we're meeting at the ballet?" I guessed again.

"Actually, the season's over so it'll be pretty quiet," said Nikki.

"And it has lots of exits including a subway and underground stage access." Dillon said. They both looked at me expectantly. It was still odd to be the leader of our little band.

"Liz has agreed to authenticate the contract but wants to negotiate her terms with Avarice herself," said Kari holding her hand over the phone.

"If she negotiates directly how will we know she isn't double crossing us?" I said.

"Have her join the conference call. It will give her secure communications as well," said Dillon. I nodded agreement and Kari relayed the number from Dillon and told her when to call.

A tremendous roar flowed from the stadium.

Dillon wiggled his fingers. "Walk off home run. Excellent! We better get moving," he said, walking toward the exit.

On the way down the stairs he said, "Kari, I need you to lift someone's cell phone." She gave him the type of look my mother had when I was in trouble.

"We can return it after we leave the message. It won't inconvenience anyone." Dillon said defensively.

The crowd was already pouring out of the stadium when we reached the sidewalk.

"Don't you think this is a little risky?" I asked.

"Oh yeah, if I was looking for terrorists it would be in this crowd." he replied sarcastically.

A large man with a Boston hat was in a cursing match with a local fan as he rudely pushed his way through the crowd that thronged the sidewalk. He turned to hurl another profanity at his opponent and slammed into me and Kari.

"Pardon me," said Kari but the man cursed her for not watching where she was going.

Kari handed the phone to Dillon. "Serves him right," she said.

"Are you a New York fan or a Boston hater," smiled Dillon.

"I'm a rudeness hater," Kari replied.

Dillon's fingers never stopped moving. He garnered more than a few looks from the departing fans as we walked through the parking garage and onto the Macomb's Dam Bridge; the bridge that crosses the East River to the Washington Heights part of Manhattan. The security fence on the bridge curves inward to prevent people from climbing over it. It felt like a steel trap waiting to snap. I felt my stomach drop when a black SUV approached, but when it reached us the family in it was laughing and smiling. I scanned the busy street again and decided Dillon was right. It was better to be part of the crowd than walking alone.

Dillon dialed the stolen phone and handed it to me.

"If you want the codex call me in fifteen minutes to discuss my terms," I said before reciting the number Dillon held in front of me.

I handed the phone back to Dillon. He dropped it through the gap in the security fence where the bridge connects to Manhattan. It bounced off the foundation and into the East River. "Oh, I'm sorry Kari, did you want to give that back to the nice Boston fan?" he said with a smile. Kari rolled her eyes. Dillon beamed.

The crowds thinned on the Manhattan side of the river as the fans headed for the closest parking lots. We walked past the apartments on 154th Street until we reached Jackie Robinson Park. The park is only a block wide, but it's eleven blocks long and sits at the base of a thirty foot high reinforced cliff in the hillside.

We followed Dillon past the heated pickup games on the basketball courts and sat on some metal benches shaded by an enormous rock outcropping. Children played on the playground that separated us from the street. Several of the children's parents stared at us. This was not a neighborhood accustomed to seeing people who looked like Nikki and Kari. I probably should have felt uncomfortable but I was absolutely confident in Dillon's direction and equally certain Kari and Nikki could handle any trouble that might come our way.

Dillon dialed each of our phones and handed them back to us. He made Kari share his head phones. There was no doubt that he enjoyed her close proximity. I didn't understand everything Dillon was doing when he called other numbers with uncomfortable beeps in our ears but eventually he gave me the thumbs up.

"Let's just hope Inicma got the message," he said. It was awkward to hear his voice echo over the phone shortly after he spoke. A moment later a musical tone rang in my ear.

"Hello?" Liz said hesitantly.

"Hi Liz, Inicma hasn't called in yet," said Kari.

"If he's not on in one minute I'm leaving," she replied. I looked at my watch and was frustrated that the second hand sat stubbornly on the eight rather than providing the information I needed.

My stomach sank as the seconds ticked by. I couldn't blame Liz if she got off the phone. Avarice had proven very resourceful in his ability to track us.

"Ok that's it..." said Liz but she was interrupted by the musical tones again.

"This is Inicma. Who's on the line?" his rough voice came over the phone. My voice caught in my throat in horror. Kari motioned that I should speak.

"This is the librarian with whom the dragon recently dissolved his agreement for protection," said Liz in a very businesslike tone. Her confidence snapped me from my fear.

"And this is JJ the guy whose mother you have," I said. I knew the words sounded stupid because they highlighted his achievements. I was certain he could hear the false bravado in my voice. "and the one who owns the codex you seek," I added trying to salvage some strength of position.

"I know who you are. Are you willing to give me

the codex?" said Inicma in a contemptuous tone.

"I am willing to trade if for my mother, but I have some conditions," my voice cracked unintentionally. It sounded much more fearful than I felt.

"I don't think you are in a position to set any conditions," he replied menacingly. I sighed at how poorly I had started the negotiations. "Why don't you bring the codex to the boat house in Central Park and I'll let your mommy go," he said. His condescension reminded me why I hated him so much

"You want to know why we won't do that? Because if we go anyplace public we're going to be arrested for everything you've done. So, until you exonerate us we can't very well meet you anywhere can we?" I replied and realized why so many people were looking at us.

There was a silent pause on the other end.

"That's my first condition. You must publicly exonerate us or there is no way for us to meet," I pressed.

"Who's us?" he asked.

I looked around, thrilled that he would consider this term so quickly. "My mom, Nikki, Dillon, and Kari," I said. Kari shook her head but I didn't understand why. "And me," I added.

"You want Kari exonerated? She's wanted in every industrialized country in the world!" he bellowed.

Kari smiled and shrugged her shoulders.

I knew I couldn't revise my request so quickly or Inicma would take over the negotiations again. "You're good at twisting the truth. I'm sure you'll find a way."

"And once I have done this you'll give me the book?" Inicma said.

"We will trade it for my mother as long as our safety at the exchange is ensured and we have a guarantee that we will not be hurt after the exchange," I said.

"Guarantees?" he said.

"That's why Liz is here," said Kari.

"Ah, Kariai Tiesos," Inicma said smoothly. "So sorry I *missed* you earlier," he said. His regret at failing to shoot her in our recent encounters was accompanied by his unsettling confidence in the implication that he would not miss in the future.

"We've been on this call too long without a verbal agreement," interrupted Liz. "The dragon will have to enter a death oath that he will cause no harm to them and that he will restore my full protection as if nothing happened," she demanded.

"The problem is that the dragon would be perfectly happy to destroy the codex," Inicma replied and my hope evaporated. "I am the one who wants the book," he said. We all gasped at the same time. "But only if it contains information that will free me from the dragon," Inicma spat the last word like a curse.

We all looked at each other in disbelief.

"Wait, you want to destroy the dragon?" said Kari.

"I am under oath to say no, but I no longer wish to be his servant. Now, if you tell me that book has information that ensures his demise, then I will meet your terms," he said.

"So, I promise to give you the book and you promise to give me my mom," I said. I hoped he wouldn't catch that I hadn't said the book had the information he wanted.

"You haven't told me what's in the book," Inicma

said.

My shoulders hunched forward in defeat. I didn't think the contents would meet Inicma's definition of information that would ensure Avarice's demise.

Then another option occurred to me. "It contains the true name of the dragon as well as a record of the early dealings of the Federal Reserve," I said.

"That's it? That's not nearly enough," he laughed.

He reacted just the way I expected. "And your true name," I added. There was silence on the line. Kari, Milda, and Dillon stared at me.

"You are implying that you are the only one who knows that name," he said.

"Yes" It was the only time I was grateful for Chan's unreasonableness. He hadn't waited for me to share the name.

"Then the agreement will be between you and me and you will swear on your life that you have never revealed my name and will never reveal my name," he said slowly. Kari shook her head vigorously.

"And you agree on your life to publicly exonerate, to ensure our safety at the exchange and to prevent anyone under your authority from causing harm to come to us after the exchange," I said. Dillon gave a thumbs up on my wording. Kari's shoulders slumped in defeated frustration.

"I believe we have a deal. You give me the codex and keep my name secret and I will return your mother and give you your pitiful lives back," Inicma said.

"Agreed," I replied.

18

Lincoln Center is an eerie scene at night when there are no performances. The enormous windows that normally allow the chandeliers to shine onto the fountain in the middle of Josie Robertson Plaza were heartless black abysses. The building's white stone columns stood before them like iron bars, restraining the abysses from flowing into the plaza and swallowing the city.

I stood on the steps that lead from the plaza to Columbus Street holding the codex under my magical suit jacket. The pristine lawn of Dante Park on the other side of the street held too many shadows to be comforting. It seemed more like a barrier than an open escape to Broadway.

I waited for Liz's call. The tension was like waiting to give an oral presentation in class. I was excited to be done with it but was nervous something would go wrong. Most of all, I was looking forward to seeing my mom.

After Liz came to terms with Inicma, we arranged to make the exchange at Lincoln Center at nine o'clock. That assumed the magical agreement had been executed.

She insisted that the deal be in writing because it made the magic stronger and more binding. The words of the contract "Upon revealing the true name of the man known as Inicma, JJ shall immediately be struck dead," echoed in my mind. As soon as I signed it I could feel the magic, like a noose around my neck, eager to enforce its penalty.

But that had been hours ago. Kari had helped me return the contract by balloon. Now, it was five minutes to nine and Liz still hadn't confirmed Inicma's written oath..

There was no doubt he had already acted on our agreement. Dillon told us about the headlines that told of my mother notifying authorities of an attempt to fence some stolen artifacts at the store where she worked. The story claimed this resulted in Chan and his terrorist network abducting me, Nikki, and Dillon while framing my mom as a criminal mastermind. Kari was proclaimed the heroic deep cover federal agent who, in the course of working to thwart the terrorist threat, had rescued us from certain death at Chan's hand. I had to admit that Inicma had a true gift for spinning lies in the media.

Kari wasn't happy about the story because she thought Chan would believe we had given him up to the dragon.

I jumped when my cell phone rang and answered it as quickly as my fumbling fingers would allow.

"Hello," I said hopefully,

"I have his oath but he's changed the words," Liz said.

"To what?"

"It says he will exchange your mother for the key

to the dragon's undoing," she said quickly.

"That isn't what I agreed!" I complained.

Nikki turned as pale as Kari, who was looking around so fast it looked like her head was spinning. Dillon's fingers were a blur.

"What should we do?" I asked.

"If you tell me you accept the new language I will put the agreement in force. If not then we have to start all over again," Liz said.

"That would mean no agreement before Chan attacks tonight, right?"

"Correct."

"Black SUV, third car from the light, at Broadway at 65th," Dillon said like he was reciting a formula in math class.

There was no way the codex would qualify as the key to the dragon's undoing. Then I thought of another option.

"Can you give me some time before I answer?" I asked hopefully.

There was silence on the line.

"Fifteen seconds until the light changes," Dillon said.

"Liz?" I asked.

The silence was probably only a couple seconds but it felt like an eternity.

"I'll buy you some time, good luck," she said.

"Thanks." I was too late, she had already hung up.

"What is it?" asked Kari.

"He changed the words," I said.

"Green light, here they come," Dillon said without emotion.

I dropped to my knees and pulled out my kamisan.

"NO!" cried Kari as I opened it.

The blackness swirled around me like a tornado. The lights shining from the windows of the apartment buildings twisted and turned. It took much too long for the foot locker to appear. Instead of a depthless black wall I was surrounded by a swirling torrent of blacks and dark grays.

I took the codex from under my jacket and placed it in the kamisan, then removed the metal case and key that had originally protected it. I dropped the quill, and the bottle of ink I had used in the library, into my jacket pocket with my father's will.

My father's image finished proclaiming his love for my mother and I closed the footlocker. The swirling mists remained. I looked at my watch to see how long it was taking, the second hand was no longer stuck, it spun so fast I could only see it when it stopped to change direction. Eventually, the blacks turned gray, the kamisan closed, and the city that never sleeps was dark.

Every light was out. The white marble of Lincoln center almost glowed in the moonlight. The traffic was silent. None of the cars were running.

"No, now everything's down," Dillon said.

"Sorry man," I said as Inicma's SUV silently rolled to the curb just up the street. I hoped they were far enough away for my plan to work.

I stood with the case in hand hoping against hope that my mom would step out of the SUV.

"They're behind us too," Kari whispered. I glanced over my shoulder. The silhouettes of suited men moving in the plaza were barely discernible against the white marble.

"I really hate that thing. I'm completely blind until everything reboots," Dillon hissed through clenched teeth, as he frantically worked his gloves.

The sound of cars starting filled the air as Inicma slowly stepped out of the SUV. He looked up and down the sidewalk. One of his goons stepped out the other side and stood in the street that was now a mass of confusion. "That was quite impressive. Is that the same kamisan your father used to cause the 1965 blackout?" he said casually.

I searched for an answer that would make sense and blurted out the first thing that came to mind. "Yeah, I figured I'd leave the codex in it until I heard from Liz then get the codex and knock out your cell phone at the same time." I was surprised at how reasonable and well planned that sounded.

Inicma smiled. "Is that it?" he said pointing to the case.

Men in suits appeared on the near vacant sidewalk to either end of the block. We were surrounded.

I nodded. My mind raced. I had to play this just right. "Where's my mother?"

His smile grew as he slowly walked toward us. "Now JJ, I'm sure Liz told you about the clarification I made to our agreement?"

He hadn't brought my mom. I tried to stay calm. "Yeah, she said you modified the language to say you want the key." I started walking down the steps to the sidewalk. I hoped I looked confident as I stared back at him.

"Basically, if this" he motioned to the case, "doesn't ensure the downfall of the dragon, you need to hope that Chan kills it so you can betray him into my custody." He grinned like he was one move from check mate. I wasn't sure he was wrong.

"Well, just so we are clear, I consider this to be the start of the exchange." I slid the case across the sidewalk.

He stopped it with his foot. From the way he paused I knew he was considering my claim. "We don't know if this is the key or not," he finally said.

"But I do know that this," I held up the key to the case, "is the key to that case, so your goons can't touch ᴜᴜ."

He took a deep breath. "You see JJ, I have certain agreements with the dragon that must be honored," his grin momentarily vanished as he sneered at the implications behind this statement. "My obligation to you does not say I can't touch you. It says I must keep you safe. I can think of no safer place than in a kamisan prison."

"We're in trouble," whispered Kari under her breath.

"Best shot is across the street," Dillon whispered.

The street was packed with cars. The traffic lights had come back on but only flashed red. The cacophony of honking and cursing rising from the traffic made it difficult to concentrate.

Inicma continued, "What a cruel twist of fate that in your efforts to save your mother you have ensured that either she, you, or your friends will die." His grin was so wide he looked like the Cheshire cat.

My mind raced. I didn't understand. His goons were getting closer. I had to make my move if we were going to escape.

Kari, Nikki, and Dillon inched toward the street.

I stayed where I was. I had to get some answers. "What do you mean?"

"You may not know that your mother inherited certain gifts from your father. She has done some marvelous work for the dragon over the past few days. Now he is keen to see how it does combating nuisances like your friend Chan. So either your mother dies defending the dragon or kills your one hope that the dragon will fall." He paused to enjoy the look on my face.

The shock wasn't that Inicma had sprung a trap. I hadn't confirmed the agreement so his trap was useless. The shock was how Avarice planned to use my mom. She no longer had the magic. I did.

Inicma swallowed like his next words were too delicious to part with. "Oh, I'm sure a mother's love for her son could be used to turn her skills against the dragon. That would probably be enough to save her, but that would make you the key to the dragon's undoing." He actually chuckled, a cold, mirthless chuckle.

I forced myself to smirk. "In which case, maybe I'll keep this." I shook the key at him the way you would tease a puppy with a dog biscuit. "Run!" I yelled and sprinted into the street.

The goon in the street was too fast for me. But not as fast as my shield. It sprang to life. The goon bounced off. I hardly felt it but pretended the impact knocked me off balance. I threw my hands in the air and let the key fly into the street. For a brief moment, the light from the cars reflected off the key as it sailed through the air. It clanged off a car before the faint metallic chime of it bouncing on the pavement was lost in the roar of the traffic.

"Get the key!" Inicma shouted.

There was no room to run between cars. Kari sprang across the hood of a cab. I followed, lost my footing, slid across the trunk of another cab, and flopped on the street. The too familiar sound of Inicma's silenced gun cut through the grumble of the traffic. We scrambled behind a bus then bolted across Dante Park.

At Broadway and 63rd I stole a quick look over my shoulder. One of Inicma's goons waved his gun at a cab and yelled at it to stop. No one followed us.

We'd run well down 63rd before a scream of agony stopped us. The wail echoed off the buildings. A sound so chilling even the horns of the New York traffic fell silent. Only then did I realize what I had done.

"I guess, Inicma opened the case," Kari said flatly. She didn't even sound winded.

"How bad will it be?" I panted.

"The poison has been out of the bottle for a while. They may have survived."

They? I had only thought of Inicma springing the poisonous trap. I wasn't ready for the realization that I may have just become a mass murderer. My knees wobbled and I felt the same nausea I'd experienced at Dillon's. I didn't have time to dwell on it.

"Do you think my agreement with Chan is enough to keep him from killing my mother?"

"Probably." She stared into the distance, lost in thought. "In fact, he will probably feel compelled to defend her from any ryders who try to retaliate when she attacks."

"But she doesn't have my father's power, I do. She

wouldn't really be a threat would she?"

"You should have listened more carefully at the library. Your mother is plenty powerful on her own."

We stepped onto Central Park West. The yellow sea of cabs that packed the street was remarkably reassuring. Not a black SUV in sight.

"Which way?" Kari asked Dillon.

"That depends on what we're doing, but I think we want to go that way." He gestured downtown.

"You think?" asked Kari in disbelief.

"Look, JJ's little stunt back there means I lost all my connections so I don't know where they are. And since our one and only plan didn't work out so well, all you get is my best guess. OK?" he said defensively.

Kari held her hands up and took a step back, "OK, you have just never been unsure of an escape route before."

"What's the quickest way into Avarice's lair?" I asked Dillon.

Nikki's eyes went wider than normal.

Dillon huffed his discontent but I wasn't sure if it was with my question or with Kari. "Looks like my best guess is pretty good. Our best bet is the Merchant's Gate." He pointed downtown again.

I started walking.

"You're not going to face the dragon?" Nikki asked hopefully as she and the others followed.

"That depends on where my mom is."

"The best option is to extricate JJ's mother before Chan's assault," Kari finished.

"Extricate? Assault? Who talks like that?" Dillon said. He wasn't look at anything but his glasses as his fingers incessantly stroked the unseen keyboard.

Kari tapped him on the shoulder and said, "The warrior princess of death talks that way." He looked at her and his fingers stopped moving. He definitely hadn't gotten over the wow factor yet.

Nikki rolled her eyes.

"If we can't *extricate* her before Chan's *assault*, then neither she nor the assault have any hope," I said.

Nikki sighed

Dillon said, "Dude, that goon must have hit you pretty hard because you're starting to sound like her" He pointed at Kari.

"Neither of you have to come, just show me the way in." It came out angrier than I had intended.

"You're an idiot," Nikki said. I stared at her in disbelief. "There is no way I'm going to sit around with Dillon wondering what happened to you. I'm coming."

I smiled.

Dillon came to a stop beneath the gleaming silver sculpture of a globe at the North edge of Columbus Circle. The only traffic circle in Manhattan was packed with cars.

"Are you leaving?" Kari asked him.

"No, I stopped because I'm not sure we want to ruin our recently cleared names by pushing past that," Dillon said, pointing to the officers who were waving he last few people out of the subway station on the other side of the sculpture.

I took a deep breath of relief that Dillon wasn't leaving.

"Is there another way in?" Nikki asked.

"Oh sure, we could walk through the front door," he said, gesturing to the enormous gold topped monument that stood between the corner of Central

Park and Columbus Circle.

"That's a little conspicuous for a front door," I said.

"Not the gaudy thing in the middle. The little stone gate houses on either side. They align perfectly with the elevators you drew at the merchant's gate," he said. I had been through Columbus Circle more times than I could count and never noticed the four stone structures that looked like empty statue pedestals.

"That looks a lot more discrete than pushing our way into the subway,' Kari said.

"In case you haven't noticed elevators don't work too well without power," he replied.

"And neither do the subways," Nikki responded, mimicking his tone.

"That's a good thing since we'll be looking for the magical entrance on the other side of the tracks," he said.

"I have an idea. Follow me," Kari said.

We followed as she confidently strode toward the officers. "Gentleman, we have an urgent need'ta investigate a possible terror threat in this station," she said to the officers with an over exaggerated Southern drawl.

"We just evacuated the station because the powers out. There's no threat here," replied the first officer.

"Hey, aren't you that undercover agent that's been all over the news?" the second one asked.

"Yep, an' these kids think they might'a seen somethin' in this station," she replied. It sounded like an awfully weak lie to me.

"I'm pretty sure they put that thing in this station. What did you call it? An EMP?" Dillon chimed in.

"Yeah, the electromagnetic pulse generator that

knocked out the lights," Kari picked up on Dillon's lead like they had been talking about it for hours.

"EMP? Not in this station," The first officer said.

"Yeah, it was in the news stand in this station." Dillon looked at me and Nikki with wide eyes, urging us to contribute.

"I thought it was more uptown," Nikki said.

"No, it was more downtown," I chimed in.

"Ya see what I mean? We've got the whole city blacked out an' these three can't agree where it is I gotta get a positive ID on where it's at," Kari said.

"Alright, You need any help?" asked the second officer, looking her up and down.

"Nah, we got it," she replied.

"Well, take my flashlight, even with the emergency lights it's pretty dark down there," said the first.

Kari flashed her smile at the officer as she took the flashlight. I thought he might swoon. She handed the light to Dillon as soon as we were out of sight of the officers.

"I thought cops were goons," I whispered to Kari as we followed Dillon into the depths of the station.

"I never said that," she replied. "Most police officers are decent people who are legitimately concerned for the public welfare."

"But you told me not to call them when Dillon was in trouble," I complained.

"Yes, because Avarice controls a few critical positions in the department. If you give good officers bad information you can manipulate them into an effective tool," she said.

The waist high security gate at the end of the subway platform was only there to discourage people from using the maintenance step to enter the tracks. At that moment it seemed to take the added role of blocking the dim emergency lighting from seeping into the tunnel.

Dillon pointed his light into the black mouth of the tunnel. At first I couldn't see anything but the thick brownish gray grime that covers everything in the subway tunnels outside the stations. But, as I stepped past the security gate, the faint outline of narrow steps appeared on the far side of the tracks.

"Now all we have to do is find the door," Dillon said as he climbed the steps to a narrow ledge that ran deeper into the tunnel. It was as high as the platform in the station but only wide enough for us to walk single file.

The rancid stench of urine and decay stung my throat and brought back memories of our journey through the sewers.

"Why would they put a door down here?" Nikki asked.

"Near as I can tell, it keeps the staff at the Merchant's gate from traipsing through the merchants lobby," Dillon replied.

I bumped into Kari. If Nikki hadn't been clinging to my shirt as she followed along the narrow ledge I would have fallen onto the tracks.

"Sorry JJ. There is a magically sealed door here," Kari said, caressing the tunnel wall. Flecks of dust fell from her fingers and drifted in the glow of Dillon's flashlight. I wondered how she knew a door was there when I hadn't felt a thing.

"Well open it and let's get out of here," Nikki said. From the nasal tone she must have been holding her nose.

Kari pushed her hands flat against the wall. She closed her eyes and held her breath. Her arms flexed and her face wrinkled as she strained against the door. Magic flowed from her, thick and powerful, but I still could not feel the door.

Her hands fell from the door and she gasped for air. "It is too strong, JJ will have to open it," she said.

The suggestion stunned me. "If you can't, I can't. You're better than me." I said.

"I am more practiced than you. You are stronger than me." she replied.

The lights in the tunnel came on.

"Now or never dude. A train comes by and we'll be subway paste," Dillon said.

He and Kari moved farther down the narrow walkway so I could get to the door. Even if Kari hadn't left hand prints on the wall I would have found the door. Standing in front of it was like standing in a running river of magic. It was warm, comfortable, and surprisingly familiar.

I touched the door and closed my eyes as Kari had. I'd expected it to be difficult to find the door's will amidst the flow of magic. It wasn't. The doors will was much different than the wind. It was smaller, harder, and unyielding but it also wasn't as aloof as the wind. It welcomed my magic like a long lost friend. I spread my will around it and tried to open it the way I would a normal door. The door seemed offended. It wouldn't move. I pushed it and pulled it in every direction but it remained stubbornly immobile.

The subway rails squeaked. After all those years of riding the subway I knew that meant a train was on the way. That momentary distraction was just what I needed to remember Pete's instructions. The key was to find a way to appeal to the door. I asked myself what doors want and decided that, more than opening or closing, doors provide safety.

The low rumble of the train echoed through the tunnel as I explained this to the door. If it didn't open, we would be killed by the train and it would fail in its primary purpose of providing safety. The will of the door did not yield, but its understanding did. It realized a different way it could fulfill its purpose. "Please open," I pleaded.

The lights of the train appeared around the corner as the door responded. The door's response felt something like, "Well why didn't you just ask in the first place?" The air horn on the train startled me. The others pushed on my back, squeezing me against the door as it silently slid back into the wall. We tumbled through the door and onto the floor. A rush of air washed over us as the train sped past the opening.

The door snapped shut. The rush of air stopped. We were locked in the dragon's lair.

19

"Get off me," I snapped as I shoved Dillon aside. I wasn't sure why I was so upset. It wasn't about invading the dragon's turf. Something else had me on edge.

"Shhh," Kari hissed. It annoyed me that she hadn't sprawled on the floor like the rest of us. Instead, she crouched behind a counter that ran the length of the room. A glass wall with small holes sat just above the counter. It looked like a ticket office.

"This must be where merchants checked in when the gate was open," observed Dillon.

Kari banged her finger to her lips so violently I thought she might give herself a fat lip. Then she pointed through the windows above her head with equal vigor.

I hadn't noticed the room on the other side of the window. Tapestries covered the walls of a room as long as a football field. The most complicated chandeliers I had ever seen hung from the polished marble arches. Four ornately carved elevator doors punctuated the far wall, each with another ticket office type room opposite it. It made the squalid little apartment I grew up in look like a garbage dump. If the lobby of the Plaza Hotel had feelings it would envy this room.

A young man stepped in front of the window. "Don't move! Hands where I can see them!" he shouted. The gun he pointed through a hole in the glass, the helmet, and the body armor, said he was a soldier, but the glint in his eyes screamed he was a goon.

Kari flattened herself against the counter. Dillon, Nikki and I raised our hands.

The goon took his hand off the front of his gun and held the radio attached to his shoulder. "Sir, this is Sal. The boy has breached the Merchant's Gate."

Kari pointed to me then to her wrist. I didn't understand.

"Is the entrance damaged?" Inicma's voice responded. Sal looked confused.

"Well I guess he's not dead," Dillon whispered.

"Silence!" Sal barked at him before responding to Inicma. "Excuse me sir?"

Kari held her fist up as if protecting her face and I realized she wanted me to use my shield. Kari was right. I could use my shield to rush Sal. I could take his gun, stash the tapestries, and pick them up after saving my mom. I wouldn't have to worry about finding work.

"The master," Inicma said the word with disdain "has made it clear that our first priority is to protect all entrances to the lair. So, did they damage the entrance?"

I was about to rush Sal when Kari held up her hand. She wanted me to wait. I scowled at her, but delayed my attack.

"Um, I'm not sure that's what he meant, sir," Sal

responded.

"Do not presume to question my authority. Your priority is to protect that entrance. By that I mean you are not to allow any harm to come to that area. Is that clear?" Inicma said.

"Yes, sir." Sal sounded disappointed.

"Now, could you safely secure the boy and kill his annoying friends without damaging the entrance?" Inicma asked.

Sal grinned. He relished the opportunity to kill. "It might get a little blood on the floor, but nothing that would be too difficult to clean up." He put his hand back on his gun.

I hated Kari for making me wait. Instead of listening to the nonsense between Sal and Inicma we could have been plundering the lair.

"Well, we wouldn't want to damage the entrance. We better not take the risk of leaving blood stains." Inicma said.

Sal's grin disappeared. Kari stood and stared at him. The color drained from his face.

Inicma continued, "Since they have no way to leave the lair I would say we have met the objective of capturing the boy. Good work Sal. Continue protecting the entrance and contact me with any further developments."

Sal ground his teeth in frustration. He whipped his gun out of the hole in the glass and stood, shaking in fury at Inicma's thinly veiled order to let us go.

Kari turned from Sal and silently tried to herd me, Dillon and Nikki toward a door at the back of the room. I wanted to stay and take out Sal but knew I couldn't do it alone. So, I followed her direction for the moment.

I had imagined the corridors of the dragon's lair being claustrophobic dirty little caves with stalactites and muddy floors. The corridor we stood in was spotless polished granite. Carved pillars on either side of the hallway supported a high, arched ceiling. The unseen source of gentle light at the peak made the hard stone look almost soft.

"What was that about?" Nikki asked.

"Inicma wants the dragon dead so he is twisting his orders to give us the opportunity to do what he cannot," Kari said. She turned to Dillon, "Can I ask which way without raising your hackles?"

"You always raise my hackles," Dillon said as he started down the corridor.

We followed as he turned right, then left, then right and down some stairs. At each turn I got more frustrated with him. His steps were too heavy. Couldn't he hear the racket he was making. He was taking too long. There had to be a better way. If he'd share his technology with us we could navigate on our own. I wanted an excuse to rip his backpack from his scrawny little shoulders. It wouldn't be hard. I was the leader I should have the best stuff. I began plotting to take what he should have already given me.

Kari waived her hands in the air frantically. She looked silly. Dillon and Nikki stopped. I sighed and stopped as well. I had no idea what we were waiting for.

Footsteps echoed down the hall. Dillon dove behind the nearest pillar. I smiled. This was my chance.

Nikki grabbed my shirt and dragged me behind a different pillar. I hissed angrily at the lost opportunity. She pulled me against her, trying to squeeze both of us into the tiny hiding space. I forgot about Dillon's backpack. The warmth of her body next to mine was intoxicating. She smelled wonderful. I ran my hand through her hair. It was soft and silky. She laid her head against my shoulder and I could feel her breath on my neck. The sensation was electric. A yearning stirred in my gut, a desire unlike anything I'd felt. I wanted her. She had to be mine. I slipped my arm around the small of her back and held her to me as my other hand moved from her hair to cheek. She stared back at me with those enormous eyes and my heart skipped a beat. Her lips quivered. I leaned forward to claim the kiss.

"Get a room," Dillon said from behind me.

"Back off!" I erupted as I reached for my ax. How dare he try to keep me from taking what was mine?

"JJ," Kari stepped between me and Dillon.

I hesitated, then resolved that not even Kari would deny me what I wanted. Nikki took advantage of my hesitation. She took my hand and peace washed over me.

"Do not let the dragon's magic get to you," Kari said.

It was weak magic. The command disappeared the moment it met my resistance. She probably didn't even realize she was doing it but I realized she was right. The magic I'd been feeling since we entered the lair was subtle, persuasive. It had taken a life of squalor and turned it into a craving for mindless plunder. It had taken my admiration for Dillon and twisted it into a need to hijack his technology. It had taken a budding passion for Nikki and turned it into a raging lust. Every drop of desire had become an insatiable thirst. I wanted it all. I wanted Nikki. I wanted Dillon's toys. I wanted the dragon's lair. I wanted to rule the Cyngor am Ryddid, no, I wanted to rule the world.

"Sorry JJ, I should have warned you." Kari said. "Dragons are not given just any name. The name identifies the primary motivation behind its magic and the emotion it will most likely elicit. You are more sensitive to magic than the rest of us and so will need to be more on guard."

I nodded and closed my eyes, focusing on the dragon's magic. It was like a gentle breeze. I knew it was there but couldn't quite tell where it was coming from. I tried to will a magic barrier into existence, but the moment I did, the desire for the wall turned into an aching need to possess all the magic in the world.

"It's ok," Nikki whispered. She gave my hand a little squeeze and stroked the back of it with her thumb.

I almost snapped at her but caught myself. It was the dragon's magic that frustrated me. Nikki didn't deserve my wrath. I wanted her to be happy.

Just like that, the magic faded. A single moment of concern for Nikki had practically blocked all of the dragon's magic.

I was shocked at how dependent I had become on my own magic. Ever since the library, ever since I had received my father's magical gifts, I had been lured into an increasing reliance on my new power. It was like someone had given me new muscles so I was stronger than anyone else. I thrilled at the thought of using the new strength. It bestowed a sense of invincibility I had never known. That power wasn't going to help me with Avarice's magic.

My whole life my mom taught me about duty to

others. I'm sure she didn't realize how important that lesson would be for her. If I was going to save her I had to do it, not because I wanted her back, but because I wanted her to be free. I had to stay focused on others if I was going to be of any use.

I opened my eyes. Kari, Dillon, and Nikki stared at me like I was a pot of water they expected to boil. I almost snapped at them. Then I remembered. I needed to focus on their happiness.

"I'm sorry Nikki," I said.

She smiled wickedly. "I'm not.'

I smiled. What I wanted made her happy too.

"It's 9:40. We have twenty minutes to *extricate* your mom before the *assault* begins," Dillon said, eyeing Kari as he mocked her. She didn't move. Dillon pursed his lips in disappointment. "So if you're quite finished with the love fest we need to get moving," he finished. I wondered if the little event between me and Nikki had ignited his own greed for Kari.

He quickly turned and headed down the hall, his footsteps no louder than mine or Nikki's. Kari was silent.

The labyrinth of corridors and stairs seemed endless. It wasn't long before I was completely lost. Ten minutes later Dillon stopped outside a window to a large room, full of computers. The door next to it had a key pad and sensor that looked remarkably similar to those I had seen at Dillon's apartment.

"Dillon?" Kari whispered.

"The lair should be a couple hundred yards up this tunnel." He pointed down the hall without looking away from the rows of computer filled cabinets.

Kari placed her hand on his shoulder. His head

turned to face her before he peeled his eyes away from the room. "You still have coms in your bag right?" she asked.

"Yeah, why?" he replied.

"Because unless you are going to start attacking harpies with your laptop I think you should stay here and see what type of support you can provide," she replied.

Dillon smiled. It was the type of smile that warns you to take cover when a person is about to explode with excitement.

For a moment I wanted to stay and plunder the computers, but I caught myself. I forced myself to focus on Dillon's joy. I wouldn't even know where to start in a room like that. Not only was Dillon the best person to have in that room but it would certainly be safer than where we were going.

He opened his backpack and pulled out four earpieces like he was in a quick draw competition. We each took one and stuffed it into our ears. Mine was just as uncomfortable as it had been the night of the bull.

"Just follow this tunnel," Dillon said. His voice echoed in the earpiece a moment after he spoke.

Kari led the way down the slightly curving corridor. I took a quick look back before Dillon passed from sight. He'd already removed the key pad and was doing something with the wires.

A moment later Kari held up her hand. We all stopped. She cupped her hand around her ear then pointed to us. She wanted us to listen. I had been so focused on controlling my thoughts, that I had completely missed the low rumble of rushing air. The sound grew, then faded, then grew again.

"Dragon," Kari mouthed without saying anything. She dropped to her knees and waved for us to follow. I wondered what she was doing but as we crawled forward it became clear. Sliding across the polished marble floor made us nearly as silent as her footsteps.

We crept forward, staying next to the wall. Sliding around the pillars that blocked our way felt like standing in the middle of street and hoping no one would see us. Finally, we rounded a column and got our first glimpse of the brightly lit opening at the end of the corridor. Most people look forward to the light at the end of a tunnel. This one filled me with dread.

Kari slid across the floor to the other side of the tunnel but held up her hand for us to stay on our side. Then she waved us forward to the next pillar.

"What is our status?" a deep voice boomed in the space past the opening. The sound rolled down the corridor.

Kari waved us forward and we rounded the second to last column before those that stood on either side of the opening.

"Inicma reports a breach at the Merchant's gate, but no griffins," a cold high pitched voice responded.

We slid along the floor to the next pillar and pressed against it like we hoped it would swallow us. Nikki crowded into the tiny space. I reminded myself that I wanted Nikki to be happy and my mom to be free.

"I'm in," Dillon's voice rang in my ear. I jumped at the sudden sound.

"Shhhhhh," Kari hissed. The sound was so soft I could see her purse her lips but could only hear it in my earpiece.

"Send your sisters to obtain a status for each entrance. The time is fast approaching and I still do not know where to send my prized weapon." The tremendous voice bellowed, a slight taunt poorly veiled in the command.

I swallowed hard. A voice that size could only be the dragon and the prized weapon must be my mother.

"Yes, master," said the high pitched voice.

Nikki leaned her head into the back of my neck and took a deep breath. The shape of her body pressed against mine. I almost forgot where I was. She ran the tip of her nose up the back of my neck. Goosebumps covered my arms.

The sound of wings filled the air. Nikki froze.

A harpy flashed past us. We both turned to face it, but it didn't even hesitate as it disappeared up the passage.

"Sorry," Nikki whispered in my ear.

I turned and placed my mouth next to her ear before answering. "I'm not."

She smiled.

Kari frowned at us then motioned us forward. My heart pounded in my chest as we scooted around the last pillar and inched toward the opening.

The space beyond was as large as any stadium. Our hall opened onto the large round floor at the bottom of the lair that was ringed with marble statues and benches. Behind these, paintings hung on a fifteen foot high marble wall. Above that, elaborately decorated and carved marble porches, balconies, and arched entries rose in tiers all around the lair. The enormous domed roof shimmered like water. Then the realization hit me. It was water. We were at the bottom of the reservoir in the middle of Central Park.

Avarice's hoard filled the center of the floor. I had pictured a jumbled pile of assorted coins and gems. This treasure was precisely organized. Gold bars had been stacked three stories high to form what looked like the base of a pyramid. The gems were separated by type and organized into distinct piles just to the right of the gold edifice. The near side of the gold platform was lined with stacks of gold candelabras, plates and statues, followed by a conglomeration of silver platters, cups and candle sticks. Suits of armor, swords, guns, and cannons were just visible to the left. In my quick survey of his hoard I could think of no treasure Avarice lacked.

"Well?" The enormous voice boomed from atop the gold plateau.

There was Avarice.

20

I wondered why the enormous green dragon wasn't the first thing I saw. Whatever my expectations had been, they were completely shattered by the sheer magnificence of the creature. Avarice was at least a hundred yards long head to tail. Every inch was covered with green scales larger than my hand. They made a slight clicking sound that accompanied the sound of rushing air, as his body rose and fell with each breath. His neck was longer than two city buses. Brilliant yellow eyes the size of large platters peered from his smooth, hornless head.

"Master, the Cyngor am Ryddid has entered the east exit. As expected they are using griffins," said the shrill voice we had heard before. It took a moment to find the harpy. It stood at a small pulpit far to our right. Its position, on the lowest patio in front of Avarice, placed any speaker at the dragons mercy.

"Nice to hear that Chan took my advice," Dillon's voice range in my ear piece.

Avarice yawned and lazily stretched his wings half way to the ceiling. His mouth could easily accommodate a small car and was filled with fangs as long as my arm. "So the fools believe they can actually beat me," he said before letting his laugh rumble through the lair. A few bricks fell from the top of the gold dais he laid on.

"Master, Inicma reports that my sister has been killed in the battle at the Merchant's gate." Equal amounts of sorrow and anger tinged the harpy's reply.

"Yeah, because Inicma killed it," Dillon said. "That happens to be one of the few areas in this place that has any type of security cameras."

"It would appear he underestimated the skill of his opponent and the value they place on this woman," boomed Avarice. He nodded toward one of the statues between us and the harpy.

"Is that your mom?" Dillon asked. Kari held her finger to her lips.

My heart jumped into my throat. I could just make out the bare feet beyond the statue. Someone was sitting on the bench hidden behind it. It had to be my mom. I wanted to see her. Nikki's hand on my shoulder stopped me.

"Yes, Master, but with his forces engaged there, the griffin riders are making good progress," the harpy bowed low.

"Engaged? Yeah, they're engaged with a stack of sandwiches and coffee," Dillon said.

I examined the space between me and my mom but saw no way to covertly rescue her. Any movement against the white marble was certain to catch Avarice's eye.

"Yes, Inicma thought the east exit the least likely entry point. I imagine the new recruits we stationed there are no match for the skilled griffin riders" said Avarice. There was a pause while the dragon thought.

The bowed harpy did not see him look over his shoulder at the large archway to our left, behind his bed. That was undoubtedly the exit under Randall's Island Dillon had talked about. It was the only opening Avarice would comfortably fit through.

"Gather your sisters and prepare an ambush for the Cyngor am Ryddid when they reach this chamber," Avarice instructed.

"Yes Master," the harpy said before taking flight toward the far side of the chamber.

"Well, that doesn't sound good," Dillon said.

"And be certain one of our new recruits notifies us of their impending arrival," Avarice called after the departing harpy.

"Stand Samantha Lee Meikleham," commanded Avarice as he dropped his head near my mother. My joy at seeing her was swallowed by my sorrow at her obedience to Avarice. She wore a white dress that was much more revealing than she would have chosen for herself. I let out a silent sigh of relief. At least there were no outward indications she had been hurt.

"I guess it is your mom," Dillon said. "Can you guys hear me?"

Nikki flicked her earpiece with her finger. I winced at the sharp sound in my earpiece.

Kari shook her finger at Nikki as if she were scolding her.

"Ow! Ok I get it. You can't talk right now," Dillon said.

"Samantha Lee Meikleham, you will destroy any enemies who enter my chamber," Avarice commanded. The potency of Avarice's magic was staggering. I was too late.

She bowed her head. "I do not want to die."

My mouth dropped in shock. Then I remembered Babat describing the power of the will to live. Avarice didn't realize he was asking her to commit suicide and that was asking too much.

"You will not die. Not with power such as you possess." Avarice coaxed.

"The power ... is not mine." She struggled under the weight of Avarice's will as she spoke. I realized she was struggling to explain that she had lost the power without sending the dragon after me.

"If you will not use your husband's magic for *me* then I shall take it from you along with your life," Avarice sneered. "Inicma will be so disappointed when he finds out you became my snack rather than his pet."

Nikki slapped a hand over my mouth muffling my screamed objection. Kari gasped at the sound. Avarice would hear us. But a gruff voice muffled the sound. "They're coming!" it called in panic.

"I suppose we can wait for your friends to watch," Avarice said. He turned away from her to peer into an opening on the far side of the lair. It was the only other opening Avarice might be able to squeeze through.

A burly goon appeared in the opening. "We couldn't hold them!" The gruff panicky voice was his.

Avarice took a deep breath that sounded like it would suck all the air from the lair.

"Wait" bellowed the goon.

Avarice didn't hesitate. He opened his mouth and a stream of fire erupted from it. The goon opened his mouth to scream but no sound came. His body evaporated in the raging inferno. The roar of the flames shook the room. Every opening on that side of the lair glowed from Avarice's fire, silhouetting the harpies, who eagerly awaited their prey.

I gasped. Chan and his ryders were doomed. Even if they miraculously survived Avarice's blast, the harpies would ambush them. It was a death trap.

Silence fell. The flames expired. Only scorch marks remained.

My chest felt like it was in a vice. I couldn't breathe. Chan had failed. Babat would have been at his side. Only then did I realize how much I'd come to like him. I watched the dragon turn back to my mother and I understood. Avarice was a horrible, nasty thing; the last creature you would want controlling anything, let alone an entire economy. He had to die.

"Perhaps I *will* have to dine alone," the beast gloated as he approached my mother.

"What just happened?" Dillon asked.

I struggled against Nikki's restraining grasp. The evil had to be stopped.

"And now you die, vile creature" Chan's high pitched squeak pierced the lair. He sat astride an enormous griffin in the middle of Avarice's exit. His magnificent steed pawed the air in front of it, as if anxious for battle. Chan waived his sword forward and the sound of flapping wings filled the lair. Griffins and ryders soared through the space over Chan's head pouring into the lair.

The dragon wheeled in place. Gold bricks flew across the lair.

Kari pushed me forward. "Move," she urged.

As we ran along the wall, harpies sprang from their concealment. Like some comic book bee swarm, they dove at the griffins rising to meet them.

Avarice snapped his jaws, plucking a ryder from the back of a griffin.

The report of automatic gun fire echoed through the lair. Harpies plummeted to the floor in crumpled heaps.

"Gun fire? But Inicma's still at the Merchant's gate," Dillon said.

"Those are ryders," Kari responded.

Avarice spun again. A new barrage of gold bricks sailed across the lair. I followed his gaze to the highest balcony opposite his exit. Ryders fed belts of ammunition through a half dozen machine guns mounted to the balconies railing.

The dragon leapt into the air spreading his wings between the harpies and the deadly weapons. The bullets ricocheted off him as if he were made of steel.

I dove behind the statue nearest my mom. Kari and Nikki followed.

Avarice landed on the balconies above us. The machine gun fell silent.

The sound of swords clashing with talons filled the lair as the mass of griffins and harpies collided. It looked like a cross between a World War II dog fight and a jousting tournament. Some ryders fired pistols at their opponents, others used spears, but most used swords.

My mom still stood obediently in front of the bench. "Mom," I called. She didn't move.

As I fumbled for my father's will, Babat swooped over the dragon's vacated bed. His griffin extended its claws, eager to reach Avarice's back. A harpy dove behind them. It was certain to catch them before they reached their target. Babat leapt from the back of the griffin, somersaulted over the harpy, and brought his sword to rest in the harpy's back. Avarice bellowed in agony as the griffin's talons opened a large gash in his back. His tail thrashed over the top of us and narrowly missed Babat as he crashed to the floor with the dead harpy.

I laid my father's will on the floor and pulled the quill and ink from my pocket. Nikki's pistol rang in my ears. I turned to see a harpy slam into the nearest statue.

Chan was barely a shadow, skimming over the balconies. Avarice snapped wildly at the griffin that had injured him. He missed but had now turned his back to Chan.

I dipped the quill in the ink and went to cross out my mom's name. Rather than make a line, the quill sucked her name off the paper.

"This is it," Kari said.

I looked up. Chan held his sword high. He was about to decapitate Avarice. Then he veered toward us, the griffin diving at a suicidal rate. I dropped the quill and raised my watch, certain they would hit us. My shield sprang to life as he flashed over our heads and slammed into the harpy none of us had seen diving at my mom. The impact threw Chan from the back of his griffin. He slid across the floor and into a stack of gold serving platters.

My mom shook her head. "Mom, your name is now Samantha Lee Jane Jones Meikleham Managito, mother of Jefferson Jones, guardian of liberty, and champion of truth," I said. I had no idea where all that came from; it simply flowed from my lips. I briefly wondered if I had been polluted by Dillon. I reached for the quill to record her new name but the ink had already flowed from it. Her new name appeared in its proper place on the will.

"JJ," my mom cried. She threw her arms around me. For a brief moment I didn't care about the battle raging around us. My mom wasn't dead, she wasn't captive, she was free.

"What are you doing? You shouldn't have come after me," she said, but hugged me even harder.

"I love you mom," I said, I could feel her smile. She broke our embrace and held me at arms distance. "Besides, it was my duty," I teased.

"Can we go now?" Nikki asked, as she squeezed off another shot.

Suddenly every harpy in the room dove toward the floor. It was then that I realized Avarice had taken another deep breath. As he leapt from the balconies, Avarice's fire spread across the top half of the lair like a sheet of lava.

I was frozen in horror. The ryders were trapped above the flames.

Black smoke swallowed the light of the flames as harpies landed safely on the floor.

Avarice landed on his bed. The force collapsed one side of the gold mesa. A wave of coins spilled across the floor. The gold brick walls were only a dam against the pool of coins that formed Avarice's bed.

Some griffins wobbled to the nearest balcony. Others spiraled to the ground in smoking heaps. Harpies pounced on those landing closest to them and quickly ensured their demise.

"I'm with Nikki. This doesn't look like my kind of party," Dillon said. He stood in the opening we had come through, gaping at the scene before him.

Avarice sucked in another enormous breath. I hesitated to make sure I wasn't about to be bar-b-qued.

"Avarice, Diluter of Liberty and Ouster of Charity I command you to stop," cried Chan. I felt the magic in the air at his command and immediately knew this was a mistake. Everyone stopped to watch. Avarice did not unleash his fire, but it was not because he was under Chan's spell. He was easily withstanding Chan's magic and everyone knew it.

Avarice laughed as he settled comfortably onto his gold. "You feeble minded fool," he growled at Chan. "Do you think your puny will can so easily drive Avarice from the heart of this city?"

"I will not only drive you from this city, but from this country, and eventually the world," Chan replied. This time the harpies joined in with Avarice's laughter. "Avarice, Diluter of Liberty and Ouster of Charity I rebuke you and command you to leave this instant," Chan cried but his magic was dilapidated.

I took my mom by the arm and we walked as silently as possible away from what I knew was impending disaster.

"Chan Long aren't you tired of being laughed at because of your voice," began Avarice. Chan took a step back at this turn in the conversation. I felt the dragon weaving its magical snare around him. "I can ensure that everyone will fear and respect you, the great Chan Long," Avarice said in a smooth provocative tone as the magic thickened. "You will live in luxury, with servants and soldiers who obey you without question."

"Chan Long, destroy all who would threaten my

dominion and I will reward you with your deepest desire," the dragon crooned. There was no doubt. This was powerful magical; more seductive and more potent than the dragon had used on my mother. Chan couldn't resist. He turned toward us and charged, sword drawn. The harpies cheered in victory and took flight, eager to finish off the last of the ryders.

"Run!" my mom cried. Nikki and I bolted for the opening where Dillon stood. Kari charged Chan.

"You'll not escape," roared Avarice. With a quick flick of his front foot he sent a pile of gold bricks and coins across the lair. Dillon disappeared behind the pile of wealth that sealed the only escape route we knew.

I backed toward the wall, pushing Nikki and my mother behind me. I raised my watch and drew my ax. Anger surged through me. If I hadn't been on guard for Avarice's magic I would have missed the ax's magic. The ax's fury flowed into me through the handle. My adrenaline surged. I blinked back the rage that had me blind to everything except the dragon. I remembered that only I stood between the dragon and the two people I loved most. I took a deep breath and pushed the anger back into the ax.

Kari and Chan collided. Their swords rang with fierce chimes at each impact. A small group of ryders clustered together in a phalanx that inched towards Avarice's exit.

"Ah, so it is the traitor's son," Avarice said. "Meikleham Jefferson Jones, drop your weapons and give me what is mine so you can live," Avarice commanded. A tsunami of magic surged from him. I abhorred being told what to do. That part of me had caused me so much trouble over the years. I was spending so much energy controlling my greed and containing the fury of the ax, that I had nothing left to contain my hatred. It erupted like a volcano. Avarice's tidal wave of magic evaporated against the mountain of my resistance.

"So, I see you have some skill," said the dragon as it crawled menacingly from its perch.

"Your best exit ... is the arch ... at the top of the rubble ... to the south," Dillon huffed.

"Are you ok?" Kari asked.

I glanced to the right. The pulpit had been smashed when Avarice attacked the machine gun. The remains formed a ramp from the lair floor to a half broken archway.

"Dillon, are you ok?" Kari demanded as she ducked under one of Chan's big swings and dragged her blade across his belly. The bottom of his shirt fell to the floor, revealing his armor. It was dragon armor.

There was no response.

Dillon was gone.

I looked at Nikki. She was just as dumbfounded as I was.

"Samantha Lee Meikleham, kill your son," commanded Avarice. The magic washed past me like I didn't exist, but it reminded me of where I was. I would have to mourn for Dillon later.

"No," my mom said flatly. I took a step toward the exit.

"My, my, this is interesting. You have been a busy boy," said Avarice.

The last remaining griffin dove toward Avarice's throat. It was Babat. Avarice recoiled from us and Babat missed his mark.

"Go," I yelled, pulling my mom in front of me and pushing her toward the exit. We sprinted toward it. There was no time to stand around watching Babat.

A frustrated roar shook the lair. I hoped it meant Babat was winning. Avarice's tail whipped toward us. I pushed my mother forward and we dove under it. A shower of gems and gold pelted us as we slid across the floor and into the ramp of rubble. I scrambled to my feet and pushed Nikki up the pile after my mom.

I looked over my shoulder, watching for the dragon's tail. Avarice snapped the griffin from its back with his powerful jaws. The lion half of the griffin fell to the ground. The dragon spat the front half at the phalanx of ryders. It smashed through the shields, knocking the ryders from their feet.

The harpies sprang at the fallen ryders. Babat leapt to their defense.

I stumbled on the debris and turned back to the task of surmounting the awkward ramp.

"I don't think so," Avarice growled. My mom had just ducked under the broken arch when the dragon's tail smashed it. The blow sent Nikki and me tumbling back to floor of the lair.

I rolled to my knees. Avarice opened his mouth and fire erupted from deep in his throat. I held my shield up and Nikki dove behind me. The intense heat and flame parted around the shield like a river around a large stone. Nikki clung to my back. Not because she wanted to be close to me, because she wanted to live. She shook with fear.

That was too much. My anger called to the ax's magic and rage overwhelmed me. At the first ebb in the fiery flow, I charged Avarice. He snapped at me. I stepped to the side, blocked him with my shield, and brought my ax down on the side of his face. At first I thought I had missed. Avarice jerked away from me and wailed in pain. Black blood flowed from the wide gash in the side of his head. My ax had cut through the dragon as if he were made of air.

"Go," I said to Nikki.

"I won't leave you," she said. I stared at her in disbelief.

The distraction was all Avarice needed. His front claw slammed into my back. My foot caught between the floor and his claw. Pain shot up my leg as my ankle twisted unnaturally. Time stood still as his claw swept me toward Nikki. Horror filled her eyes as she realized she couldn't avoid Avarice's swipe and the pain it would bring. My stomach wrenched at the sickening thud of the claw hitting her. She gasped at the impact. Then she looked at me. Her eyes lit up and she smiled. I closed my eyes. How could she smile while Avarice swept us into oblivion? Then it struck me. She was smiling because we were together. She and I would be crushed by the same dragon's claw.

I opened my eyes and she was gone.

The dragon held me pinned, upside down, against his hoard. The edges and corners of the treasure dug uncomfortably into my back. The pressure was like a hammer on my hands. I gasped in agony. If not for my armor, I'd be dead.

"How many more of Barry's toys do you have?" Avarice asked.

Gold coins cascaded over my, throbbing, and now bare, feet. They were free, on the other side of the dragon's claw.

Avarice looked at me so closely I could spit in his eye. I did.

Avarice blinked, then chuckled.

I searched for my ax. Its silver capped handle gleamed from under a pile of coins. I struggled to free one of my hands but only succeeded at changing the pain from horrendous to overwhelming.

"Now, you die." Avarice drew a deep breath.

Death would be welcome if it would stop the pain, but I knew better than that. I wanted to live. There was no other option. My only hope was magic.

"OK!" I bellowed.

"Ok what?" Avarice asked.

I had to get him talking but couldn't focus through the pain. I latched onto the only opening he had given me. "You want my father's toys and I'm the only one who can get them for you."

The pressure eased and the agony dulled to mere misery. "So?" he encouraged.

I had to be careful not to get into another magical contract. "So maybe we could work out a deal where you get the toys and we get to live," I said. Avarice's eyes flickered. I'd seen that look before. It was the same look Dillon had at Tony's. Avarice wanted to deal.

"Haven't we had enough failed agreements," Kari called, side stepping Chan.

"Oh, do hurry and finish her off," Avarice said to Chan, annoyed that Kari still lived.

Kari had used a contraction while thrashing Chan. Dillon would have loved it. I sighed.

Avarice heard me. "That's right. You better make that deal quick or your friend will die."

His magic surrounded me. It wove an

impenetrable net and captured my desires. I wanted my friends to be safe, but Dillon and Nikki were gone. Kari was the only one left. I watched as her blades lashed at Chan one more time. She had hit him so many times that he had no clothes. Only his armor remained. His knees wobbled as he struggled to heft his sword. If someone killed her it wasn't going to be Chan.

I smiled.

"What are you smiling at," Avarice growled as he ground me into the hoard.

The increased weight didn't hurt at all. In fact, the twisting motion let my hands find some gaps in the treasure. My armor was working. I still wanted to live. With a little more time, maybe Avarice wouldn't. I had to keep him talking. "I just think it's funny that you think Chan could beat Kari." It was the first thing I thought to say and I regretted it the moment it left my lips.

"Oh, Kari will lose," Avarice said.

As he spoke someone touched my foot. The warm deep power of Nikki's compassionate will flowed through me. I suddenly felt sorry for Avarice. He was surrounded by violence and traitorous henchmen. I wondered if anyone had ever cared about this pitiful beast.

He lifted his other claw to reach for Kari. All of his weight bore down on me.

"Avarice please ..." I was surprised at how calm and tender the tone was. The combined force of my will and Nikki's compassion flowed from us in a slow unstoppable tide that buckled the dragon's defenses and swallowed his will in a warm depthless pool of magic. "...show mercy."

Avarice froze.

He wheezed.

The room fell silent. Only the halfhearted clash of Kari and Chan's swords disturbed it.

Avarice gasped.

The warmth of Nikki's compassion disappeared.

Avarice bellowed in agony. He reared onto his hind legs lifting the claw that had held me pinned. Nikki crouched at my feet, my dagger in her hand. The dragon's black blood covered the blade she'd thrust into the beast's foot.

I rolled to my ax and pulled it from the pile of coins. The rage surged through me. I welcomed it. The dragon's claws dropped toward me. I raised my arm and my watch burst into its shield. The crushing blow glanced off it and slammed to the pile of coins next to me. I whirled with my ax. It effortlessly sliced the heel and rear talon from the dragon's foot.

The leg buckled at the pain. Avarice stumbled. His body crashed into the hoard. Nikki dove to the floor. My armor wouldn't keep my head from being crushed. I swung the ax the other direction. It ripped through the dragon's chest. Avarice recoiled from the pain of my strike and crashed to the floor.

"Claim your destiny," Kari ordered.

As Avarice whipped his head across the floor to breathe fire at me, Chan vaulted from his place next to Kari. He slammed into the dragon and plunged his enormous sword into Avarice's neck. The inferno erupted from the new opening, engulfing Chan and the dragon's head in flames. Avarice's anguished scream shook the lair.

Chan fell to the floor.

Avarice thrashed about scattering his trove like waves in the ocean.

A strangled plea of "Help me," bellowed from his throat as he struggled in vain to remove the sword from the back of his neck. The harpies sprang to help, leaving the few remaining ryders to flee the lair.

The harpies did more harm than good. As they reached for the sword the dragon's gyrations pushed his neck against their claws, opening fresh wounds. The chaotic swarm of the thrashing dragon and slashing harpies disappeared over the crest of the hoard. The tumult continued unseen.

My fury compelled me to follow. The first step was excruciating. I had to make sure he died.

Nikki caught my hand and my thirst for Avarice's death evaporated in the warmth of her affection.

The cries of the dragon's agony faded as Nikki helped me hobble to where Kari leaned over Chan. His hands looked like charred twigs. The blackened skin on his face oozed from cracks where he had opened his eyes. I forced myself not to look away from the gruesome sight. His pristine armor rose and fell with each breath. The sticky sound that accompanied the labored movement told me the rest of his body did not fare much better than his face.

"Can you heal him," I asked.

"No, I can close cuts but this is beyond my ability," Kari replied.

"I … fulfilled …our agreement," Chan choked. The motion of his mouth opened new seeping cracks in what used to be his cheeks.

"Thank you." It was all I could think to say. My mother certainly would have died if not for Chan.

"I wish … we never …. made that agreement," he said. He gasped for breath. "It cost many lives."

I wondered how many of the ryders would have been saved if Chan had taken his shot at Avarice rather than saving my mom. My throat ached and tears filled my eyes; tears of gratitude that we had saved my mom and tears of sorrow that it had cost so many lives.

"I'm sorry," Chan choked, looking at Kari. "My love … of power … and luxury … eclipsed … my love … of liberty." The fluid crackled in his throat as he struggled to get the words out.

"Shhh, don't speak," Kari said.

"Thank you … for … helping … me … fulfill … my … destiny." He gasped and closed his eyes for the last time.

The sound of tinkling coins in the hoard reminded me we were not alone. I turned.

Avarice lay on his hoard; only his head and neck visible at the summit of his treasure. A dozen harpies stood on either side of their wheezing master. "Kill them," rasped the dragon.

I raised my shield. Nikki drew her gun. Kari brandished her blades.

We had no hope of survival.

But, the harpies didn't move. They weren't looking at us. They were looking above us.

I followed their gaze to find Inicma standing on a balcony high above us. His neck more mutilated than Chan but not as black. His eyes burned with hate. He cocked his gun and innumerable identical clicks echoed through the chamber.

"Prove yourself. Kill them," Avarice bellowed, raising his head. The exertion was too much. He collapsed into his coins, his breathing raspy and irregular.

Inicma made a motion like flipping a switch and gun fire erupted from balconies all over the lair. I pulled Nikki to me and closed my eyes as we huddled under my shield, but no bullets came near us.

A moment later the gun fire ended. I opened my eyes to find the remaining harpies lying in motionless heaps.

A guttural laugh shook Avarice as he stared at Inicma. "You traitorous leech, did you grow a conscience or get too greedy?"

"Do my ears deceive me? Don't tell me Avarice, Diluter of Liberty and Ouster of Charity, suddenly thinks there is such a thing as too much greed?" Inicma mocked. "I am now the most powerful man in the world," he declared. I shuddered at the thought.

"The other dragons will destroy you," Avarice said, his eyes shutting and opening as he fought for consciousness.

"I doubt that very highly," Inicma said as he walked down the steps toward us.

Avarice's eyes opened, "If not, then they … will" he said, looking at us.

"They can't touch me," Inicma replied in disgust.

"Compassion … can … touch … anyone," Avarice said with his last breath.

21

"**P**owerful, but stupid," said Inicma as he sauntered toward us. His gun toting goons fanned out behind him, taking what Babat would have called a flanking position. "I didn't appreciate that little surprise you left me with," Inicma said as he gestured to his neck. "Do you know how I am going to return the favor?"

I had no doubt he would kill me. Chan was dead so I couldn't give him the key to the dragon's undoing.

"I'm not going to kill you," he said, reading my face. "I'm going to make you watch as I torment your friends in ways you can't even imagine." I shuddered, trying to wipe the worst possible images from my mind. "And I'm going to start with your mother."

"Leave him alone Inicma," my mom called from a balcony behind him as she struggled against the grip of the goon who held her.

I should have been upset at his threat. I should have been horrified. But, I was just happy she was alive. "And then you'll kill me," I stated the obvious.

"No, it turns out that the case you gave me is indestructible but the key for it is not." He made a motion with his hand and a goon carried the open case forward; the key a melted glob in the lock.

"So?" I should have been scared. But somehow, after Avarice, Inicma didn't frighten me.

"So once I am done filling your head with the sights and sounds of your friends begging for death, I'm going to stuff you in that kamisan of yours and lock it in this case." He paused to smile. "That way you can dwell on those memories for eternity."

"I'd pass on that one if I were you," a familiar voice called from a balcony half way up the lair. Nikki squeezed my hand. I smiled and let out a sigh of relief. Dillon was alive.

"Yes, I think we are going to have to pass on Inicma's offer..." Kari started, then raised her voice, "...So I can KILL DILLON."

"Now why would you do that?" Dillon asked like he was hurt.

"Because you let me think you were DEAD," Kari replied.

"See? She does care," he said to me.

Inicma looked nonplussed. "As amusing as this is, neither of you have any part in this. My deal was with JJ," Inicma said.

"No part, except torment beyond imagination and the fact that the contract says you can't harm us at the exchange," Dillon corrected. I wondered what he was doing. He knew there was no contract.

"Except there is no exchange to be made." Inicma replied.

"Inicma, you are the one who changed the language of the deal," said Liz as she emerged from behind Dillon. She stared at me without blinking. "JJ need only give you the *key* to the dragon's undoing." The words of my father flooded my mind. I'd heard them every time I was in the kamisan.

"You stay out of this old lady. Chan was the key and he is dead," Inicma called to her.

Liz scowled but didn't take her eyes off me. "First, I am *not* an old lady. Second, Chan was *not* the key to slaying the dragon. And third, I will *not* stay out of it. The agreement between you and I is part of that same contract so I am here to ascertain compliance with it."

She really was marvelous at choosing just the right words. She had just asked if I accepted the contract right in front of Inicma and he had no idea. I nodded my agreement to Liz and she turned her gaze on Inicma.

"Since I have agreed to the contract, I will give you the key." As soon as I said it, the security of the magical contract wrapped around me. Inicma couldn't touch me as I recited my father's message, "The heart of any beast, man, dwarf, elf, or dragon is the key to its undoing. Those with enough love in their heart to fight for the life and liberty of others will have the courage to bring about the eventual downfall of the dragon. That is how it has always been and is how it will always be."

"There, now you have the key to the dragon's undoing. Now *you* can't touch *them*," Liz said.

Inicma clenched his teeth. He looked around the room for any way out of the contract. "I will get even with you for this," he said gesturing to his neck. "You know, your father thought he was clever too; right up to the point where I suckered him into facing Avarice without any of his magical accoutrements."

Nikki squeezed my hand. I raised my ax. Inicma grinned. I placed the ax on my back where I knew it would be safe and grinned back.

"Come on, avenge your lying, good for nothing father. He used to complain about how grumpy your mom was when she was pregnant with you. He wished you hadn't been born."

His childish rant hurt, but I just smiled at his obvious lies. I knew precisely how much he loved my mom and me.

"He is just trying to goad you into attacking him," Kari said.

"If we don't do anything he can't hurt us," Dillon added.

"But those words hurt," Nikki replied.

"The contract ensures he will not harm you after the exchange. During the exchange it only ensures your safety," Liz called.

"You may have given me the key but the exchange is not complete until my men release your mother," Inicma sneered. "I think perhaps the best way for me to ensure your safety would be to keep you in the dungeon."

"Let me remind you," Liz said. "JJ swore he had told no one your name before the agreement and that he would not reveal your name after the exchange. There is no guarantee he won't reveal your name during the exchange."

"My men are loyal," he said calmly. The fear in his face betrayed his rebuttal.

"Yes, but I would be obliged to record it in the archives," Liz called.

Inicma looked at us as if he were deciding if keeping us was worth the price. I did my best impression of his check-mate smile.

"I suppose I have hurt each of you enough," he

said. I wondered what that meant, then remembered I still didn't have a home. "Let them go," he said.

Nikki's phone rang. She handed it to Kari without answering.

Kari scowled at the display before answering it. "I really am going to kill you." She paused. "For directions out of the lair I will commute your sentence to a simple maiming." She smiled. "You're going on speaker," she said.

Dillon spewed endlessly provide directions but Nikki and I didn't pay much attention to them, we just followed Kari. I put my arm around Nikki's shoulders and leaned heavily on her as I shuffled from the Dragon's death chamber.

Our pace was painfully slow, mostly due to my aching ankles. Inicma had goons rushing through the halls. It seemed like forever before we were alone in one of the elaborate corridors.

"So, how does it feel to be the first dragon slayer in a millennium to actually survive slaying a dragon?" Kari asked.

The comment didn't make sense to me. "I didn't slay the dragon. Chan did."

"Oh, Chan might be the reason you are alive, but there is no doubt Avarice was done for before Chan expedited his demise," she replied.

"Ugh, and I thought we'd made such progress mellowing our stodgy Brit." Dillon's voice chimed from the phone.

Both Kari and Nikki rolled their eyes.

"Did I get an eye roll?" he asked.

"Double eye rolls." I said.

"Yes!" he exclaimed.

Kari and Nikki smiled.

"You *didn't* answer my question." Kari put extra emphasis on the contraction.

I thought about her question for a moment. "Other than saving my mom, I'm not sure I did any good. I mean, won't Inicma be just as bad, or worse, than Avarice?" I asked.

Her head bobbed from side to side as she considered her response. "Perhaps, but he has a much shorter life span than a dragon."

"Incoming," Dillon said. Kari drew her blades. They weren't needed.

My mom rushed around the corner and threw her arms around me. I almost fell over from the impact. She hugged me so tightly I wondered if the armor was protecting me. "Don't ever do that again," she said.

"Don't worry mom. That is definitely on my list of things to avoid in the future," I replied.

Dillon appeared a moment later.

My mom hugged Nikki and thanked Kari profusely before ducking under my other arm. I had to admit it was much easier to walk with the added support.

"All of you are suffering from a deplorable lack of curiosity," Dillon said.

"And why's that?" Nikki asked.

"Because, I am the man," he proclaimed. Nikki rolled her eyes. Dillon pumped his fist.

"Do tell," urged Kari.

Dillon blustered non-stop the rest of the trek to the merchant's gate. He bragged about the piece of equipment (the one he stole from the warehouse two nights previous) he had installed in Avarice's computer room. I didn't understand much but it sounded like he would know about everything Inicma did going forward. He claimed a near death experience when he was nearly buried under the riches Avarice had flung at him. He boasted of dodging goons and contriving to get Liz into the lair like he had scaled Everest.

"Very nice," said Kari as we reached the ticketing room.

"That's it!" Dillon cried indignantly. "I do all that and all I get is very nice?"

"Well, it's not like you had to face the dragon. What did you want?" Nikki asked.

"A date," he screeched. Nikki rolled her eyes. Kari smirked. Dillon didn't pump his fist.

It was only after we stepped out of the merchant's gate and into Columbus Circle that I realized I didn't know where we were headed.

"You know, we never had that celebratory Chinese dinner," My mom said.

"I'm buying," Dillon said. We all looked at him in shock.

"A generous dwarf?" asked Kari.

Dillon smiled. "Well, I did just come into a sizeable sum." He held his backpack open. It was full of coins and gems.

"That would fund the Cyngor am Ryddid for years," Kari said.

"Then maybe we should take some to them," Dillon replied.

"We?" Kari said.

"You did not think I would allow us to part ways so easily, did you?" Dillon asked in his best Kari impersonation.

"Very well, you rapscallion, you may accompany me to my debriefing with the Cyngor am Ryddid," she said. Dillon beamed.

"All well and good but can we get something to eat before you two fly off into the sunset together?" I asked.

"Since our names are cleared can we please take a cab instead of the subway," Nikki asked.

A dark SUV pulled to the curb and the passenger side window opened. "Oh come on! As if this guy hasn't tormented us enough," I complained, expecting another of Inicma's surprises.

"Actually, I believe one school year in my class is enough torment for anyone, but I'd be happy to quiz you if you would like?" Mr. Morgan said from the front seat of the car.

"What are YOU doing here?" my mom asked.

Mr. Morgan looked at the floor.

"He's a ryder. Oh, and he asked me to tell you he said 'Hi'," I replied.

My mom sighed. "Just when I was really starting to like him too," she mumbled. I suppressed my gag reflex at the thought of my mother spending time with Mr. Morgan.

"So is that why you talked her into sending me to college in Utah, so you could make your move on her?" I accused Mr. Morgan.

"Absolutely not," he genuinely sounded insulted at the accusation. "I was trying to help your mom. You can't beat that school for the price."

"And it's relatively goon free," my mom added without missing a beat.

"What do you want, Mr. Morgan?" pressed Dillon.

"I was wondering if you needed a ride?" he replied.

As we piled into the SUV I realized it was dark blue rather than black.

"You know this looks like a goon-mobile, right" Dillon said.

"I know but it's great for camping trips."

Nikki and I sat in the back seat. She leaned her head on my shoulder.

"So where to?" Mr. Morgan asked

"Well don't look at me. Inicma destroyed my dad's place," Dillon said. Then under his breath he mumbled, "I wonder if he's even back from San Francisco yet."

"Um," said Mr. Morgan, as if he was trying to find the right way to say something.

"What?" Dillon asked.

"Your father was arrested for embezzling from MegaBank this evening," Mr. Morgan said. Everyone fell silent. "We think Inicma arranged it," he added.

"Oh, I'm so sorry dear," my mom said. "You can stay with us. Broome St. please, I want to change into something more presentable before we eat," she said. We all looked at each other.

"Um," Mr. Morgan began.

"We live right next to the Holland Tunnel," she tried to clarify.

"Mom, Inicma torched the apartment," I said.

"Literally, to the ground," Mr. Morgan added.

My mom sighed, shook her head, and covered her face with her hands.

"I'm sure you can stay at my place for the night," Nikki offered.

"Um," said Mr. Morgan.

"Oh come on. Her dad's like the most powerful criminal on the East Coast," I said.

"And someone just happened to give the Feds a complete run down of his operation, including financial statements," said Mr. Morgan.

"Let me guess, Inicma," said Kari.

"Well, yeah we think so," said Mr. Morgan.

"Any other news we should know about?" I asked.

"Um," said Mr. Morgan.

"Just spit it out," Dillon demanded.

"Jane ..." he said.

"You can call me Sam," my mom interrupted.

"Sam, the antique shop you worked at burned down. They found the owner and are claiming it was suicide by arson," he said.

"That's Inicma for you," Dillon said.

"Do you have any good news for us," I asked.

"Sure, you, Nikki, and Dillon all passed your exams, so you'll be able to attend the commencement ceremony in a little less than ten hours." The three of us looked at each other in disbelief. After what we had been through in the last four days, graduating from high school seemed pretty insignificant.

"In case you haven't noticed, none of us will have a cap and gown," Dillon said.

"That is why I went to great lengths to secure a cap and gown for each of you," Mr. Morgan said with pride.

"That still doesn't give us a place to stay," Nikki said.

"Since the caps and gowns are at my place you're welcome to stay there for the evening" he said with a smile. I rolled my eyes.

Nikki laughed.

"I can't believe we are talking about graduation," Dillon said.

"I can't believe a couple Manhattan kids took down Avarice," said Mr. Morgan.

"You mean the love of a couple Manhattan kids," corrected Nikki.

"Love?" I asked.

"Oh, shut up and kiss me," she said.

And I did.

📖 📖 📖

"Well that was certainly a graduation to remember," my mom said as our cab turned onto Broome St.

I smiled. The auditorium at the nearby college had been filled with all the dull monotony of graduation until just after I received my diploma. That's when the fire alarm went off and the sprinklers doused the stage. Everyone had evacuated and they had promised to send the rest of the diploma's by mail. Security said it was an accident, but the look on Dillon's face had told me different.

Nikki, my mom, and I had stayed at Mr. Morgan's apartment. He had given us a ride to the ceremony but had to stay to help clean up the mess. The cab seemed indulgent, since the only money we had was half of the delivery fee Dillon had given me. But, my mom and Nikki had nixed the subway. They didn't want to go underground again and there was no way I was going on another bus.

I'd seen burned apartment buildings before. Usually, the inside was gutted while the outside structure remained intact, although blackened by smoke. This was different. From the cab all we could see was gray ash swirling in the summer breeze. The empty lot was as obvious as a missing front tooth. I asked the cabbie to stop in front of Our Lady of Vilnius church. We hadn't come to see the remains of our home. We were here to fulfill my father's wishes.

The cabbie stared at the scrub brush in my hand as I paid him. That morning, my mother had insisted that we personally deliver it to Pete and thank him for his help.

My mom knocked on the church doors and a moment later Pete answered.

"Hello JJ, Nikki... What name are you going by now?" he asked my mom.

"With the dragon dead and Inicma bound by the contract, I've decided to go back to Sam," she replied.

"Wonderful, that will make things so much easier," he said jubilantly.

"What things?" my mom asked skeptically.

"Didn't JJ show you the will?" he asked. I wondered what he was getting at.

"Actually, no. We just talked about it," she said.

Pete looked disappointed in me. "Barry willed you the Broome St. property" he said.

"But if I own it why have I been paying rent for the last eighteen years?" she asked before I could get the words out of my mouth.

"Because for the last eighteen years you have been Jane Jones rather than Barry's widow. Of course, now that you are using your real name, you can claim the property at any time."

We all stood in silence. I wondered why he hadn't told us that before it had become an ash pit. "It doesn't look like there's much to claim," I said.

"I'm sure the law firm who managed it maintained current property insurance. Barry paid them a handsome sum to keep it in its original condition, but with the insurance you can rebuild it however you want," he said.

"I always wondered why the rent was so low," my mom said.

"Yes, well it did take some effort to convince them to take you on as a tenant," Pete smiled, then noticed the scrub brush. "What's that?"

"Oh, the message in the kamisan said if you had kept your end of the deal I should tell you to take a bath with this," I said, handing it to him. "I figure you've probably kept your end of the deal."

He stared at the brush for a minute, then said, "Let's go look at your property."

Nikki held my hand as I reluctantly followed him to the charred remains of my home.

The cell phone Dillon had given me rang. It was Babat's number. "Hello," I answered.

"Hello JJ," Liz said. "I heard your employment plans fell through."

"Yeah, but given the criminal connections that's probably a good thing." I gave Nikki's hand a squeeze and she smiled at me.

"Well, it just so happens that I am in need of a new adjunct librarian and I would love to have one that can read dragon script."

I didn't want to become the next Tom but with such little cash I couldn't pass on the opportunity. "Does it come with a place for us to stay?" I asked.

"Absolutely. Nikki and your mother would be

most welcome. Does that mean you're interested?"

"Well, it would have to be just a summer job. You see, I'll be going to school in the fall." This time Nikki squeezed my hand.

"Really, I thought you were dead set against college." Liz said.

"Well, an encounter with a dragon made me think I should learn a little more about financial and monetary systems." I tried to make the statement sound ordinary but it just sounded silly.

"Very well, a summer job it is. Can you make it to Tarrytown on your own or shall I send someone to pick you up?"

I was confused. "Tarrytown?"

"Yes, it's very difficult to explain the disappearance and reappearance of two houses so I moved the library entrance to Tarrytown," she said.

"Well that's better than Hicksville," I replied without thinking.

"Don't knock Hicksville. It's much nicer than the name implies. Now do you need a ride or not?"

I had managed to offend my first boss before I even started. "We'll take the train."

"Very well, call me when you get to the station. Good bye." She hung up without waiting for me to say good bye.

I was so focused on the call with Liz I hadn't noticed that we had reached my old home. I watched from the side walk as Pete traipsed through the ash covered depression. I had always said our apartment was a hole. Now that was literally true

Pete stopped at the only part of our home that was still recognizable, the old cast iron bathtub and the tile wall beside it. As soon as he ran the brush around the edge, a single tile fell from the wall to reveal a small hole. He pulled something from the hole and practically danced back to the sidewalk. He handed a piece of paper to my mom. I wondered if it was another kamisan.

She burst into tears.

"What is it?" I asked.

She couldn't answer through her tears.

"It is the information your mother needs to access the numbered bank account Barry left for her," he said. He held up a second piece of paper. "And this is the numbered account old Barry left for my payment," he smiled.

"That makes no sense. Why didn't he tell Sam about it?" Nikki asked.

"He did," my mom said, between gasps as she regained her composure.

"What? Why didn't we use it then," I asked.

She took a deep breath. "Because, I didn't know how to get to it. Your father's last gift to me was a set of bath lotions. I could never bring myself to use them because it reminded me of him too much. I assume I would have found this paper if I had only used his gift."

"I'm sure that's true," Pete said.

"JJ," Dillon called through the window of the Town Car that was pulling to the curb.

"What's up?" I said as he and Kari got out of the car. Other than nodding to each other across the room at commencement, I hadn't talked to Dillon since he refused to spend the night at Mr. Morgan's and left with Kari to find a hotel.

"I just wanted to say goodbye and make sure you're all right. I just sold a couple diamonds to Tony and didn't want you living in the gutter while I'm cruzin' around the world with my girl," he said. I involuntarily raised my eyebrow. Nikki just smiled. Dillon looked disappointed.

"I am not your girl and do not mislead them," Kari scolded. She turned to us and said, "We had separate rooms last night and nothing happened."

"It's only a matter of time," Dillon said.

"At this rate, it is more likely I will kill you," Kari said. Nikki laughed.

"So are you ok," Dillon asked.

I looked at my mom, who was talking with Pete about how to get at the numbered account. "Yeah, I think we're going to be just fine."

A black SUV stopped on Broome St, double parking next to Kari and Dillon's Town Car. The back door opened and Inicma got out.

"I thought the deal was clear. You need to leave us alone," I said.

"Please," Inicma said, "I need your help…"

THE END

AFTERWORD

In 2011 the occupy movement captured headlines and inspired this book. I found it interesting that the occupy movement was keeping score of who was winning by how many dollars they had without paying much attention to who determined how many dollars were available. They talked about getting a bigger piece of the pie without acknowledging that the size of the pie changes at the whim of a dozen people in the Federal Reserve (and at the time only ten people).

So I embarked on the ludicrous task of writing a book for teens that would provide an engaging story while causing them to ask questions about how the monetary policy of the United States is managed. We are taught that it is handled by congress but the Federal Reserve's own website says that they make monetary policy for the United States and are separate from the government. I hope this book will lead people to ask questions and that people smarter than I am will find a way to introduce some accountability for those who make our monetary policy.

History has shown that when a position exists with great power and inadequate checks and balances, someone will eventually abuse that power. I want to be clear. I do not claim that the power held by of the Federal Reserve has been abused. I am simply pointing out that it is ripe for such abuse to occur.

The fictitious actions described in this book were created for entertainment only. I in no way advocate any type of violence. On the contrary, I believe that civilized discussion is needed between intelligent individuals who care about this great country and recognize the peril of our current system for establishing monetary policy.

Made in the USA
Lexington, KY
01 May 2013